Bootcamp
For BROKEN
Hearts

Bootcamp for Broken Hearts

Joanna Bolouri

Bookouture

Published by Bookouture in 2022

An imprint of Storyfire Ltd.
Carmelite House
50 Victoria Embankment
London EC4Y 0DZ

www.bookouture.com

ISBN: 978-1-80314-633-1
eBook ISBN: 978-1-80314-632-4

For Olivia

CHAPTER 1

'Victoria, can you go and tell Romeo and Juliet over there to calm down before I turn the hose on them? There's a time and a place for everything. I don't want their teenage hormones dripping all over my nice café floor and I need to get these invoices finished.'

Victoria stops loading the dishwasher and turns to peer over the coffee machine. She snorts as she spots the teenage couple fused together at the mouth.

'Ah, young love,' she responds, wiping her hands on her apron. 'They're not doing any harm, Nora. I seem to remember you and Mark Davis getting pretty hot and heavy after school in Burger King...'

And during school, I think, briefly allowing myself to fall down a particularly nostalgic rabbit hole. My high school boyfriend was spectacular. A tall, dark-haired rugby player with the bluest eyes I've ever seen, while I had the nastiest discount specs and a blonde, spiral perm. I punched way above my weight back then, no idea how I managed to snag that one.

'That's not the point,' I reply, snapping back to reality. 'This

is a café, not a bloody nightclub... Are they... Oh, no chance...
HEY! HANDS WHERE I CAN SEE THEM, CHILDREN!'

'Stop being a bore.' Victoria sighs, making her way to the
other side of the counter. 'Sometimes you act like such a mom.'

'I am a mum.'

'You know what I mean.'

The now suitably startled teens slide six inches apart and
begin wiping the saliva from their faces. Ugh, *that* I don't miss.
The inexperience of youth. Kissing like a fish until you eventually get it right. They glare at me like I have ruined their lives
and I go back to my invoices.

'Time to go, guys,' I hear Victoria say behind me, no doubt
giving them an apologetic look for my uncool behaviour.
Victoria and I are the same age and yet sometimes I feel about a
million years older than her... not necessarily wiser admittedly,
just older. She still shops at Topshop and is organising a trip to
Ibiza with her husband for her fortieth birthday, while I'm planning a quiet, uneventful meal with my daughter where I will no
doubt wear a nice cardigan and get an early night. Even though
our completely different life paths led us to the same place,
Victoria's still living hers to the full, while sometimes I feel like
mine is passing me by.

'This place is shite anyway,' I hear the teenage girl mutter as
she stands up. 'It's like an old folks' home in here. Let's go,
Oscar.'

Oscar makes the grunting noise of his people and shuffles
obediently after her.

'Miss you already!' Victoria sneers as I hear the door slam
behind them. 'Cheeky little madam.' She laughs. 'I *was* going to
tell her she had lettuce between her teeth, but I changed my
mind. Oscar should definitely be the one to break it to her.'

'An old folks' home?' I mutter, shaking my head. 'How rude!
Were you that obnoxious at sixteen? I don't think I was.'

'Probably,' she responds. 'I think I still am.' She lifts their glass latte mugs from the table before hesitating. 'But maybe...'

'What?'

'... she has a point?'

Victoria sees my face and makes a *yikes* one of her own. 'Relax, Captain Death Stare!' she exclaims. 'I only meant maybe she—'

'Our café is not shite,' I reply, calmly closing my laptop. I can tell that the girl's comment upset Victoria more than it should have, whereas I feel relatively unbothered given that I have a sardonic teenager at home who thinks everything is shite by default. 'In fact, our café is whatever the opposite of shite is.'

'Un-shite?' Victoria offers.

I nod. 'Precisely. We have an un-shite café.'

I wait for Victoria's resounding support, which eventually appears in the form of a quiet 'hmm.'

'What does *hmm* mean?' I ask, my eyes narrowing.

Victoria flips the sign on the door to closed and turns the lock. 'Look, I know it's not shite exactly,' she begins. 'But you must admit, it's a tad old-fashioned. Could maybe do with an overhaul? Something more modern? Less, well... beige.'

'Café 12 is not old-fashioned!' I exclaim, now firmly joining her in the *bothered* camp. 'How can it be old-fashioned when we've just got this new, beautiful contemporary coffee machine, for goodness' sake! It's three grand's worth of bloody modern,' I say, gesturing to it like a home shopping network host.

She holds her hands up. 'Jeez, I'm only saying that we haven't changed much in the past decade. Yes, we have the new machine, but the look of the place is kind of twee. We don't have our own stamp. It's the kind of place my mom would approve of and that troubles me.'

Victoria's mother frames photographs of random cats from the internet and hangs them on her wall, like it's the most normal thing in the world. She also paints everything beige or magnolia. We hang photos of cupcakes we don't even sell here. I see Victoria's point.

She watches me sulk beside the coffee machine while I make my usual end-of-shift cappuccino. She is as unsure of my upcoming response as I am. I take the portafilter from the machine and begin banging the used grounds against the Knock Box, internally arguing with her.

This place is not twee. This place is quirky, damn it. Quaint perhaps. I love our little round tables and the booths are cosy. So, the walls are a little dated and maybe the cupcake photographs aren't the trendiest choice but—

'Nora, you're going to break that filter...'

'What? Oh.' I stop banging and start rinsing it off. 'So, why didn't you say anything before? We're partners in this place!'

'I own forty-two percent, so technically you're my boss.'

'That's only on paper. We are a team. You don't need to wait for my permission!'

'Nora, I changed the brand of handwash in the bathroom and you freaked that I didn't consult you first.'

'That's only because that particular liquid formula can be harsh on delicate skin!' I exclaim.

'Delicate skin or old folks' skin?'

A stupid grin appears on Victoria's face, and I start to laugh. We've known each other since high school when she moved here from Chicago. I find it very hard to argue with her because she's rarely wrong about anything. She's a petite, American business whizz, with the best smile I've ever seen and the worst taste in footwear. When we bought this place, neither of us were entirely sure what we were doing. One former barista with a six-year-old and an inheritance from her late grandpa plus a bored investment banker with a redundancy payout did not exactly equal ideal candidates to run an independent café – but eight years later, Café 12 is still going strong.

'Change isn't always a bad thing,' she adds while I select a cup from the shelf. 'Everything needs to evolve, or it'll just stagnate.'

I warm my cup, tamp the coffee grounds and wait thirty seconds for the shot to pour.

'Fine,' I finally concede. 'You're right. *She's* right. Our clientele is ninety-five percent coffin-dodgers and the occasional tourist or schoolkid. We never used to be this lame.'

'Come on, we're not lame!' Victoria insists, clearing the last of the tables. 'At the end of the day we make a good living, and the old dears enjoy coming here. We're not Starbucks and they appreciate that! We know their names, which admittedly is easy as they're all called Mary and Bill, but you get my point.'

I nod while I steam the milk and pour it into my coffee. It might be 6pm, but I still have heaps of stuff to do when I get home and the caffeine will keep me going.

'I know, I know,' I reply, 'I'm sounding utterly ungrateful, aren't I? Poor Marys and Bills. I'd take a hundred of them over that silly girl from earlier any day.'

'Exactly.'

'Sorry for being so bloody obstinate,' I say softly. 'You know what I'm like, pay no attention.'

Victoria stops wiping down the table, her hand moving to her hips. 'I do know what you're like and *this* isn't like you,' she asserts. 'You OK?'

I nod, rubbing the back of my neck. 'I'm fine. I'm just tired. I was up—'

'—*and* you're doing the invoices today; you never do the invoices,' she continues, ignoring my reply. 'You hate invoices. There's something going on here.'

'Vic, no one likes doing invoices, it's hardly a cry for help! I'm allowed to be tired. It's not unheard of.'

She goes back to cleaning for a moment. 'Wait... is this because you're turning forty next week?'

'What? No!' I reply, perhaps a little too quickly, 'But thanks for reminding me.'

The truth is that it has been playing on my mind somewhat. Mainly because I am clearly still in my twenties and this 'forty' nonsense is obviously just some birth certificate misprint.

'Nah, something's up,' she continues. 'Are you sad? Worried? Lonely? I know you have Charlotte, but she's hardly a substitute for—'

'There's nothing wrong!' I insist. 'I'm perfectly happy with my lovely daughter, my job, my flat and even my increasingly irritating best friend. I have everything an almost-forty-year-old woman could possibly need.'

'But you need—'

'Don't say it!' I implore.

'A man.'

I sigh. She said it. 'I really, *really* don't, Vic.'

She shrugs dismissively. 'A woman needs more than a coffee filter to bang,' she mutters as she resumes cleaning. 'Just saying.'

'No, what I *need* is this cappuccino and then I *need* to get home and make dinner for Charlie.'

Victoria pauses and tilts her head to look at me. 'You know, Faith was telling me about some guy she met who would be perfect for you.'

I already know. I had been in the middle of the lunch rush yesterday when my younger sister, Faith, rang my phone so incessantly, I became convinced that someone was dead or getting their last rites.

'Faith? What's wrong? Is everything OK?'

'Yes, yes. Now listen; I'm at a press launch for a new client and there's an amazing guy here. How do you feel about project managers?'

'I don't know how to answer that.'

'He's fit, under fifty and no wedding ring. Shall I give him your business card?'

'Faith! I'm up to my eyes in it here today... why are you whispering and... wait, why do you have my business cards?'

'I'm in the loo, I didn't want him to hear me. Well? Shall I?'

Balancing the phone between my ear and shoulder, I began plating a salmon and avocado salad.

'NO! Don't you dare. I don't want some random guy calling me. What if he shows up at the café? He could be weird. Victoria, can you take that coffee to table six? I'm doing eight's salad.'

I heard Faith sigh louder than she probably intended. 'Eleanora Brown, the problem is you don't want *anyone* to call you. You've completely given up. You must get back out there. If you—'

'What? Sorry, you're breaking up. I'm going into a tunnel. A big underwater one. Speak later.'

'Yep, Faith told me,' I finally reply to Victoria. 'And for the eightieth time this month, I'm not interested. You both need to cool it with the matchmaking.'

For the past couple of years both Victoria and my sister Faith have made it their mission in life to set me up. To them, the idea that I could possibly be perfectly content on my own is utterly ridiculous and therefore must be corrected as soon as possible. Victoria tends to set up dating profiles on my behalf without telling me, while Faith's method is to secretly scout out all the available men she meets and assess them for marriage suitability. It doesn't help that she's head of marketing for a huge media agency and meets new men roughly every seventeen seconds. I've pretty much given up telling them to leave me alone. I figure they'll get the message soon enough.

'But you need some company, Nora,' Victoria says softly. 'Everyone does. Maybe a few dates? A couple of dinners or—'

'I don't have the time or the inclination to start dating again,' I say firmly. 'Besides, the perfect man – the one who will give me emotional support, great sex, kindness and access to his Netflix password – doesn't exist.'

'You have your own Netflix account.'

'Yes, but I hate paying for it. Ninety percent of the films are terrible. All I'm saying is, I don't need anyone. I'm fine just as I am.'

Victoria lets it go for the time being and we finish closing, before stepping out onto Bread Street. The harsh November wind bites my cheeks as we briskly walk towards the bus stop under a sky so dark, it feels much later than 6.30pm. Edinburgh is charming at night, and as much as I never tire of seeing the beautifully lit castle, it always feels just a little too crowded. Thankfully tonight isn't Edinburgh Fringe crowded (Edinburgh's famous festival and three weeks of zero-personal-space misery), but it's busy enough that I'm tripping over tourists on the narrow pavements while giving weary nods to fellow workers who look as glad to be heading home as I am.

Victoria wraps her red scarf around her neck before linking arms with me as we cross the road. For someone with no children, she is the most maternal person I've ever met. I swear once she tried to clean my face with spit.

'You should start bringing your car to work,' she suggests, body-swerving some tourists who stop suddenly in front of us. 'It's too cold for this shit.'

'It costs me £3.40 a day on the bus. I'm not paying idiotically expensive parking rates just so I can have the pleasure of driving you home afterwards,' I reply, smirking. 'You know how to drive, why don't you buy your own car?'

She sniffs and shakes her head. 'Nah, I just use Benjamin's. Besides, it might interfere with my wine time. Damn, there's my bus already – see you tomorrow!'

Twenty minutes later I arrive in my neighbourhood of Broughton, and after a five-minute speed walk, I'm home, where my fourteen-year-old daughter Charlotte has already increased the central heating temperature from 'comfortably warm' to 'stifling as hell'. She gets home from school at four and while I'm usually home by six, I still feel like a terrible parent for leaving her alone. Charlie, on the other hand, relishes the independence.

'Hey, Mum!' she yells from her bedroom. Even when I'm not there, she prefers to hang out in her room with the door closed. 'What's for dinner?'

'Pizza,' I reply, throwing my coat in the hall cupboard. 'Did you have a good day, honey?'

Her door swings open and she appears, school shirt half tucked in and hair like a burst couch. She gives me a huge hug. 'You're late tonight. I'm starving.'

'I know, honey, I'm sorry. I had to finish off some invoices.'

'But you never do the invoices – Victoria does.'

Why is everyone so suspicious of my invoicing today? I'm a businesswoman doing business things. I bet Alan Sugar doesn't have to put up with this crap.

'Well, today I did. Anyway, how was your day?'

She shrugs. 'We're doing badminton in PE and I'm really rubbish but home economics was cool. We made scones.'

'Amazing! Did you get to bring them home?' I ask, then notice the crumbs on her cardigan.

'The thing is...' she begins.

'Yes?'

'Annabel burned her scones, so I gave her two of mine and then I got hungry waiting for you to come home so I ate them. Sorry!'

'It's alright,' I reply, 'I had one in the café earlier, anyway.' A complete lie of course, but I don't want her to feel guilty. It's bad enough that she comes home to an empty flat after school, the least I can do is not moan about a scone. 'I'll call you when dinner's ready.'

I turn on the oven to preheat while I pull the pizza and

some seasoned potato wedges from the freezer. Not exactly the most nutritious meal I've ever thrown together but it'll have to do. *I'll make a meal from scratch tomorrow*, I tell myself, *one consisting entirely of organic, corn-fed, free-roaming vegetables.* In reality, I know I'll end up taking one of the lasagnes from the café home and heating it up. I sigh as I spot the breakfast dishes from this morning sitting in the sink and make another mental note to start insisting Charlie helps out more. I'm not talking cleaning the house from top to bottom, but rinsing a bowl and spoon isn't breaking any child labour laws.

As the food cooks, I whizz around the flat with the hoover, throw some washing into the machine, bleach the toilet and set the table while I mentally run through the ironing I'll do after dinner and factor in time to help Charlie with her homework. There isn't a day that goes by when I don't want to scream at the banality of it all, but I never do. What would be the point?

Once a week, I let Charlie eat in her room, but tonight she's sitting with me at the table, playing with her pizza crusts and telling me about her day.

'Before I forget, I have drama club tomorrow, so you'll need to pick me up at half five.'

'Is there a tidying-up-your-stinking-room club, you could join?' I ask. God, this pizza tastes like cardboard.

'Very funny. I'll tidy it after my homework.'

'Good. It smells like there's a dead body in there... Are you not liking mushrooms this week? If you're not going to eat those, give them here.'

She hands me her plate. 'Mushrooms are weird, I'm not a fan. No idea why you like them so much.'

I happily add her little pile to the top of my pizza. 'What homework do you have?'

'Maths and history. I might need help with maths.'

I tell her it's no problem, but I know I'm going to have to google every question she's unsure of. I hate maths. To me, maths is for orderly people who make their beds every morning and own a Dungeons and Dragons–themed chessboard. Having a daughter in high school only reminds me of how little information I've retained since I attended myself, mainly because I've never had to use most of it. Any person who says they frequently use Pythagoras's theorem is a liar.

At 10pm I knock on Charlie's door to say goodnight. She's sprawled out in bed with her headphones on, her face highlighted by her phone screen. Surprisingly, her room is now at least thirty percent tidier.

'Night, honey.'

She takes her headphones off one ear. 'Dad texted earlier to see if I want to go and watch that *Harry Potter* spin-off film at the weekend.'

'That'll be fun!' I reply enthusiastically.

'Fun for people who like *Harry Potter*, maybe,' she responds. 'I've suggested we see *Bohemian Rhapsody* instead so he's now checking to see if it's age appropriate. It's 12A! I'm fourteen!'

'I'm sure he'll say yes.'

'I doubt it. He's freakishly into wizards. I honestly don't know what you saw in him!'

'Lots, as it happens,' I tell her. 'He was extremely funny, he was clever, handsome and I loved him very much! You wouldn't be here if I hadn't.'

'I guess,' she replies. 'He's just soooo annoying sometimes.'

'And that too,' I reply, with a wink. 'Listen, sweetie, being annoying doesn't make him a bad dad. It just makes him a dad. One who loves you a lot. And if he doesn't take you to see *Bohemian Rhapsody*, I will. Deal?'

'Deal.'

I also have no idea if it's suitable, but I'm too tired to

continue this. I need to sit down. My back hurts almost as much as my feet.

'Thanks, Mum.'

I lean over and kiss the top of her head, unashamedly sniffing her beautiful brown hair. She smells of apple conditioner and the burned toast she made earlier. But most of all she smells of something that I can't describe with words. It's a smell only my heart can define.

I make my way into the living room and sink into the couch, determined to have an hour to myself before bed. Just me, the television and the half a glass of wine that remains in this bottle. It's not even that good, but it will help me sleep.

The living room is my favourite room in the flat, mainly due to the fake flame-effect fire which gives off a most delightful glow. The walls are entirely white, interrupted by splashes of colour from the artwork hanging there, the floor is wooden beneath a large patchwork rug and the couch is midnight blue. I'm surrounded by books and photos and odd knick-knacks I've collected over the years; things that remind me of where I've been and who I used to be. The cat postcard on the mantelpiece reminds me that I was once eighteen and on holiday in Greece. The large silver candlestick reminds me that I was once twenty-four and in a bazaar in Tunisia and the blue-framed photo of Charlie as a baby reminds me that I was once twenty-six and part of a 'we.'

It's not often I think about what life would have been like if Stuart and I hadn't split up – if we'd simply muddled through for the sake of Charlie. But on days like today when I'm feeling a bit weary, the thought makes its presence known, like an unwelcome whisper in my ear. Thankfully, it creeps back out just as quickly because, well, screw him. He'd been clever enough to hide an affair for three long years, then suddenly stupid enough to get caught. Stuart Jamieson let me plan my entire life around him. A life that he didn't want to be part of but didn't have the balls to tell me himself.

That was his mistake. Mine was staying with him, thinking I could carry on, even when it was clear that his love for Julia resulted in nothing but contempt for me. It was like he thought I had intentionally gotten pregnant just to trap him and prevent him from living his best life. I mean, really? I rarely plan what I'm having for lunch, let alone the systematic destruction of someone else's happiness. I have no doubt that if we were all still under the same roof, Charlie would be stuck in the middle of two people who couldn't love each other less if they tried. And I would have tried.

So, ten years on, we chat politely in front of her, she stays at his house a few nights per month and goes on holiday with him and Julia once a year. She knows her parents as two, separate happy people and that's how it will remain. He's not a bad father, he's just not a particularly good man.

Sometimes I picture what it would be like to have someone else, someone new... and then ninety-nine percent of my brain rejects the idea within seconds. After a decade, would I really be able to play nicely with another grown-up? One who takes up half of my bed, uses my toilet and notices when I don't shave my legs for weeks at a time? It's doubtful. I don't want to share my home with anyone else except Charlie, and I don't expect her to make room for someone new either. She doesn't need an additional father and she doesn't need a mother who moves some guy in because she's fed up watching the telly alone.

However, there is still that one percent that believes life might be better with someone to laugh with. I don't laugh nearly as much as I used to. The truth is, I have no idea if I'm truly content on my own or if I've become so used to it that I've become numb to it.

Maybe Faith is right, perhaps I have given up? If I have, it certainly wasn't intentional. When I was younger, the fairy-tale, knight-in-shining-armour, *someday my prince will come* bullshit was still conceivable and even the prospect of meeting someone felt like a bright light inside of me, bursting to get out. But every failed relationship or unlit spark caused that light to slowly fade. All I know is that after years of dating and kissing frogs, there were never any princes. Only frogs.

I turn on the television and pour the last of my wine.

CHAPTER 2

Friday mornings are always hectic and this one is no different. I usually start at ten, but employee of the year Tracey has a dental appointment so I'm going in earlier than normal to give Victoria a hand.

'Have you seen my gloves?' I shout through the bathroom door, but my question goes unanswered due to the music blasting from Charlie's Bluetooth speaker. I mum-dance my way through the house to Billie Eilish, continuing my glove search, eventually finding them on top of the fridge.

Five minutes later, a wild Charlie zips past me from the bathroom, looking as dishevelled as she did when she went in twenty minutes ago. Quite the achievement.

'The hairbrush is your friend, sweetheart!' I inform her as I grab my bag. 'There's some serum in my room if you need it. It's the good stuff from—'

'I've already brushed it!' she interrupts, irritated. 'It's just frizzy, Mum, it's fine. No one cares, except you.'

I feel a jolt of shame in my chest. She's right. This is the kind of garbage my mum used to frequently say to me, when she became exasperated that I was not as groomed as she'd like.

'*Would it kill you to put some makeup on, Eleanora? You might not care but you're not the one who has to look at you all day.*'

'You're right,' I reply, angry that my mother's bullshit has left a great big dirty smear on my psyche. 'Ignore me, you're perfect exactly as you are.'

Charlie looks a little surprised that she's won this battle so quickly. 'You OK?'

I laugh. 'Yes, I'm fine. Tired but I'm good. I love you very much.'

She pulls on her blazer and kisses me on the cheek. 'Do something fun while I'm at Dad's, will you? You work too hard.'

'I have to work hard,' I tell her, 'Someone has to pay for this mansion we've grown so accustomed to living in. Those ponies won't feed themselves...'

She rolls her eyes, but I give her a hug to reassure her that I'm not dismissing her suggestion entirely. 'I will,' I say softly, 'In fact, by the time you come back tomorrow, I'll be known across Edinburgh as *Fun Mum*.'

'God, I hope not. That's terrifying.'

'Gotta run!'

I kiss her on the head and dash out the door, making the bus with seconds to spare. Unsurprisingly there are no seats, so I'm forced to make a power stance in the aisle, like some filthy upright manspreader. As we trundle along, I begin to feel a little uncomfortable about Charlie's request. The fact that she might even be a smidgen concerned about me, makes me uneasy. That's not her job – her job is to be a kid, not to worry about her mum. It gnaws away at me for the rest of the journey, only dissipating when I reach the café and see Vic mouthing along to whatever she has playing on the radio. She looks nice today, her curly hair pulled into two puffs on top of her head.

'Morning!' she chirps, opening the door for me. 'Cuppa?'

'Please, my face is frozen. Did the pastry lady come? I've been dreaming about her chocolate twists.'

'Yup,' Victoria replies. 'We're actually organised for once. Even Brian the bread man was early.'

I throw my coat and bag in the back and wash my hands while Victoria makes me a tea.

'Meant to say,' she shouts over the noise of the machine, 'I have some clothes that are too small for me. Think Charlie might want them? Some really cute tops and skirts.'

'Maybe, I reply. 'Though currently she's going through an emo/goth phase. Got anything with skulls or parental contempt?'

'Always,' she replies. 'God, I love that kid.'

'Well, according to *that kid* I work too hard,' I inform her, enjoying the warm water against my skin. 'I've been ordered to have more fun.'

Vic places my tea on the counter as I emerge from the bathroom. 'She's not wrong, you know.'

'Hey, I watched the first three episodes of *Schitt's Creek* the other night!' I reply indignantly. 'That was fun! Took me ages to realise that the woman who plays Moira is actually Kevin's mum from—'

'I think Charlie means something you don't do every evening, Nora.'

I lift my burning-hot tea and sip cautiously. 'Really? Wow. So, crying uncontrollably is out of the question as well then?'

Vic's face drops.

'I'm kidding, lighten up. This needs more milk.'

She tuts loudly and picks up a large jar of gherkins. 'Listen, Benjamin's at some dental conference until Sunday, fancy doing something tonight?'

I glance over as she wrestles with the lid. 'Hmm, like what?'

'Oh, I dunno,' she replies, her forehead breaking into the

tiniest of sweats. 'Whatever we like! Skydiving, salsa dancing, road trip to Vegas—'

'New Tom Cruise at Cineworld?'

She frowns. 'Anyone but him. You know how I feel about him.'

I smile because I do; she cannot stand him, but she rarely says it out loud in case someone overhears and informs the Church of Scientology. 'OK, a different film then.'

The jar lid finally comes away with a disappointingly quiet *pip,* given the amount of energy she's just expended. 'I'm sure we can come up with something a bit more exciting than the bloody cinema,' Victoria insists. 'Remember the fun we used to have pub-hopping around the Grassmarket? We should totally do that.'

'I do remember.' I reply, 'But we were at uni, Vic. We also used to crash house parties, wear checked shirts and gracefully throw up in bus stops. Shall we do that too? Ooh, alcohol poisoning sounds exhilarating.'

'I'd rather do that than watch Tom Cruise,' she mumbles, flipping the door sign to open. 'But come on, Nora, don't you want to do something just a little wild? Be spontaneous, like the old days?'

I shake my head. 'No, thank you. These days I prefer my fun to be planned, completely predictable and preferably with easy access to parking and popcorn.'

I hear Vic chuckle because she thinks I'm joking, but she doesn't understand. I may be acting flippant, but I'm entirely serious. The choices I made as that carefree spontaneous idiot are still haunting me to this day, choices that resulted in a broken heart and a broken home. Victoria's choices led her to an amazing job in New York and a husband who's king of clear braces or something equally lucrative. She was never naïve like I was, and now that naivety has been replaced with something far colder and guarded. So, no I do not want to relive my former glory days. I do not want to ever be that person again.

My inner turmoil is thankfully interrupted by three sixth-year students entering the café for takeaway vanilla lattes and croissants. I happily oblige – if only to give myself a rest from the *fun* conversation which has become anything but. To their delight, I throw in the croissants for free, thus proving once and for all that our café is indeed un-shite.

Victoria finally relents and agrees to the cinema, but only if we see Olivia Colman be *the Queen that she is,* if I don't drive and if I buy her a beer and hotdog combo.

'Why can't I drive?' I ask. 'We could go to the place at Fountain Park.'

'Because you'll need to go home and get the car,' Victoria informs me, 'and when you get home, you'll get all comfy and warm and then you'll cancel.'

It's a fair point. I might have previous for this.

'Fine, we'll go after work then? Happy?'

She grins. 'I've never known anyone as reluctant to have a social life as you are.'

I do have a social life, I think to myself. *I just choose to socialise indoors, alone.*

CHAPTER 3

There's already a queue forming when we arrive, but it's mainly for Tom Cruise so we get decent seats in a relatively empty screen for the latest Olivia Colman film. I buy Victoria her beer and hotdog, choosing some nachos and a Diet Coke for myself, knowing that if I drink booze in a dimly lit room, I'll be asleep in twenty minutes. Vic also buys some popcorn and a large bag of peanut M&Ms because the woman has the metabolism of an Olympic athlete. It's been forever since we went to the cinema and as the trailers begin, I remember why. Victoria likes to talk as much as she likes to eat.

'Hang on, wasn't she in the—'

'This trailer looks terrible, who commissions this garbage?'

'Can I have a nacho?'

'She looks like Pauline from my hair salon. Ooh, did I tell you that—'

'SHHHHHH!'

We turn to see a man behind us, glaring and it seems to shut Vic up for the time being. I push the button on the lazy-boy chair and settle back.

By the end of the movie, a disgruntled man behind us has

moved eight rows back and I've learned that Pauline from the salon once mistakenly bleached a woman's fringe clean off and now Pauline no longer works there. I've never met this Pauline in my life.

'Great film,' Vic states as we head out. 'I would pay to watch Olivia Colman read a Domino's menu.'

'Yeah, it was brilliant,' I reply, 'Though your cinema etiquette still needs some work, my friend. You made that man move seats.'

'I whispered!' she insists, with a grin that says otherwise. 'Anyway, you know I get restless in cinemas. I only came for you.'

'And Olivia Colman.'

'Well, obviously. Listen, I'm going to nip to the toilet, be two secs.'

Once in the foyer, I see the disgruntled shushy man. He looks miserable and much balder than he looked in the dark. I'm sure he had more hair. Did we cause that?

Then I hear a voice behind me.

'Hello, love. I was just saying to Mary, there's Dora and here, I was right.'

Dora. There's only one woman who's gotten my name wrong at least three times a week for the past six years. I turn and she greets me with the huge smile I'm so used to seeing.

'Jean! How lovely to see you!'

Jean is one of our café regulars and must be nearly eighty but she's still a lively old bird. Her green wool coat is buttoned to the neck, but I know that underneath she's wearing the same set of pearls she always wears. She's extremely well spoken, well mannered and possibly a little bit lonely. I wave hello to her friend Mary, another regular who's heading towards the same bathroom Victoria's currently using. Mary is far less put together than Jean, preferring a sensible short haircut to Jean's curls and a blue waterproof coat, which is slightly too long in the arms.

'Are you coming or going, Jean?' I ask. 'We're just heading home.'

'We're going to see the Tom Cruise one. My son, Wilbur, recommended it. He was at the premiere in London, you know.'

'Oh, really? Was he working on the film?'

'I don't think so,' she replies, fiddling with the strap on her handbag. 'I'm not quite sure what he does these days.'

Jean loves to talk about her son and is very proud of him, despite lumbering him with the name Wilbur. From what I've garnered from various conversations in the café, Wilbur was a 'late baby', lives in England, is married and apparently goes to film premieres. Given Jean's very demure and proper exterior, I imagine Wilbur to be the same, only taller.

'Great, well, I hope you enjoy the film,' I say, spying Victoria leaving the bathrooms. 'You can tell me all about it when I see you next.'

'Bye, love!'

She walks across to the bar area, greeting Victoria as their paths cross.

'Is Jean getting her drink on?' Vic asks, grinning. 'You love to see it. I heard Mary humming to herself in the toilet, too, I think she's already three sheets to the wind. When I grow up, I want to be just like them.'

'I think we are already,' I reply. 'Jean is a talker, like you. The whole cinema will be hearing what bloody Wilbur's been up to this week.'

'Well, if I'm Jean in this scenario, that makes you Mary, the half-cut toilet hummer.'

'I've been called worse.'

Victoria laughs and links her arm into mine as we head back towards the car. It's been a really nice evening. Charlotte was right. I did need to have more fun.

CHAPTER 4

The people who proclaim that you're *only as old as you feel* are liars. The fact that I still feel the same way I did ten years ago will not halt the ageing process, a process that in three days will have me turn forty against my will. FORTY. It's not the actual number which upsets me, it's the reality of what it represents.

People in their forties have joint mortgages and life insurance and hold dinner parties for all the other forty-year-olds who have their shit together. They have reliable cars and dependable spouses and know how to adult. None of these people are me.

'Eleanora?'

My sister, Faith, sits in front of me in her Marc Jacobs blouse, looking at me like I'm the most annoying individual she's ever met in her entire life. She's the only person, except for Mum and the doctor's receptionist, who calls me by my given name. Faith hates my nickname.

'I know you think it's cute, but Nora makes you sound plain.'

'Well, Eleanora isn't any better. I feel like I should be doing Victorian needlepoint while sitting on a chamber pot.'

'Your birthday is on Saturday,' she continues. 'What do you want? Are you even listening to me?'

'Yes,' I reply, 'I'm just a little distracted, you know, WITH BEING AT WORK. Victoria's at the suppliers, don't you have work to do? Somewhere else to be? I need this table for paying customers.'

'I'm at lunch, it's raining and I'm not moving.'

Even though she's shaking her head in frustration, her brown bob hasn't moved an inch. Her hair is as inflexible as she is.

I call Tracey to take over for five minutes and pull out a seat at Faith's table. Tracey has been a godsend since we hired her. She'll open the café early, work overtime and even came up with the idea to hold events after hours. We have mainly hosted book clubs, but they eat a surprising amount of profitably marked-up cake.

'I haven't even thought about my birthday,' I lie. 'I honestly don't care. Get me a fancy candle or something.'

'It's your fortieth,' replies the thirty-one-year-old who still thinks forty is something to be celebrated. 'You should do something special.'

I see the glint in her eye. She's planning something and I intend to put a stop to it right now.

'Don't you dare! I do not want a party or any kind of social gathering. You know I get uncomfortable in large groups. All that bloody small talk, bleh.'

'Oh, relax,' she replies, 'I have no intention of throwing you a party.'

I suddenly feel insulted. Why isn't she throwing me a party? I deserve a party. A huge one. Just not one where other people also have to be there.

'But we should have dinner or something at least,' she insists. 'This is a new chapter in your life! Seize it! Embrace it!'

'Jeez, calm down, Tony Robbins.'

'Who?'

'The self-help guru? He's very famous. He was... never mind.'

The café door opens and what looks like a Saga bus tour begins traipsing in. 'Uh-oh, I have to go. Look, I'll have a meal or a takeaway with Charlie or something. I don't want a fuss and NO PARTY. Promise?'

She doesn't. Faith's one frustratingly admirable quality is that she never makes a promise she can't keep. 'I'll see you on Saturday, sis. Go deal with your pensioners.'

I don't trust her. Not one little bit.

———

After a long and busy day, I catch the bus as usual, planning out my evening in my head. It's Wednesday, so Charlie's dad will collect her from school, which means I can either spend my evening productively sorting through café paperwork or I can eat chips and watch box sets in bed. By the time I've shown the driver my day ticket, chips are already the clear winner because the paperwork can wait. The paperwork can always wait.

Thankfully, it's not too busy and I sit near the front. I've never liked the back of the back of the bus; I prefer to gracefully exit, rather than pinball off everyone when the tyres hit a pothole.

I watch a woman in her mid-twenties who sits in the seat in front of me. She's wearing the cutest red and gold-flecked bobble hat with matching gloves and she looks incredible. She looks like a woman whose life is as sparkly as her winter accessories. I wonder what she has planned for tonight. I bet it's far more electrifying than what I have planned... of course, that wouldn't be hard. I bet there are prisoners in Barlinnie with more exhilarating evenings planned.

When I first broke up with Stuart, I used my free time

wisely. I'd organise dinners with friends, I'd go to the cinema alone, hell, I even tried to learn Spanish online, but none of it lasted. While I was busy starting again, everyone else was busy settling down. Girlfriends became wives and wives became mothers who I saw less and less of. I was the single mum and secretly every married friend was grateful it wasn't them. I tried dating, but nothing ever quite stuck. Most dates never made it to a second and those that did, fizzled out quickly. So, dates turned into hook-ups and sometimes hook-ups turned into flings, but after a while I realised that I'd stopped being flung completely. It's been three years since I had sex and I'm not even sure that I miss it.

The driver beeps angrily at a cyclist, snapping me out of my melancholy. I'm two stops from home and the wind and rain has picked up, clattering loudly against the window. In front of me, the bobble-hat girl begins a loud, shrieking conversation with someone called 'Babe' causing passive-aggressive tuts from everyone, as I glare at the back of her head. I might not be young, or particularly perky, but at least I'm not an inconsiderate bus arsehole. I secretly hope her hat blows off.

Once home I delight in the fact that for an entire Charlie–free evening, I have nowhere to be and no housework to catch up on. I pull the blinds, turn on some music and head to the bedroom to plug in my electric blanket so I don't have to deal with cold sheets later. As I turn on the bedside light, I look around my room. It's a space that hasn't been used for anything other than sleeping for a long time. The charity shop clothes pile in the corner is reaching new heights, filled with pre-weight gain purchases I can no longer fit into, nestled against a dressing table covered in makeup and toiletries I rarely use anymore. A bedroom can speak volumes about its owner and this one belongs to someone sad. When did I become so sad?

I catch myself before my chin starts to wobble. *Enough! You*

*have a happy child and your own business. You just need a hobby
or something.*

I march myself into the living room and sit on the couch,
fuming. This is all their fault – Faith and Victoria's – with their
ooh, here's a great man for you and *ooh, forty is special except
when you're alone* bullshit. They know I will dwell on this,
that's why they do it. I've managed ten years without dissolving
into some weepy single stereotype and I don't intend to start
now. I might have had my wobbles, but I'm still treading my
tightrope, trying not to look down. If they think I'm waiting for
some big strong man to catch me, they're very much mistaken.

CHAPTER 5

Thursday is 'pie, chips and peas' day at the café, which always sells really well, especially to the local tradesmen, but stinks the place out. Some people remark that the smell reminds them of school dinners in the seventies, making me very grateful that I didn't start school until 1983.

'We only have twelve left,' Victoria informs me, sliding the last tray of pies into the oven. 'Then we're out. Table two should be ready to order if you want to get them.'

I nod, grabbing my notepad, while Tracey plucks two lunch order tickets from the stand and begins working on them both at the same time. Despite our fancy coffee machine, the rest of our operation is pretty much old-school. We still write everything down and ding a bell when an order is ready.

After a particularly deaf pensioner at table two asks me to explain the difference between lattes, cappuccinos and flat whites several times, I return with their order for two pots of tea and some scones.

'Do you know what popped into my head last night?' Victoria says, filling up a bowl with tiny packets of white and brown sugar. 'Those ugly pyjamas you used to wear at uni.'

I'm instantly bombarded with flashbacks of pink flannel. 'Hey, those were warm as hell and probably lifesaving considering our digs didn't get central heating until the year we left.'

She laughs. 'I know, but they were hideous! They had red wine and pot noodle stains all over them. I kind of miss those days.'

'You miss being poor and cold?' I ask, as the memories flood back, not all of them welcome.

For four years, I'd studied drama and English while Vic studied business and economics. We'd shared a pokey three-bedroom flat in Fountainbridge, along with a German girl, Lena, who studied chemistry and was a complete poker shark. It was grim, cheap and we had the best time. I must look up Lena on Facebook. She's either a millionaire now or in jail.

While Vic might miss them, those were the days when I'd worked in a coffee shop part-time to keep me in the aforementioned red wine and pot noodles while I studied. It was where I continued to work between acting auditions after we graduated at twenty-two, and where the handsome, older engineer I served every morning asked me out and eventually knocked me up aged twenty-five. Vic went off to work in America, I never went to another audition again.

'Those pyjamas are the only thing I miss,' I finally respond. 'Weird thing to remember, though. Do you often think about my nightwear?'

'Never,' she replies. 'Must be an age thing. I'll forget my own name eventually, but never those bloody pyjamas. Take these peas to six, will you?'

I nod and reluctantly pick up the dish of lumpy green slop, knowing I will be spending the rest of the day trying to put the past back into its little box at the back of my brain.

'Here's your peas, Jean,' I say, setting them on the table. 'Sorry if you've been waiting, we're a bit manic today.'

'Don't worry, Dora,' she replies, passing them to the woman

on the right. 'They're not for me, anyway. Mary likes to take them home for her Great Dane.'

I glance at Mary who's scraping the dish into a Tupperware box and wonder how someone who's barely five foot and approaching eighty copes with a Great Dane.

'My Wilbur used to hate peas,' Jean begins. 'But then, at his wedding – what did they serve? Pea puree with the scallops! I couldn't believe it... Mary... hold it steady... that's going to spill all over your carpet bag if you're not careful.'

I slip away unnoticed while they deal with their pea crisis.

————

I get home at six and after a disappointing dinner, I settle down on the couch with the new John Grisham novel that Victoria lent me while Charlie retires to her pigsty. However, ten pages in, she appears at the living room door.

'Hey, Mum, do you prefer white, dark or milk chocolate?'

'Milk,' I reply, looking up from my book. What is it with the weird questions today? 'I mean, I like white too. Never dark. It's a bitter waste of cocoa beans. Why?'

'Um, we're making this pavlova thing in home economics,' she replies. 'You like pavlova, right?'

My eyes narrow as I watch her hover, phone in hand. Last week she made basic scones in Home Economics; I'm pretty sure something as complicated as pavlova isn't on the third-year curriculum.

'I do,' I reply. 'Pavlova, huh? Who's teaching the class, Michel Roux?'

'Who?'

'He's a... never mind. Do you need money for the ingredients?'

'Nope,' she replies, smiling sheepishly. 'School provides them. Thanks!'

'Your Aunt Faith actually makes a mean pavlova!' I yell as she darts back to her room. 'Pretty sure she'll give you some tips if you—'

I pause as the proverbial penny starts to drop. Faith does make a good pavlova. In fact, she made an exceptional one for her friend Rona's birthday two years ago and she made me help carry it in. *Birthday pavlova.* I have a horrible feeling that she's using my child as a pawn in her pavlova games. For a moment, I consider grilling Charlie until she tells me Faith's plans. but I stop myself. She actually looked quite excited. Do I really want to be the mean, old woman who ruins her own birthday party? I go back to my book and hope that whatever they have planned, it's painless and brief.

CHAPTER 6

'Faith, I hate your client launches. I'm always stuck talking to the other people who also hate your client launches.'

'Oh, just come for goodness' sake,' she insists, sighing down the phone at me. 'It's free booze and Charlie's with her dad. It's not like you're doing anything else.'

'I could be doing something,' I reply huffily. 'You don't know my life.'

God, she's infuriating but correct. My only recent accomplishment is becoming the reigning Queen of Netflix.

'Look, Victoria and Benjamin are coming. Besides, I fought hard for this client. They nearly went to Saatchi. It's a big win for me. Their rum brand could be huge by next year.'

'Fine, OK. But I'm only doing this because you're emotionally blackmailing me... and, well, I like rum.'

'Perfect. Half eight at the Blue Rooms. We have an hour and a half before they open the doors to the public. Your name's already on the list.'

I haven't been to the Blue Rooms in years, and quite rightly so – I'm almost forty. Still, maybe throwing on a dress and having a dance on a Friday night isn't the worst idea in the world. I'll leave before the twenty-somethings come in and start wondering who brought their mum. Vic's husband, Benjamin, very kindly offers to drive. He drops Vic and I at the door while he parks the car in the nearby multistorey. When Victoria first started dating him, I thought they were a little mismatched. Her unique sense of style is far removed from his, which mainly consist of plain shirts, sensible ties and the occasional pullover when it's chilly. I always thought she'd end up with some tech entrepreneur or a Ferrari-owning media mogul, but instead she fell for a gentle orthodontist with a Honda. It's unusual to see him dressed down. For once, tonight he doesn't look like he's going to court; instead he's wearing a pale grey shirt and some jeans. Vic's wearing a blue-and-black bodycon dress which was obviously designed to make women like me feel bad about themselves.

'You look stunning,' I say miserably. 'I look like I should be busking outside Waverley station.'

'Oh hush, you look great,' she reassures me. 'You've always suited that grunge look. I could never pull that off.'

I peer down at my black tea dress, matched with chunky ankle boots. It appears, for me, the nineties are still very much alive and well.

Benjamin joins us and we head inside, navigating the badly lit stairway to the private function area in the basement. It's busy already, a blend of corporate types mixed with the target demographic of cooler, young professionals who've moved on from Smirnoff Ice and Bacardi Breezers.

'Welcome to Red Rum's launch night,' greets a woman in a tight white T-shirt. I can feel the heavy bass from the DJ vibrating in my boots. She hands us tiny shot glasses of blood-coloured liquid as we move through the entrance. 'Our full range is available behind the bar.'

Victoria immediately necks her shot, declaring that it's 'effing awful.' She then does the same with Benjamin's drink because he's driving and it would be a shame to waste it. I hold off and decide to mix mine with a Coke.

'You guys grab some seats,' I suggest. 'I'll head to the bar. Want anything?'

'Soda and lime,' Benjamin requests. 'You want a beer or something honey?'

'Better not mix,' Vic replies. 'Though I need something to wash this god-awful taste away. I'll stick to spirits. Just a G&T please, Nora.'

I don't know the track the DJ is playing but it still makes my head bop as I push my way into the bar queue. I try to catch the barman's eye but to no avail. I'm not even on his radar. God, I feel old. Twenty years ago, I would have flirted my way to the front of the queue, now I have to jostle for my place with every other loser.

I spot Faith at the end of the bar with a tall woman in a coral jumpsuit, who appears to be hanging off her every word. She waves to me before signalling that she'll be five minutes. I'm always a little in awe when I see Faith working. Unlike me, she is incredibly professional and there is a charisma that radiates from her. It's electric. She's the only person I know who can stand beside someone in a garish coral jumpsuit and still be the one you're immediately drawn to.

'Coke, G&T and a soda and lime please,' I shout to the barman when he finally looks in my direction. He dances his way through my order before handing me my drinks in record time. I pour my rum shot into the Coke and carefully manoeuvre my way out of the queue and look for my friends. Thankfully, they've managed to find a table. A win for the oldies.

Half an hour later, Faith finds us sitting near the back and plonks herself down beside us. 'Well, look at you lot all fancy,' she compliments. 'So glad you could come. Have you tried the rum?'

We all nod and tell her how delicious it is, but Victoria was right. It is effing awful. It tastes like spiced foot.

'You look pretty,' Faith tells me, scanning my outfit. 'Are those Charlie's boots? They're... interesting.'

'No, they're my boots,' I reply, childishly scrunching my face at her. I'm two sizes bigger than Charlie and she knows this. 'But thanks for noticing.'

'No problem,' she says, 'It's good to stand out when you're single.'

'I'm here to support you, Faith,' I remind her, somewhat amused by her tactless comments, 'not to wow men with my footwear.'

'Can't you do both?' she asks. 'I mean, what about that guy? Green shirt. Looks reasonable.'

'Reasonable? Gosh, nothing but the best for your sister, eh? Faith, do you think we could have one evening without trying to marry me off?'

'Nope. Twelve o'clock. Look now.'

I reluctantly glance behind me towards Faith's imaginary clock hands before returning to my starting position with a sigh.

'Wedding ring,' I inform her. 'And if that's his wife sitting beside him, she could definitely take both of us in a fight. Everyone here is probably married, Faith. Give up.'

'Hey, I'm not married!' she replies, indignantly but we both know it won't be long before her boyfriend, Daniel, pops the question. 'Besides, people get divorced all the time, it doesn't hurt to lay the groundwork—'

'Next you'll be telling me to scope out potential widowers from the obituaries.'

She grins. 'Everything's an opportunity.'

I can't help but laugh. I know deep down Faith means well, but she's relentless. The thought that I could be perfectly happy alone is alien to her. She won't stop until I'm trussed up in white and hurtling down the aisle towards anyone with a pulse... and even that might be optional.

CHAPTER 7

On Saturday morning, Charlie announces that, despite it being my birthday, she absolutely and immediately must have new jogging trousers for school on Monday, even though she's spent the past three years not caring what she throws on her tiny backside for her thrice-weekly physical education.

'We can't do this tomorrow?' I ask, clicking the kettle on. 'I'm barely awake.'

She shakes her head. 'No, I have loads of homework to catch up on.'

'But I was going to make a fancy breakfast for us,' I complain, glancing at the pastries I had put aside from the café. 'Can we just go later?'

'You know how busy the mall gets on a Saturday,' she replies firmly. 'Come on, we hardly ever go shopping together. It'll be fun!'

It will not be fun. Charlie prefers to buy her gear online because clothes shopping with me frustrates her dark soul beyond belief.

'When have I ever worn a pink crop top, Mum? Or wedges. Have you met me?'

'Not everything has to black, Charlotte. Even Satan wore white at one point.'

She shiftily looks at her phone and I start to realise what's going on. She wants to get me out of the house. But why so early? Surely people have better things to do with their Saturday morning than gather in my flat and make me uncomfortable. Charlie's somewhat anxious face makes me reconsider my initial plan to be obstinate and ruin everyone's fun, so I smile and play along. Besides, I could buy myself some new concealer for the spot that has sprouted on my chin during the night. Even my skin is still stubbornly clinging on to its youth.

'Fine,' I reply. 'Give me half an hour to—'

'Fifteen,' she interrupts quickly. 'You have fifteen minutes.'

We take a drive out to Ocean Terminal, which sits right on the waterfront. It's only half past ten but I struggle to find a parking space. Why is it so mobbed? Is everyone having a surprise party?

Once inside, my suggestion to buy some good-quality gym trousers from a sports shop is met with a look of disdain as Charlie drags me towards New Look. If anywhere makes me feel old, it's New Look, a shop filled with teens, all dressed the same despite the wide range of clothing obviously available to them. This is clearly not the year of individuality. Charlie spots the leisurewear near the back of the store, and I follow behind.

'When I was in high school, we had to wear navy gym skirts with navy knickers underneath for PE,' I tell her as she grabs a pair of black jogging trousers off the rack. 'It was humiliating. Trampolining was just a mid-air blur of stretch-marked thighs and stray pubic hair.'

'Jeez, Mum,' she exclaims. 'The 1950s sound rough.'

I nudge her in mock offence and laugh. 'Our school was horribly old-fashioned but I'm not that ancient! See all that grunge shit that's coming back into fashion? My generation invented that. We ripped our jeans so *you ingrates* could enjoy the trend twenty years later.'

'Thank you for your service,' she replies, smirking. I smirk too, secretly thrilled that I have successfully raised such a cuttingly funny little smart-arse. Pretty sure she must get this from me, because her father is charming but not particularly funny. That should have been a red flag – who the hell wants to spend the next fifty years with someone who doesn't make them laugh? In my twenties, a silver convertible and West End flat were the more attractive draws in a relationship. These days, I'd overlook a lot for someone who really makes me laugh.

'We good here?' I ask Charlie as I pay for her trousers. 'Do you need anything else?'

She peeks at her phone, looking for an update. 'We don't need to go yet, do we? Wait, didn't you want to get makeup?'

My hand instinctively touches the blemish on my chin. 'I think I'll need a flamethrower for this beast. OK, we'll go to Boots and then home?'

'Sure, take your time.'

By the time we leave Boots, I've bought tea-tree oil, two different types of concealer, and a lipstick I don't need but claims to stay put for seventy-two weeks or something equally outlandish. Despite her ulterior motives, the hour Charlie and I have spent together has been really fun. Not the sitting-on-my-arse start to my birthday I had planned, but enjoyable none-theless.

We arrive home to a street as empty with cars as it was when we left. Unless Faith bussed a whole load of folk in, this is a good sign. Charlie throws a look up at our living room window before bouncing in front of me to open the door.

'Happy Birthday, Nora!'

Oh, thank God. I internally rejoice when I see that it is only Victoria and Faith standing in my living room, not everyone I've ever met or worked with and certainly not a surprise visit from Mum and her obnoxious husband, Darren. Saying that, I haven't seen Mum in twelve years, and she married Darren without telling anyone, including her own children, so nothing she does would surprise me anymore.

My living room is quite a spectacle. A bright pink fortieth-birthday banner hangs unevenly above the television, balloons and party streamers cover the entire floor while Cliff Richard croons 'Congratulations' from a tinny-sounding mobile phone. I bet Victoria chose this. She knows I hate it. Still, it could have been a lot worse.

Faith notices my look of confused relief.

'Ha, don't worry, sis!' she chirps, already halfway through a glass of champagne. 'I know you didn't want a big party.'

'I believe I didn't want *any* party—'

'But if you think you're turning forty on your own, you're mistaken,' she continues. 'You have the rest of the year to feel regretful about being an ageing human woman. Today is not that day. Charlotte, honey, can you bring some glasses?'

Charlie gives me a satisfied *this was all my idea* look before skipping off through balloons to the kitchen, leaving me alone with her co-conspirators.

'Fine,' I concede, dropping my bag beside the couch. 'This I can handle. Charlie tried so hard to pretend everything was normal, but I swear I thought she'd organised a bloody flash mob or something equally fussy.'

'But you should want a fuss!' Victoria insists, pointing to the vast amount of food they've laid on. 'I feel bad that you're not being whisked off to New York by some jet-owning billionaire. It's the least you deserve. Even Benjamin took me to Paris for my thirtieth... I mean, I'd rather have gone with you guys, but the thought was there.'

I smile. Victoria's been married to Benjamin for nine years and although she insists it's all just a great big bore fest, I know she'll be married to him for fifty more. There are women like my best friend and sister, who are destined for marriage, but I am not one of them.

'I like your earrings,' I reply, changing the subject. 'Are they new? I can't wear giant hoops. They make me look like a fortune teller.'

'H&M!' she replies. 'I accidentally shoplifted them, but I'm not sorry. They fell into a pair of boots I was also buying and well, here we are. I'm sure they'll recoup the massive £4.99 loss without laying staff off.'

Charlie returns to the living room with a wine glass for me and some orange juice for herself. I know that Faith will ask her if she wants a sip of champagne and Charlie will decline because she's the most sensible female in the room and then I'll tell Faith to stop offering my fourteen-year-old booze at noon and she'll scowl like I'm being unreasonably overprotective. I try to body-swerve this inevitable scenario by raising my glass before anyone else does.

'Thank you for organising this but—'

'What are you doing?' Faith interrupts. 'We haven't toasted you yet. Stop trying to get this over with. Charlotte, honey, you could have a little champagne with your orange juice if you like?'

'I'm fine, Aunt Faith.'

I bite my tongue as Faith smirks at me. I'm not playing.

'To my sister, Eleanora!' she begins. 'May the next forty years be filled with joy, laughter and a handsome man with a huge—'

'FAITH!'

'—wallet! I was going to say wallet!' But her face says otherwise.

Charlotte starts laughing like a drain, swiftly followed by Victoria. God, my sister is so inappropriate at times.

She throws her arms around me. 'Love you, sis. Happy

birthday.'

As Charlie and Victoria turn it into a tight, group hug, my no-birthday resolve starts to crack. Maybe I don't feel special enough to celebrate, but my family does. I feel physically squished but extremely lucky.

Charlie breaks her hold first and heads towards the food. I join her, pouncing on the mini samosas which smell incredible. Charlotte points out the items she's responsible for making with her own two hands, while Faith points out the food that she's responsible for buying from Waitrose. Victoria changes the god-awful birthday music to a playlist they've all collectively made consisting of songs that remind them of me.

'"Islands in the Stream"? Who picked this?'

Faith, already dancing, raises her hand.

'How on earth does this remind you of me?'

'That time we drove to the spa at Gleneagles. You don't remember?' She turns to Charlotte, who's currently making her way through the finger sandwich platter. 'Your mum was pregnant with you at the time and had bought me spa vouchers for my seventeenth birthday, so I dragged her and her *desperately in need of a pedicure* feet, along with me.'

I smile as I remember that day; it seems like a hundred years ago now.

'We had the most fun,' Faith continues. 'She was so excited to meet you, even though you'd been kicking the hell out of her for weeks. Anyway, I remember on the way home, watching your mum sing this song as she drove and thinking she was the absolute best person I knew and how lucky you were. I mean, she practically raised me, but you would get the honour of calling her Mum.'

Our eyes lock and my heart almost ruptures. Our own mother, Natasha, a very beautiful, half-Swedish interior designer, left the country when Faith was sixteen, but in reality, she'd been absent long before then. I was eight when Faith was born, ten when Dad died and twelve when I finally realised that Mum had no intention of doing any of this alone. Instead of taking care of us, her focus shifted to finding someone to take care of her. I lost count of the new 'uncles' we were introduced to, each one a little wealthier than the one before, until 'Dubai Darren' showed up and Mum found her older, overweight, egotistical millionaire in shining armour. He wooed my mother while I mothered my sister.

'Who even sings this?' Charlotte asks, her voice snapping me back to reality. 'It's so... ancient.'

'Dolly Parton and Kenny Rogers,' I reply, 'and the word you're looking for is *timeless*. This song will still be around long after Calvin Harris or DJ Shithead or whoever else blares from your headphones constantly.'

'There should be a DJ Shithead,' Charlie agrees, 'but I listen to Twenty-One Pilots. Nice try though.'

I used to know bands, I think to myself. Now I probably couldn't identify one song in the top 40. Do they even still have a top 40?

The track changes and I watch Victoria pull Charlie towards the middle of the floor, where Faith is still dancing. I hear the opening bars to 'Since U Been Gone' by Kelly Clarkson.

'And this one?' I ask. 'Who chose this?'

'You always used to play this when I was a kid,' Charlie replies, being spun around by Faith. 'You haven't in ages though, it's a good song!'

'It's a brilliant song,' I remark, nodding. I played this a lot after I broke up with Charlie's dad, Stuart. I stopped playing it when I stopped caring. I think the way to truly know when you're over someone is when love songs aren't about them anymore. I brush the food crumbs from my hands and join in the dancing, kicking balloons as I go. Despite not wanting any of this, I'm having a really great time.

A few songs later, we all collapse on the couch and give my neighbours some respite from the ceiling thumping they've had to endure.

'Aren't we going to do the presents?' Victoria asks. She bats a balloon towards Charlie who swats it away.

'But we haven't finished eating.' Faith replies, throwing Victoria a look, which instantly arouses suspicion. She gets up and grabs the large tray from the table. 'Sandwiches! Please, do eat. Waitrose do a lovely smoked—'

'What's going on?' I ask. 'Why are you being the weird sandwich lady?'

Faith looks at Victoria and then both look at Charlie, who stops mid-sandwich grab and smiles. Whatever this is, she's in on it too. I narrow my eyes, until she cracks.

'It was Aunt Faith's idea!'

'What was?'

Victoria lifts the gift bag from the side of the couch and places it on the coffee table. What the hell did they buy me? A blow-up boyfriend?

'This one first?' she says, handing me a small box wrapped in brown paper. It's too small to contain anything that requires a foot pump. Thank God.

To Mum, love Charlie x

'You didn't have to get me anything, sweetie,' I say, carefully removing the paper. This statement is true. All I require from Charlie is a daily hug, but the other two better have bought me something I can drink from a shot glass. Inside is a Body Shop travel set of almond milk toiletries. If walking from the living room to the bathroom constitutes travelling, I'm into this. 'I love it!' I gush. 'How thoughtful.'

Next, a slightly larger package is handed to me. It's squishy and obviously contains clothing – hopefully that red, fluffy jumper from ASOS I showed Victoria a few weeks ago. It isn't.

'Oh. Pyjamas!' I remark, holding them up in front of me. This is why she thought about the flannel pyjamas. But these are a soft pink satin, with frilly shorts and a matching camisole. It's November. These are the pyjamas of a much warmer woman who cares about how she looks like in pyjamas. My flannel days should have cleared up any confusion years ago.

'It makes a change from those old jogging trousers you wear to bed,' Victoria comments. 'I've seen them. Those things need to be binned.'

'They're beautiful!' I reply, and I'm not being insincere, but I don't see the point in looking fancy just to sleep alone. I want comfort, not a wedgie.

Finally, Faith hands me an A4-sized, official-looking envelope. It doesn't look remotely birthday-ish and it certainly isn't housing a bottle of tequila.

'Am I being served?' I enquire, staring suspiciously at it. 'Please don't give me a lawsuit for my birthday.'

'Just open it,' she insists. 'It's nothing like that.'

'... OK.'

'And don't freak out,' Victoria chimes in. 'Remember, we love you.'

'Oh God, WHAT IS THIS?'

'It's exactly what you need,' Faith asserts.

My finger slides under the fold and stops. I don't think I want to know. Are they having me adopted?

'Open it, Mum!' Charlotte bounces on her chair in anticipation as I take a deep breath and open the envelope.

Holistically Yours presents

ROMANCE REBOOT

(Friday 30th November – Friday 7th December)

Where even the most broken hearts can heal.

Dear Eleanora Brown,

Please find enclosed your travel and accommodation information for our exclusive six-day romance bootcamp retreat.

We look forward to meeting the old you.

I read the cover sheet twice because I'm not quite sure what I have in front of me.

Six-day bootcamp retreat.

Bootcamp?

I look up at Faith who is poised on the edge of her seat, fists clenched, practically pissing her pants, waiting for my reaction.

'What is this? A bootcamp? Like in the army? I don't get it?'

'Remember I called you from the toilet to tell you about that guy who was at the launch I was at?'

'Vaguely...'

'Well, the launch was for this company. They're huge in the States. Everyone is into that mindfulness stuff. You know, being present, paying attention to your feelings. They basically rewire your brain to think about love and relationships differently. For people like you who've become jaded with the whole relationship thing.'

'I think you mean realistic... so, what, they brainwash you for a week and then hand you a special drink? Who are you trying to set me up with? Charles Manson?'

She laughs. 'No, it's nothing like that! It's like a conference with workshops and meditation and roleplay and —'

'And nooooo, thank you.'

'I knew she wouldn't go for it,' Victoria says. 'Way too close-minded.'

'I am not!' I reply. 'I'm just not remotely *new age*. Besides, this is next week. I have a business to run and a child to look after!'

'All sorted,' Victoria responds. 'Tracey is covering your shifts and Charlie is staying with her lovely auntie Faith.'

Faith waves at me like I've forgotten who she is.

'Mum, I think it sounds really cool!' Charlie insists. 'It'll be like a little holiday. You can take your new toiletries!'

Ah, now it's starting to make sense. The new pyjamas, the travel shampoos – they're part of this plan. God, even my daughter wants to send me to cult camp. I take out the rest of the information from the envelope, but there isn't much: a separate sheet with travel and contact information for a place called Cairn Castle Lodges and an email address for the organisers. 'Where's the rest of the info? Oh God, is it some kibbutz in the middle of a field? Am I going to have to share a bathroom? Are there even bathrooms?'

'I would imagine so, given that it's the twenty-first century. Stop being such a drama queen.'

'Look, maybe this hippie stuff works for people who believe in it. I don't need to sit cross-legged in a forest clearing making "ohmmmming" noises in order to know myself.'

'It's much more leading edge than that,' Faith insists. 'They charge five grand for the bootcamp.'

'Five thousand pounds? Are you serious?'

'Yes, so it's hardly camper-van-loving tree huggers who'll be there. Apparently, Lady Gaga attended one in New York.'

'Don't you try and use my love of Gaga against me, although to be fair, for five grand I'd expect Lady Gaga to be included in the price. How the hell did you afford this?'

'I didn't.' Faith smirks. 'It's amazing what you can wrangle for free when you're very good at your job. But it's all arranged, and you cannot say no because they need equal numbers. I promised them you'd be there.'

I look at Victoria for help, but it's futile. They've made up their minds. I stare at the contents of the envelope again.

'I'll go on one condition,' I say. 'And you have to agree, otherwise I'll call them right now and cancel.'

They all nod in unison.

'I will go to this bootcamp, and I will chant the chants and drink the Kool-Aid and when I return, you will drop all of this.'

'All of what?'

'This idea you have that I'm not happy because I'm not with someone. I'm so tired of hearing it! And, Charlie: your part of the deal is that you cannot tell your dad where I am. I cannot bear the thought of him thinking I'm so dysfunctional, that I've had to seek professional dating help. I'm at a business conference, that's all you know.'

'You shouldn't care what Dad thinks,' Charlotte replies. 'But I wouldn't tell him anyway.'

'Do we have a deal?' I ask.

'Deal,' they respond, in unison.

'Fabulous,' Faith replies. 'Now, who's for pavlova?'

As she brings out the cake, with one large sparkly candle instead of forty and they begin singing 'Happy Birthday', my stomach is in knots. I feel like the control I've worked so hard to maintain has been ripped away from me. The thought of not knowing what the next week holds is terrifying. I don't want to navel gaze myself into oblivion with a bunch of strangers.

'Happy birthday, Mum,' Charlie says, and hugs me tightly. 'Love you.'

But most of all I don't want to leave Charlie for an entire week. Yes, she's fourteen and yes, she'll be fine... but it's not her I'm worried about. It's me. I'm not entirely sure who I am without her.

CHAPTER 8

With only a few days to plan and pack, I feel a tad shell-shocked when it's suddenly the morning of my trip. I don't feel ready for this at all.

'Ugh, don't get all weepy, Mum,' Charlie pleads, rolling her eyes. 'It's only for a few days!'

I lift my glasses and dab my eyes gently before turning to face her. She grins at me, flashing a mouth full of metal. 'You didn't get this emotional when you went to London for the week with Aunt Faith.'

'I did, you know,' I confess, sniffing. 'But I waited until I drove away... Did you remember to pack the elastic bands for your braces? Please don't break them while— Charlie, what are you fiddling with?'

'This stupid thing!' she replies, pointing to the keyring on her school bag. 'I hate this kind of keyring; I can't open the round bit.'

Charlotte's love of keyrings is obvious in the way she jangles like a jailer with every step she takes. She must have hundreds. As I lean in and help her pull apart the tiny metal rings, I notice her name tag on the inside of the bag.

Charlotte Jamieson. Broughton Grammar School.

I always feel a little odd, not having the same surname as my only child. Having to constantly correct teachers and doctors who assume I'm Mrs Jamieson never fails to remind me that at one point in my life, I assumed I would be too. Still, we have the same mouth, the same nose and even the same hands. She's undeniably mine and besides, Jamieson is better than *Brown*. Charlie Brown? No kid needs to be a ready-made cartoon character.

As we step outside, the morning breeze quickly dries the few tears which have defiantly escaped my eyes. Ugh, I don't want to be this needy. 'It's cold, honey. Did you pack your hoodie? Will you be alright with just one jacket?'

Charlie nods. 'I'll be fine, Mum, stop worrying. I feel like I should be checking if you're OK!'

I laugh. 'All mothers are like this, Charlie. We cry when you're not within cuddling distance for longer than six minutes.'

'That's embarrassing. I'm fourteen.'

'You are never too old for cuddles. Pretty sure that's the law.'

Charlie smirks. 'Fine, one cuddle now and one when I get to school. Deal?'

'Deal.'

I hug her tightly and kiss her cold cheek repeatedly, like a woodpecker. *Get a grip, Nora. You'll see her next week. It's only a bootcamp, not bloody war.*

'Um, I have to go, Mum,' Charlie says, trying to carefully peel me off. 'I don't want to be late. Our maths teacher gets annoyed if anyone arrives after she's taken registration.'

'I know, I know. I'm just getting my fix,' I reply. 'You won't be late.'

Charlie probably would have been quicker walking to school, given the traffic, but I want to drive her. I want to spend every second with her before I have to leave for this idiotic bootcamp.

Ten minutes later, I drive into the school car park as the first bell rings. It's filled with equally tired parents who lovingly boot their children out into the cold without stopping. Charlie unclips her seat belt and grabs her backpack.

'Have fun!' she says. 'You can phone me anytime, you know.'

'Since when did you become the mum?' I ask, as we both step out of the car and walk towards the gates. 'I'm supposed to say that to you.'

She leans into me, and I keep my word. One respectable hug, one cheek kiss and one great big joy-filled '*I love you, have a brilliant time with your Aunt Faith*' speech as she runs off into the school building. I take a deep breath. She'll be fine. Faith will spoil her, Tracey will make sure Victoria doesn't burn the café down and, after this week, I'll finally be free from the constant nagging and matchmaking. Everything will be fine.

I walk back to my car, trying to plan my day ahead; Faith took Charlie's suitcase last night, so all I have to do is tidy up and then, in a couple of hours, I'll be driving to a cabin on the outskirts of Loch Cairn. *Maybe a few days of no responsibility will be good for me*, I think as I pull on my seat belt. No work, no roadworks, just me and fifty strangers who clearly have too much money and time on their hands. I start the engine and turn on the radio. *One week*, I tell myself. *One week and I'll be back in Edinburgh and back with Charlie.*

It's 9.20am when I arrive home, still trying to shake the feeling that I might be about to embark on the most expensive week of self-centred, unscrupulous bullshit ever.

Where even the most broken hearts can heal.

I cringe. It's like a tagline from a Hallmark movie. My life is not a romcom and my perfectly functioning heart is not in need of repair. I'm already judging the people I imagine will be there: rich widows, socially awkward hipsters, yoga bores... Ugh, I bet there's an entire group of people who talk incessantly about juicing and coffee enemas.

I shuffle into my bedroom and peer into the suitcase on my bed, already filled with clothes I hastily packed last night. Comfy trousers, T-shirts, underwear, black suede heels... *Really, Nora?* From what I've seen online, the lodges are situated beside a small loch, surrounded by trees and rough gravel roads that even my car might struggle on, never mind my kitten heels. Surely my sturdy, all-weather boots will be more appropriate? *They'll probably make us walk about barefoot anyway,* I think, reluctantly throwing my heels back into the wardrobe – *barefoot and brainwashed.*

I slump down onto my bed and grab the very limited information sheet they've provided to see if they've mentioned anything about dress code or romantically conducive footwear, but of course there's nothing. It does, however, mention an end-of-bootcamp soiree on the final evening in the main house, *to celebrate your hard work and success.* I laugh. *Congratulations! You're now five thousand pounds poorer and still single. Have a vol-au-vent.* Still, at least my kitten heels are now back in the game. I remove them from my wardrobe along with my dependable little black dress, which hasn't seen the light of day since Charlie was six and Faith forced me to accompany her to some dull industry awards ceremony in the hope of setting me up with her colleague. Her colleague was a man called Rav who repeatedly said the word 'yeah' while I was speaking. He wasn't even listening to me; I could have been saying anything.

'So, I live in Broughton—'
'Yeah.'
'And my daughter—'
'Yeahyeahyeah.'

'...is the chosen destructor. Prepare to die.'

'Yeahyeahyeahyeah.'

On my dressing table, I spy my birthday gifts, still all unused and with tags on. I throw them into my case, thinking that if I take pictures of them in the cabin, Faith won't courier them up to me during the week in case I've made the horrific mistake of sleeping in an old T-shirt like the rest of the planet. I sweep the contents of my bathroom shelf into a plastic bag, zip my case shut and then spend twenty minutes sitting on the couch, giving myself a pep talk.

It has a hot tub, Nora. You like hot tubs!

There's bound to be one normal person to hang around with. Maybe someone else has a pushy family member and a pair of pink pyjamas hidden in their case.

Oh, for God's sake, Nora, it's a free trip and you don't have to serve anyone coffee for a week. So, you might be out of your comfort zone, but so what? Suck it up.

By 10.45am, my car has entered the A9 with Stevie Nicks blasting from the stereo, and I'm promising myself that if anyone tries to 'audit' me or cleanse my bowels, I'm leaving.

CHAPTER 9

Four hours later, my rickety grey Peugeot makes its way along an exquisite tree-lined driveway, and I catch a glimpse of the spectacularly imposing Cairn Castle. It's a huge grey-brick Baronial mansion which is most definitely home to at least one ghost and possibly a deranged housekeeper who'll make me wear the former mistress's clothing. Nerves rush through me and I begin to sweat, peering through the windscreen at the house ahead. What the hell am I doing? I'm forty years old and I'm about to spend the week with a bunch of singletons who have paid five grand to have some new-age wankers tell them they're worthy of love. I know I'm worthy, I just choose not to get involved with all the bullshit that goes along with it. If I wanted to date someone, I would! If I really wanted to fall in love and get my heart broken again, I'm perfectly capable of organising that without the help of a 'life coach' with a pseudo-degree in breathing in and out a bit slower than usual.

There's a road off to the left of the house, so I follow the signs for reception and Cairn Castle Lodges. As much as I'm against this whole ridiculous set-up, the idea of having a lodge with a private hot tub is very appealing, as is not having to wash clothes, iron, cook or be responsible for anyone else except me. No work. No school run. No boring bloody routine. No children. My thoughts stir a pang of guilt which forms a knot in my stomach. Charlie isn't a chore. She's the reason I have a routine and I wouldn't change it for the world. I know she was happy for me to go, but that's because she won't miss me half as much as I'll miss her.

I curse Victoria for putting this idea in everyone's head. She is the ringleader. She is the intervention stager. She is the one who will get an astoundingly awful Christmas present this year. In fact, everyone is cancelled, well... except Charlie. She's just grounded.

I pull into the car park and turn off the engine, rubbing my clammy paws over my jeans before looking at myself in the mirror and then immediately regretting my decision. This morning's makeup has evaporated, and my hair looks like it's harbouring a terrible secret. Thankfully, I'll have the rest of the evening to myself before I'll be forced to mingle with the great unloved tomorrow.

Alongside the car park, near the banks of the loch, stands a quaint, homely-looking reception and shop, with another small dirt road leading down to the right. Wooden lodges are dotted everywhere, all overlooking both the loch and the impressive mountains which surround it. I walk over to reception to book in, still feeling at odds with the week ahead but marginally better having seen the view I'll be admiring. It certainly beats having to look at my neighbour's ever-present wheelie bins and scattered fag ends.

The reception is at the back of a fully stocked and completely free store, which is heaving with everything from the essentials like bread and milk to junk food, health food, wine, local handmade gifts (available at an extra charge) and a huge pile of dry logs for the wood burners.

'Can I help you?' asks the young woman behind the

counter. I nod, reaching into my bag to find my booking details. She's wearing a dark green bodywarmer and riding boots, her hair tied up in a high, messy bun.

'I have a reservation,' I say, rummaging in my bag. 'Nora... Eleanora Brown... It's in here somewhere...' Soon my arms are elbow-deep in the lining of my large weekend holdall, tipping it in various directions. Red-faced and flustered, my fingers finally grip the invite and whip it out through the massive hole.

'Found it!' I exclaim. 'Sorry about that.'

'No problem,' she responds, like a woman who's just stepped in fox shit. 'One moment please.'

I watch as she inputs my details into the computer. Her name badge says Persephone, because of course it does. She oozes private school disdain. She is someone who owns a horse and has the phone number of at least two investment fund managers in her address book, while I must look like someone who once owned a budgie and sleeps in a hedge.

'Ah yes, you're here for the romance bootcamp,' she confirms, a little too loudly for my liking. 'Did you receive your welcome pack in the post?'

'Yes,' I mutter sheepishly. 'I'm all set.'

'You're in lodge thirteen. Follow the road to the right and your parking spot is numbered. Wi-Fi codes, log burner and hot tub instructions are all in your cabin, but we're here if you have any problems. Here is your site map, emergency number and your itinerary for the week. Have a great stay.'

Damn, her tone is ice-cold. She hands me an envelope and a key with an oversized wooden keyring attached and I'm certain that her parting smile is one of absolute pity. I'm tempted to explain that my friends (and daughter) forced me to come to this bootcamp and I am not some lonely, dusty desperado who can't get a man but given my current appearance, I decide to get the hell out instead, so she'll just stop looking at me.

Key in hand, I scurry back to my car and see a red sports car pull up beside me, its tyres crunching noisily on the gravel. Is everyone on earth more impressive than me? I watch as the driver jumps out and jogs into reception. He's tall, well-dressed, mid-thirties perhaps, and I see Persephone cock her head to one side as she chats to him. There's no way he's here for the same reasons I am. He's obviously here for some other event. Perhaps there's a 'Handsome as Hell' conference going on? Maybe he owns the place? But I see him take a key and head back out to his Porsche, while I pretend to look for something under my seat so he doesn't have to accidentally behold the Old Hag of the Loch.

I find lodge thirteen easily, noticing that every parking space in the neighbouring lodges is taken up with expensive cars, including Porsche man who's staying in number six. It would make sense that I would have the shittiest car given that there's no way in hell I could afford this under normal circumstances, but it doesn't stop me feeling like the poor scholarship kid from a boarding school novel. I want to call Victoria. She'd make me feel better and remind me that not giving a shit is one of life's greatest gifts. Unlike me, Victoria mastered this at the grand old age of twenty-one, regularly dismissing anything that doesn't benefit her existence. Like the time she broke up with a guy because he owned a parrot:

'I mean, he's a great guy, but those things live for eighty years. I just don't see that in my future.'

Once inside my cabin, I lock the door and begin investigating my new lodgings. I'm delighted. It looks exactly like it does on the website. It's small but perfectly formed: open-plan kitchen and living room, small double bedroom with en-suite bathroom and underfloor heating throughout. Double patio doors from the living room lead out onto the decking which looks over the loch, and has a barbeque area and a large, eight-person hot tub. This beautiful cabin might just make my stay here tolerable.

I place my case beside my bed and hang my coat in the wardrobe because when I'm not at home, I'm *tidy* Nora. The Nora who doesn't leave everything lying around, hoping that fairies will pick it up at a later date. I might even become *starts drinking before dinner* Nora, who knows.

It's already getting dark outside, but I step out onto the deck anyway to admire the view. The site map indicates that there are fifty cabins in total, which I'm assuming means forty guests plus staff will all be staring bemusedly at each other first thing tomorrow morning. I can see the glow of the hot tub lights from several cabins and hear a woman laughing in the distance. The loch is very still, almost eerie, making me fully aware that I'm a woman, alone, in a remote cabin by a lake with a pretty terrible phone signal. I might as well be wearing a T-shirt saying FINAL GIRL.

Slightly unnerved, I move back inside, lock the patio doors and connect to the Wi-Fi. If I'm going to be murdered out here, they can wait until I've made sure that Faith remembers Charlie's orthodontist appointment tomorrow. Her phone rings twice before she answers.

'Hey! Are you there already?'

I plop down on to the beige couch and kick off my boots. 'I just arrived. It's gorgeous,' I reply, feeling the warm floor through my socks. 'Spookily quiet though. Like Camp Crystal Lake but with accessible roads and internet.'

I hear her snigger before she covers the mouthpiece and yells at someone across the office. 'Sorry, it's crazy in here today.'

'I thought you were taking time off?' I almost yelp. 'What about Charlie?'

'Oh, relax, Eleanora,' she snaps back. 'I'm picking her up in half an hour. I just popped into the office to take care of something. And no, before you say it, I haven't forgotten she has the orthodontist tomorrow.'

'I didn't think you had!' I reply, totally thinking that she had. 'I was only checking in. Tell Charlie to call me later?'

She agrees and hangs up, leaving me with only my warm feet for company. I don't quite know what to do with myself, it's pathetic.

I turn on the television for background noise and take the itinerary out of the envelope, curious to see what lies ahead.

Meditation with Brad, Healthy Dating Workshop, Group Healing, Manifestation & Visualisation, Eye Energy Transfer, Redefining Love, Affirmation Workshop

The list goes on and on. What the hell have I let myself in for? Who the hell is Brad? What exactly is Eye Energy? Oh God, I feel a bit sick. It seems intense – 9am to 5pm every day with a couple of breaks and there's even a mentor thrown in for one-to-one support. Why the hell would I need individual support? What are they going to do to me? It won't be long until I find out as the first class, 'Welcome to the New You', is at 9am tomorrow in the main house. I hope the new me has a smaller arse.

CHAPTER 10

BOOTCAMP: DAY 1

My alarm goes off at 7.30am.

There's a small chink in the bedroom blinds but it's still dark outside, the morning silence only interrupted by the stirring of birds and a breakfast van dropping off its continental contents outside the door of each cabin.

I switch off my alarm, text Charlie good morning then count to five before throwing back the covers, reluctant to leave this very expensive, very comfortable bed.

How bad can it be, really? I think, my feet slipping into a pair of complimentary flip flops. I'll simply show up, participate and then scurry back here to binge my way through the seven hundred true crime documentaries on my phone. It'll be fine. *Think of it as a holiday, Nora, everyone deserves a holiday.*

I take a quick shower and throw on one of the heavy white bathrobes before retrieving my breakfast from outside the door, delightfully presented in a small, woven picnic basket. I'm not particularly hungry yet, but don't want to be the phantom stomach growler in a hall full of strangers. I force myself to demolish a croissant before taking my coffee out onto the deck to admire the view because that's what people do in the movies.

I can hear the rumble of next door's hot tub running but the cabins are cleverly positioned so that no one can see each other, for which I'm grateful. No one needs to view me flailing around in last year's swimsuit. I attempted to work my hot tub last night before discovering that lifting a heavy lid on my own in the dark was trickier than expected. It's ironic that I've come on a singles' retreat which requires two people to access the fun stuff. I'll tackle it again after dinner when I can see what I'm doing. As beautiful as the view is, I last approximately four minutes in the cold morning air with no knickers on before retreating inside.

Deciding that jeans and a T-shirt are a good option for the first morning, I pull my hair back into a high ponytail, praying that everyone else won't turn up in yoga pants and crab-walk past me while I stand there looking like a frumpy soccer mom. I pull on my coat, leave the cabin and start the ten-minute walk to the main house. I'd preferred to have driven but according to the literature, the walk will *help remove any morning worries or negativity*. I could argue that walking anywhere makes me intrinsically more negative, but I'm not looking to cause trouble on my first day.

I stick in my earbuds and begin plodding up the road, noticing at least ten other guests doing the same. Perhaps Nirvana isn't the chilled vibe I should be aiming for, but I'm going with it. Charlie always makes fun of my musical tastes, despite the fact we share a lot of the same tracks on our playlists, but I get it. A song instantly becomes less cool when your mum sings along.

Thankfully, there's not a yoga-panted arse in sight; in fact, everyone is dressed relatively normally – hoodies, jeans, skirts, boots – except the one guy in a fedora. Well, there's always one. The only thing that hints at the calibre of the guests are the handbags. I've never seen so much designer leather in my life.

We all nod politely at each other, some listening to music, some striking up conversations with whoever is closest, and by the time we reach the main house, we join the others inside the main doors. It's a varied group, from late twenties to fifties, lots of lip fillers and brow work and certainly not the new-age, socially awkward undateables I was expecting.

The entrance lobby of the house is stunning. A huge white staircase to the left, polished wooden floors, fresh flowers in every corner and an archway to the right where a woman in her thirties with shiny brown hair stands, beaming at everyone.

'A warm welcome to you all. My name is Miranda. If you'd all like to follow me through to the hall please, we can get started.'

Miranda has clearly never met a workout she didn't like. Even through her heavy jumper, I can still see her abs. It's times like this where I wish I'd followed through with that plan I had to go to Zumba once, back in 2010. She bounds off through the archway and we all follow, sucking in our stomachs.

As I walk into the main hall, I spot a podium at the front with a large projector screen, displaying the company logo and white chairs set out in rows, each with a notepad and pen on the seat. To the side are tea and coffee machines, bottled water and what looks like sandwiches and finger foods all neatly laid out and covered in clingfilm. I watch as the seats fill up quickly, some people scrambling to get near the front. I choose to sit near the back where I won't be picked on to participate in anything weird. I spot an empty chair between a woman in her fifties wearing a patchwork skirt and a man in a polo shirt with a heavy beard and plonk myself down, placing my notepad and pen on my lap. I tighten my ponytail and breathe a sigh of relief. My anxiety was for nothing. I'm here. It's fine. So far so—

'This is a nightmare. Even being in the same room as you makes me want to vomit.'

I turn towards the direction of the growling voice to see patchwork woman looking furious. But she's not looking at me. She's looking through me to the bearded man on my right.

'Did you do this on purpose, Kenneth?' she continues. 'How did you know I'd be here? Did Patrick tell you? I knew I shouldn't have mentioned it to his bloody wife. I cannot *believe* you came to this.'

'I did not know you'd be here, Patricia,' he whispers harshly, leaning across me. I'm so uncomfortable right now, I want to leave. I look around for a spare seat, but they're all taken. There's no escape.

Kenneth shakes his head. 'It's a coincidence – a horrible bloody coincidence.'

Patricia makes a *pfft* sound and crosses her arms, mumbling, 'I hate your beard.'

'Yeah, well, your legs imply that I'm not the only one who gave up shaving after the divorce—'

Before they can continue, plinky-plonky music can be heard from the speakers at the side of the stage and Enya becomes the reason this argument stops and the bootcamp begins. I've never been so grateful to hear 'Orinoco Flow' in my life.

As a tall woman in a peach dress steps on to the stage to a huge round of applause, I quickly check the day's schedule to see who she is.

Anna Adams. Clinical hypnotherapist, counsellor and holistic healer. Originally from Alabama, Anna has been working with clients from all over the world since 2001.

Has she now? I think, half-heartedly joining in the applause. That's a long time to bullshit for a paycheck...

'Thank you, you're very kind,' she declares, walking across the floor like she's hosting a TED Talk. In the corner of the room behind her, I notice five people, all busy checking through papers and working on laptops, including Miranda and the handsome man in the Porsche I saw at reception when I arrived. He works here?

'Welcome to the Romance Reboot! The first we've held in Scotland. We're all so thrilled that you've chosen to join us this week.'

I continue to look down the list of support staff running the bootcamp, starting with handsome face.

Brad Hyde. Counsellor, life coach and yoga mentor.

Miranda Grant. Life coach and meditation instructor.

Lewis Crow. Life coach and holistic massage specialist.

Claire Dalton. Life coach and energy healer.

Sally Foster. Administrator and personal assistant.

As I sit there wondering what the hell a life coach does, Anna continues speaking.

'Now, I realise it wasn't easy for some of y'all to come here but let me reassure you that if you put the work in, it'll be one of the most important weeks of your lives.'

That's a bold claim, I think while everyone applauds themselves for being brave enough to attend a luxury retreat. I like Anna's accent though. It's very endearing. I can see why people might pay to hear her speak.

'Nine years ago, I found myself twice divorced and finished with love at the age of forty-one,' Anna proclaims, adjusting her little radio mic. 'I didn't see the point in pursuing another relationship, when every single one I'd been part of had failed. I was exhausted thinking about love, exhausted wondering why other people managed to maintain meaningful relationships, yet I couldn't. I concluded that some people just don't get to be romantically fulfilled, and I was one of them. And I can see from looking around this room, that this resonates with a lot of you. You too are one of those people who doesn't get to be happy, right?'

There's a murmur of agreement, combined with a sudden coughing fit from a man in the third row.

'There's over seven billion people in the world,' she continues. 'Sixty-six million in the UK and five million in Scotland, yet you're still alone. Why? Why do you think that is?'

She points to a man in a black T-shirt. 'You, sir. Why are you single?'

He shifts uncomfortably in his chair. *This* is exactly why I didn't sit near the front.

'I'm not sure...' he replies, shrugging. 'I just am.'

Anna smirks and walks over to stand beside him. 'Honey, every single person in this room has a theory on why they're single – hell, I had more than one! Let's see; I was too independent, too emotional, too weird, my chin was too pointy, even my hair was too frizzy. But now, here I am, married again and happy as hell. I didn't change my face and, as you can probably tell, I didn't change my hair; all I changed was *my mind*. Now you've been smart enough to come here, be bold enough to start your journey.'

'Um...' he begins, his face now flushed.

'Yes?'

'Well... I guess, all the good women are taken.'

She high-fives him.

'We have our first reason! Though, I'm pretty sure every single woman in this room would disagree, but yes! All of the good ones are taken. Who's next? You. Lady in the yellow scarf.'

'I'm not conventionally "attractive",' she replies hesitantly, air-quoting the word attractive.

'In what way?'

'I'm fat.'

'Good!' Anna exclaims. 'Let's keep this going. Next!'

And with that, the entire room starts revealing the reasons they're single, some even shouting out without being prompted.

'I can't find anyone good enough for me!'

'I have a dodgy leg!'

'I'm ugly!'

'I only attract arseholes.' (That one was Patricia.)

'Men only want sex!'

'I'm too busy to meet anyone.'

'I get bored quickly.'

I'll give Anna credit. In only half an hour she's managed to whip a relatively quiet room into a frenzy; people yelling and laughing, even hugging, until finally everyone has vented. Well. everyone except me, because I'm not here for the same reasons they are. I'm not single because there's something wrong with me, I'm single because I choose to be.

Anna gestures to everyone to quieten down. 'Those reasons you gave – you're absolutely right, those are the reasons why you are single.'

At least half of the people in this room now look horrified, the rest mildly offended.

'You see, it doesn't matter whether those reasons are true or not because y'all *believe* them. You tell yourself the sky is green for long enough, you'll start to believe that too. Keep saying *no one loves me* over and over, that's exactly what you'll get. You manifest exactly what you think about. The universe doesn't understand sarcasm, or wit or nuance. You say *I'm too ugly to find love*, the universe will say "OK". You say, *I only attract assholes*, the universe will say, "Cool, here's another asshole". You see, in every aspect of our lives, we get what we think about, and love is no different. If you continually think about what you don't have, that's exactly what you'll get. This week we're going to teach you how to attract what you want by believing you already have it. We're going to teach you how to reprogram your subconscious to shift your paradigm. Think you can't be loved? We're *literally* going to change your mind!'

While everyone else applauds, cheers and whoops, I look for the emergency exits. The universe? Paradigms? Reprogramming?

What on earth has Faith signed me up for?

CHAPTER 11

After a coffee break in which three-quarters of the bootcampers go outside to smoke, we're divided into four groups of ten, consisting of five men and five women. I'm in Group Two.

'This will be your team for the week,' Anna explains, while everyone assembles at their designated area. 'Each team has been allocated a mentor who will work with you individually and collectively throughout the bootcamp. Of course, you'll still be participating in larger group activities, but consider your group your family for the week.'

That might not be so terrible, I think, sending Charlie yet another message she won't reply to. I'll be looking to replace Faith with a better sister anyway, when I get home from this circus. I place my phone back into my bag and smile civilly at the rest of Group Two. They just stare back at me. My new family appears to be mute.

'Nora,' I pipe up, breaking the ice. 'Lovely to meet you all.'

'Hi, Nora,' they all reply in unison. God, this feels like an AA meeting. As we go around the group, I learn that my new female family members are Allison, middle-aged redhead; divorced Patricia, blonde, last seen insulting her ex-husband's beard; Jillian, dark hair, darker eyes; and Meg, pink ombre hair, has a 'welcome to my channel' YouTube vibe about her. While my male siblings are Paul, middle aged, bald, man jewellery; Tim, early sixties, looks startled and also like a potato – a thin-lipped potato; Russell, fedora owner; Will, tall, dark hair, dishevelled; and Nish, cute face, reminds me of a guy I went to school with whose name escapes me.

'I wonder who our life coach is?' pink-haired Meg chirps, looking around. She appears bubbly and confident, but the way she's nervously picking her nail varnish, leaving tiny white specks on her black skirt, makes me think otherwise. I'm guessing she's in her early thirties, perhaps younger; it's hard to tell under the sheer volume of makeup she's wearing. I'm not entirely sure when the go-to makeup look became Drag Queen Chic but it's hard to find someone under forty who isn't contoured to within an inch of their life before they leave the house.

'I think it's that guy walking towards us,' Nish replies, his gaze lingering on Meg for a little too long. I turn to see Brad striding towards us, his biceps like baseballs, and I silently groan. His face looks like it's been sponsored by Armani. How the hell am I supposed to concentrate with THAT all up in my business? This is probably how Nish is feeling about Meg.

'Hello, everyone. I'm Brad. Everyone well?'

His accent is also American, but not Southern like Anna. California, perhaps? I nod to indicate my wellness, while everyone else is able to form actual words. What the hell is wrong with me?

'Great!' he replies, pulling over a chair. WITH THOSE ARMS. *Oh, for God's sake, Nora, calm down, you've seen arms before.*

'My role here is simple. As a life coach, my job is to help and encourage you to make changes in your life. I'm not a thera-pist, so I won't be making you lie down and tell me about your childhood, but I will be inviting you to look at past behaviours and patterns which have brought you to where you are now. I also teach yoga, eye energy transfer, mindful dating techniques and—'

'Do we have to participate in yoga?' Tim interrupts. 'I'm really not too fond of that idea.'

'Yoga and meditation are powerful allies,' Brad replies. 'Calming your body and mind is essential to raising your vibration. We'd highly recommend you don't skip either unless it's for medical reasons?'

Tim shakes his head in defeat. I feel bad for him. He's obviously the oldest in the group and it must be intimidating. My initial reaction is to spring out of my chair and remind Brad that we do not live in North Korea, and we are free to do what we want! But on the other hand, I want Brad to love me one day, so screw you, Tim.

'Great, then your first meditation session is in the room opposite, if you'd like to follow me?'

I nod again and watch him walk towards the door. As I rise from my seat, I hear a voice say, 'You can put your tongue back in now.'

I turn to see Will smirking at me.

'Excuse me?'

'Our life coach?' he replies. 'Listen, no judgement. I'm straight as an arrow and even I'm rethinking my preferences. But you might want to make it less obvious.'

Wow. Is everyone here as blunt as he is?

'I have no idea what you're talking about,' I insist, manoeuvring around him to catch up with the others, but my burning cheeks tell a different story. I scurry away, mortified.

We meet up with Group One in a smaller room, empty except for a plush red carpet, floor cushions and the distinct aroma of sandalwood. Brad instructs us all to remove our shoes before he leaves and closes the door behind him. The first woman we met, Miranda, fiddles with a sound system at the front of the room.

'Welcome, everyone,' she says, 'I'll be leading our love-focused guided meditation this morning. If you're new to meditation, don't worry. It may take you some time to be able to clear your thoughts, but with regular practice, this will come. Please find a comfortable position and we'll begin. If you need to use a chair for back support, please feel free to collect one from the front.'

Several people scurry to the front for a chair, including Patricia who mumbles something about *not sitting cross-legged with an effing skirt on*, but I can handle sitting on a cushion with my eyes closed for half an hour. I see Will, who cautiously moves towards me, looking awkward.

'Erm... listen... back there, I didn't mean to make you uncomfortable. Just trying to break the ice. I have no idea how these things work.'

'You didn't make me anything,' I lie, 'but maybe just open with *hello* next time.'

He scrunches up his face. 'Yeah, sorry. My sense of humour isn't for everyone. Can we start again?' He extends his hand. 'Will Thomson. Happy to meet someone who perhaps feels as out of place as I do?'

'Is it that obvious?' I reply, thawing slightly as my hand meets his.

'Hmm, a little,' he replies. 'It's not a bad thing. Listen, if you—'

'Let's go, everyone!' Miranda insists. 'Places please.'

'Better get on with this,' I say, 'but apology accepted.'

Will gives me a small nod of gratitude, before lying down and resting his head on the cushion.

'We don't recommend lying down,' Miranda informs him. 'It's far too easy to fall asleep.'

'I'm fine with that,' he replies, but she stares at him until he reluctantly assumes a sitting position. Once everyone is ready, Miranda sits crossed-legged on her own cushion and clicks play on a small remote.

'OK, nice straight spine, eyes closed and deep breath, everyone. In for four through the nose, out for four through the mouth...'

The sound of trickling water and pan pipes fills the room as people whoosh air out of their bodies.

'And again. In for four... out for four...'

'*Whoosh.*'

Well, this is utterly ridiculous and not remotely comfortable. I try to focus.

'Just breathing out all that negativity and focusing on this moment. There is nothing but this moment.'

Someone's nose is making a whistling sound. Oh God, is it mine?

'With every breath, you're going deeper. Allow any thoughts to come and go.'

I wonder what Charlie is doing right now. I hope she has lunch money in her account, I can't remember if I topped it up.

'As you begin breathing normally, imagine a lavender-coloured light beaming down from the ceiling directly into your head.'

Hang on, what?

'This beautiful light travels down through your head, your neck, your shoulders...'

Why is it lavender? That's very specific.

'All the way down through your body, so relaxed now.'

Lavender's blue, dilly-dilly...

This is useless and now these water sounds are making me want to pee. I shift position and take another deep breath. Why can't I bloody relax like a normal person?

'Imagine yourself walking through a garden, filled with beautiful flowers and—'

Wasps. Thousands of wasps. No. Focus, Nora.

'Feel the soft grass under your feet. Appreciate the beauty of nature. Thank the universe for providing you with such a magnificent canvas to—'

Still need to pee.

I open one eye a little and look around the room. Everyone is perfectly still and perfectly quiet and obviously far more experienced in meditation that I am. Until I see Will scratch his head and check his watch. He catches me looking, makes his fingers into a gun shape and pretends to blow his own brains out. I smirk, grateful someone else isn't getting this. I feel slightly less of an uncultured prick now.

As Miranda goes on to ask us to imagine meeting our ideal partner in the now wasp-infested garden of my mind, I realise that this bootcamp is going to be every bit as weird as I anticipated.

Let's hope the universe has provided gin.

CHAPTER 12

I leave my first meditation session feeling completely demoralised, while everyone else seems to be gushing over how relaxed and centred they feel. Either they're lying or their heads were empty to begin with. All I feel is slight backache and bladder pressure. I head towards the bathroom at the end of the corridor and avoid eye contact with the women inside, shutting myself in a cubicle. The bathrooms are as lovely as the ones in the cabins, with marble worktops, polished wood floors and pristine cubicles which smell like almonds.

'What do you have next?' I hear someone ask. The sound of hairspray can be heard clanking on the marble sink area.

'Cosmic ordering,' a voice replies. 'Should be interesting. Ask and ye shall receive... I think everyone is participating in this.' I hear voice number one check her itinerary and agree.

I pee and roll my eyes at the same time. Cosmic bloody ordering. I remember when cosmic ordering was all the rage a few years ago. People thought you could ask the universe for a new car and the universe would have bugger all else to do except ensure you got that shiny black Mercedes with heated seats.

I exit the cubicle and realise that the first voice was Allison from my group. She's openly vaping while she types on her phone, despite the no smoking sign on the wall behind her, but she's not the only one. I count four women puffing on their e-cigarettes, while applying makeup or sorting their hair. I feel like I'm back at high school, only no one is keeping edgy for the teachers.

Hands washed in peach blossom soap, I make my way towards the main hall, where everyone is taking their seats again. Determined not to be stuck between Patricia and Kenneth again, I sit near the back at the end of a row. I have a good view of the grounds from here, overlooking a huge boating pond at the back of the house. The trees are bare and perennial flowers are scattered intermittently but I imagine in spring, this garden becomes something quite spectacular. It's like a location from a Jane Austen novel and it's strange to think that this was once someone's home. Someone woke up to this view every morning. I hope they appreciated it as much as I do.

The buzz in the room is quite different from when we first arrived, groups of people laughing or deep in conversation, and I seem to be in the small minority of people not engaging with the rest of the guests. One meditation and now they're all BFFs? I take out my phone and check my messages, determined to appear busy rather than unsociable. I have two new messages. One from Charlie.

Hi mum! I'm good! Ttyl x

And one from Faith.

Café is fine. Charlie is fine. Stop pestering us, woman.

I smirk and place my phone back in my bag, just as Anna appears back at her little podium.

'Well, I hope you're all relaxed after meditation,' she says, smiling. 'I want your mind as clear as possible for this next task, as it's an important one. Cosmic ordering. Take out your notebooks.'

We all obey, turning to a blank page, awaiting further instruction like good little sheep while Anna waits.

'Show of hands please if you keep dating the same person over and over?'

There's a confused silence among the audience with only one man raising his hand cautiously in the front row. Anna laughs. 'Let me put it another way. These people may have different names and faces and jobs, but they bring the same issues or problems?'

More hands start to shoot up.

Anna starts to strut around the stage. 'You find yourself thinking, "Why can't I meet someone great? I know what I want, but I keep getting let down or bored after a few weeks or something seems to be missing?" You're just really unlucky in love.'

By now, almost everyone's hand is up. Mine isn't. In the past decade I've probably dated for a total of seven hours, hardly long enough to draw comparisons. Though they *have* all had dark hair...

'*This*, ladies and gentlemen, is the reason.'

She taps her laptop and gestures to the screen behind her which is now displaying the words WHEREVER YOU GO, THERE YOU ARE.

'The problem isn't that you're unlucky, the problem is *you*. If you keep approaching relationships with the same mindset, and patterns of belief but expect a different outcome, you'll never get what you want.'

There's a collective *ahhh*ing in the audience and for the first time, I join in. It's a good point. Not relevant to me of course, but credit where it's due.

'Now, I know you've all heard the old cliché "How can you expect someone to love you if you don't love yourself?"'

Anna clicks this up on to the screen behind her and reads it again.

'I can guarantee, some of y'all aren't very kind to yourselves, am I right? The love and affection you show others, doesn't apply to you. Raise your hands if you have children.'

I raise mine without thinking, but thankfully she picks on someone else.

'Lady in the pretty green sweater. What's your name? OK, Kathy, how would you feel if you knew that your child felt that they'd always be alone? For whatever reason, they weren't loveable?'

'I'd be horrified,' Kathy replies, placing her hand on her heart.

'Why?' Anna asks.

'Because she's wonderful!' she answers. 'She deserves all the happiness in the world.'

'But why? Is she an exceptionally gifted child? Earth-shatteringly beautiful? What makes her so superior, that she deserves *all* of the happiness in the whole darn world?'

Even though I can only see the back of Kathy's head, I can hear how perplexed she is. If Anna had asked me this about Charlie, I would have replied that she's the greatest human being ever made, and I will fight anyone who disagrees. But Kathy is less of a maniac.

'No... not exactly... um... well, she deserves it because I love her so much. I want the best for her.'

'EXACTLY!' Anna yells, making half of the audience jump. 'You are all capable of so much unconditional love but only when it's not pointed in your direction! Take even a small fraction of that love and keep it for yourself. You too are someone's child, and you are just as deserving as your own.'

Oh God, I think Kathy is crying.

'We are all spiritual beings having a human experience and human beings need love. We need comfort. We need to connect. Why on earth would any of you be somehow excluded from this? Tell yourself, every day, that you are worthy! That you are beautiful! That you are enough! Tell everyone!'

'I am enough!

'I am beautiful!'

People are standing and declaring their worth. Oh, sweet lord, is this really happening? In Scotland? People here don't behave like this. We don't have sudden outbursts of self-esteem, declaring how great we are, unless football – or whisky – is involved. We're the ones who'll tell you to *sit doon* and then make fun of you until you regret ever being born. People are hugging now. Is this the part where we all sing a hymn or something? Will Anna make that man with the cane walk without a limp next?

'By the end of this bootcamp y'all are going to love yourselves so much that anyone else loving you is just gravy. Now, I want you all to draw a circle in the middle of your page, like this.' Anna points to the screen behind her, displaying a circle, in case we were confused about simple shapes. 'And inside the circle, write "My Ideal Partner".'

I hear faint mumbling as everyone proceeds to draw, including me. I wonder if I can just stick a photo of Brad in mine and toddle off for lunch.

'Now we all have a physical type, don't we? Tall, thin, dark, curvy, blonde, etc. but that's not what I want you to focus on. I want you to focus on their character traits for now, not their physicality.'

I can see a few of the men slink down into their seats and I don't find their reaction unreasonable.

'Relax, fellas, you'll get to add in the vital stats later,' Anna informs them with a wink, and they all laugh before resuming a more upright posture. Ugh, they're so predictable.

'Now I want you to imagine that the circle is the sun and from it, you'll draw rays, each one representing a quality you want from a partner. You'll see examples here: on this ray, I've written kindness, on this I've written sense of humour, this one says ambition and so on, you get the idea.'

People are already scribbling. What are they writing? I've never put much thought into what I want from a partner, yet everyone else seems to have some sort of checklist.

'Remember, be specific. If you want someone who loves animals or goes to the gym every day or writes poetry, then include it. If it matters to you, it goes on the sunray. You wouldn't order something from Amazon and just ask for whatever! You'd be specific about your order, so be specific here.'

I look down at my rayless sun. I have no idea what I want from a boyfriend because I don't bloody want one. Besides, you can't just invent a frickin' person. I could write 'has a library of over four thousand books and lives in a houseboat near a Tesco Express' but that doesn't mean he actually exists. This is pointless but I guess could have a little fun with it...

Sponsors children in Africa. All of them.

Is disgustingly wealthy and likely to hand it over in large bundles.

Has siblings with ridiculous names like Beetroot and Windfarm.

Shags like a champion/is actual shagging champion, has many awards.

How is anyone supposed to take this seriously? Everyone wants someone who's kind and funny, smart but not pompous, warm and loving, but most of all, all anyone wants is someone to watch box sets with.

Time ticks on and I manage to throw a few platitudes onto my sheet of paper. I watch people consider every word they write with such resolve that it makes me a little envious. Hope must be a wonderful thing.

'How are we all doing?' Anna asks. She's spent the last five minutes whispering to Brad. I start to idly wonder if they're having an affair, for no reason other than it's more interesting than ordering an imaginary man via sunbeams.

'Great. Now, hold on to these and work on them during the week. You can make as many versions as you need to before we release them on our last day.'

Release them? Like doves? Like hounds? Like little paper inmates? I'm scared to ask.

'We're going to stop for lunch now and resume again at half past one. We have provided a cold buffet for those who would prefer to remain in the main house or hot food is available at reception which you can take to your cabin. Thank you all.'

I have no intention of hanging around to chat, I'm going to be stuck with these people all week. I grab my bag and make for the door with the sole mission of getting back to my cabin to finish off the rest of my breakfast basket.

It's bright but bitterly cold outside as I trudge back down the hill towards my cabin. I see people with handfuls of finger food strolling off towards the east side of the loch, but I continue north, happily embracing my 'me' time.

'Not in the mingling mood either, I see?'

I turn to see Will a few steps behind me, pulling on a pair of gloves. I wish I'd had the foresight to bring some, my hands are freezing.

'Not really,' I reply coolly as he catches up. 'I just need some respite from all the... well, weirdness.'

'Likewise,' he responds. 'I don't think I've ever felt like such an outsider in my entire life.'

'Yup,' I reply. 'I think I'm far too rooted in reality to be a viable team player here.'

As he grins, little dimples form in his cheeks which softens his increasingly attractive, chiselled face. He is not well-groomed, unlike most of the other men here, and I have no doubt that he literally rolled out of bed and came straight to the welcome meeting. His salt-and-pepper stubble places him around my age, but the Joy Division T-shirt he's wearing under his jacket implies that he's mentally the same age as Charlie.

'Yeah, I thought you looked a bit bewildered in there,' he says, nodding. 'You don't seem like the type of person who'd go to one of these events.'

'Why?' I ask. That insecure feeling I had earlier is now making an unwelcome return. It's my lack of designer everything, isn't it? Do I look like I've been crowdfunded to come here?

'I dunno,' he replies. 'You just seem too normal.'

For some reason, this feels like the worst compliment anyone has ever been paid. *Normal. Unexciting. Ordinary.*

'Well, you don't look like you belong here either,' I snap back. 'Everyone else brushed their hair.'

Way to go, Nora! Offend the only person remotely interested in talking to you on day one. Good job!

He holds his hands up, surrendering. 'Woah, relax. It's a good thing. I saw you sniggering while you were cosmically ordering your ideal partner. It comforted me to know that I had a fellow doubter.'

'Sorry,' I quickly reply. 'It's been an odd morning. But you're right. I don't belong here. Long story, but this was a birthday gift from my family.'

'Why does your family hate you?'

I laugh. 'My sister works for the PR firm handling this.

They needed to make up numbers, the birthday part was just coincidental. I'm very happy being single, they just can't accept it.'

We pass by the reception which is starting to fill up with guests looking for lunchtime sustenance. The smell of home-made soup wafts from the open front door, revealing a flustered-looking Persephone in a brown apron.

'Weirdly enough, I am also here for free,' Will replies. 'Though it wasn't my birthday. My editor paid for me to come. Eight hundred words on what it's like to attend the exclusive new-age love bootcamp that's taken America by storm.'

'Who do you write for?' I ask, rubbing my hands together for warmth.

'*Incel Quarterly*.'

'Very funny.'

'I write for lots of different publications but this one is for *FMQ*.'

I make an impressed face. It's one of the better-known men's magazines. 'The interview they did with Bill Gates was excellent. Very probing.'

He nods. 'Not one of mine but yeah, it was. They have a fascination with self-made millionaires, like the CEO of this set-up, Larry Wilde. I hear he's insufferable and smells like sandal-wood. Look, you're the only one who knows I'm undercover here and I'd like to keep it that way.'

'Sure, Will,' I reply, 'if that's even your real name...'

'It is... though you can call me "staff writer" throughout these proceedings.'

'This is me,' I say, pointing at my cabin. 'Lucky thirteen.'

'I know,' he responds, smirking. 'I'm next door. I saw you freezing your ass off in your dressing gown earlier.'

'Oh, for goodness' sake. I thought no one could see into the hot tub area!'

'You can't, the tubs are lower level, but the decking is a free for all. Anyway, neighbour, I'm going to eat and grab a drink. Fancy coming in for a quick beer?'

'Um... no, I'm good,' I say. *Strange man I've only just met*, I add in my head, edging towards my house. Why on earth would I follow him into his cabin for afternoon booze that he might have spiked? Hasn't he ever seen *Law & Order: SVU*? He notices my reluctance.

'Good God, woman, I'm just being friendly! Look, I think it'll be a long, boring week without someone to trash-talk with. I say we buddy up and get through this as unscathed as possible.'

'Erm...'

He shrugs. 'Think about it... but not for too long, we're only here for a week. I don't want to see you in my rear-view mirror, chasing my car, yelling "I ACCEPT YOUR OFFER", while I'm driving out of your life for good.'

He's insane, but I can't help but be impressed by his bravado. And his dimples.

'Right, I'll see you back at the manor for round two,' he continues. 'We're covering *gratitude scripting* and more meditation. I'm so excited, you have no idea.'

Without waiting for a response, Will walks off, talking to himself. 'Yep, so very excited. Fifteen years in journalism to spend a week chatting to the bloody universe.'

I make my way inside, laughing. I have no idea what to make of him, but I'm not unhappy that we've met. Maybe this week won't be so mind-numbing after all.

CHAPTER 13

By the time I've finished off the remainder of the morning's breakfast (a sticky cinnamon roll and some powdery, bland muesli), I wish I'd picked up some of that soup I smelled on the walk back. I'm still famished. It must be all the unpolluted air and unnecessary walking that's increased my appetite. I scramble around in my case and retrieve my emergency packet of instant noodles, along with the bag of M&Ms I was saving for my Netflix marathon. I'll replace them with something from the store later. Like wine.

Noodles microwaved, I sit at the dining table and swipe to my contacts on my phone. I could call Victoria, but it'll be the lunch rush at the café, so she won't have time to chat. Faith is the only one left and I have no intention of complying with her request that I stop pestering her or Charlie.

'Hey, sis!'

'Eleanora! How are you? Is it going well?'

It's... different,' I reply, stabbing at the noodles with a fork to let them cool. 'We've done some meditating and worked on placing an order with the universe. People are really getting into it, it's so surreal.'

'But not you?'

'You really have to ask?'

'I guess not,' she replies with a chortle. 'What are the people like? Anyone interesting?'

By 'people' she means 'men', and by 'interesting' she means shag-worthy.

'Yep, they're all unbelievably arousing,' I reply, eating my first forkful. 'It's like one big cock-fest. I expect to be pregnant by Wednesday.'

'Excellent,' she replies dryly. 'I'm sure all the wealthy single men will be lining up to bang the sardonic loner who's calling her sister instead of mingling.'

'Actually, there's a journalist here and he wants to be my friend *and* he's one of the only men who isn't sockless and in loafers.'

She perks up again. 'Good-looking?'

I continue eating. 'I guess,' I reply, giving nothing away. If I say he's attractive, she'll only drive up here and give him my business card. 'He's kind of Negan from *The Walking Dead*-ish, if Negan was into depressing eighties bands and scared of hair-brushes. You know – rugged. Not really my type.'

'What? You love a rugged type, you liar. Negan's not really *my* type though, I'm far more Team Rick.' She sighs. 'He's better dressed.'

There's a brief silence while I eat, and she takes sides in an imaginary zombie war where only the well-presented survive.

'Anyway, I need to get going soon. Tell Charlie I'll call her tonight.'

'Will do. Though, I might take her for dinner somewhere nice. Maybe the cinema too?'

'Faith, she'll have homework! Don't start messing with her routine, she'll—'

'Loveyoubyeeeee!'

She hangs up. Dammit. If I return home and find that

Charlie has a detention, has missed class or pierced something, I'll murder Faith.

I scroll through Facebook, killing the last ten minutes before I need to trudge back up the hill to the main house. Geraldine Palmer, a girl I went to school with, is asking anyone if the chemist is open, Wendy Smith has posted her twelfth selfie of the morning and Derek MacDonald thinks he might have bird flu. I sigh and close the app. I'm not even friends with these people. It should change its name to 'Acquaintance-book' or 'I'm-too-polite-to-block-you-book.' When did I become such a misanthrope? I'm not like this at the café, but then again, my customers don't bombard me with game invites or make me look at photos of their toddlers.

Steeling myself for bootcamp round two, I tidy up my pony-tail and apply some tinted lip balm. My foundation still looks fresh and hasn't started to settle into my under-eye lines yet, so I feel relatively protected against judgemental glare. I open my front door to be unexpectedly greeted by Will who's propped up against my wheelie bin.

'How long have you been standing there?' I ask.

'About five minutes.' He sniffs and rubs his hands together.

'There's this thing called knocking,' I say, locking the door behind me. 'It's really useful and far less stalkery.'

I commence walking up the road towards the house.

'True,' he replies, following behind, 'but then you would have invited me in and well, I think we both know how that would end.'

'With me asking you to leave?'

'Exactly.' He grins. 'I'm too fragile for that kind of rejection.'

Normally, this type of arrogant behaviour would annoy the hell out of me, but for some reason, I'm not mad. I'm more intrigued. I feel like I've been sparring with Will my entire life, which is both heartening and a bit unsettling.

'You're extremely sure of yourself, aren't you?' I remark.

'I'm fifty-nine,' he replies. 'It's a bit late in life to be unsure, don't you think?'

I stop in my tracks. 'You're *fifty-nine*?'

He shakes his head. 'Nah, I just wanted to make you slow down. You walk like the bloody Terminator. I'm actually forty-two.'

'Shame, I was going to say you looked good for your age,' I retort. 'Not so much now.'

'Touché.' His dimples make themselves known again as he laughs.

'Look, I'm happy to buddy up with you this week,' I say as we begin walking again, 'but if you're looking for something more meaningful, I'm probably not your woman.'

He nods. 'Heard and understood. I mean, I won't lie. I'm totally up for some naked hot tub action, but my wife might not share my enthusiasm.'

I stop again. '*You're married?*'

'I am. I told you, I'm only here for work. Nothing else.'

I glance at his left hand. 'Bullshit. You're not wearing a wedding ring.'

Now he's the one walking in front. I trot to keep up. I see him reach into his jacket pocket and hold up a small gold band. 'Would kind of blow my cover if I did.'

'But... but... you've been flirting with me since we met!' I stammer, peering at the wedding band. 'Why would—'

'Flirting?'

He squints at me like he has no idea what I'm talking about. Oh God, now I feel like an idiot. I purse my lips and quicken my pace.

'So, you're essentially tricking everyone?' I ask, hoping the cold air will block my flourishing flame face. 'What makes you think I won't tell?'

He turns to face me. The dimples are gone. 'Look, keep this between us, yeah? I get the feeling I'd be ostracised for invading everyone's safe space or whatever the hell goes on here. I'm not here to trick anyone, or sleep with anyone, or do anything remotely underhand. Just work.'

'Fine. No problem.'

There's a little knot in my stomach that's hard to ignore. Not only do I feel stupid for mentioning the flirting, but I am also a little disappointed that he's married. I mean, it's not like I planned on having a meaningless fling, but it might have been nice to have the option.

As we get nearer Cairn Castle, I can see Kenneth actively avoiding walking anywhere near Patricia whose eye daggers strike him hard.

'You know, you could have just *not* told me,' I say quietly to Will, breaking the silence. 'Peculiar that you'd trust someone you've only just met. I could be a professional snitch.'

'True,' he replies. 'But you're not taking this any more seriously than I am. People here have spent thousands to fix their love lives and here we are, making a mockery of the whole thing. Besides, if I'm going down, you are too, Miss Freebie.'

'Damn. Fair enough.'

Kenneth pushes open the main door and we all file in behind him, some more eagerly than others. Miranda greets us again and instructs us to make our way to the main hall for gratitude scripting, which my powers of deduction lead me to believe will be 'write down things that you're grateful for'. This should be easy.

Anna has had a costume change and now appears at the front of the room wearing a dark brown poncho and long black boots, while the rest of her team remain dressed in the standard bootcamp uniform of white T-shirts and combat trousers.

Will and I are sitting together near the back. He's drumming his pen on his notepad while I watch everyone take their seats.

'I trust you're all reinvigorated and ready to go?' she says to an enthusiastic audience. 'Great. Now for this part of the afternoon, we're going to participate in scripting. Scripting or journaling is a very useful, very powerful technique used to attract and manifest the life that we want. Your very own journals are now being passed out, please keep these safe.'

I see Brad and Sally, the administrator, walk down the ends of the rows, passing along A5-sized white bound books. Sally looks like an elderly fairy, with wispy grey hair and a long, kaftan-style dress.

'Within these books you will narrate your life as you want it to be, more specifically, your love life.' Anna waits as everyone continues to receive their books. 'By doing this you will attract exactly what you've been desiring. However, before we begin, it's important to understand that everything you desire must come from a place of gratitude and not from a place of lack.'

'Here we go,' Will mumbles under his stupid, married breath.

'We only want what is absent,' she continues. 'Think about it. We don't go around wishing we were healthy when everything's in perfect working order, or for money when we're financially abundant, we only want what we do not have. If you say, "I want to meet the love of my life," your vibration is coming from a place where that love is nowhere to be found and the universe doesn't understand words; the universe understands vibration because we live in a vibrational frequency. We are all energy and energy is…?'

'Vibration,' we all reply like robots. There's a rumbling of approval from the audience and a groan of scepticism from Will, followed by a chuckle from me. 'She's seriously using physics to try and legitimize this?' he whispers. 'Einstein is turning in his grave.'

Anna presses her projector-screen clicker.

'Even Albert Einstein said, "Everything is energy and that's all there is to it. Match the frequency of the reality you want, and you cannot help but get that reality. It can be no other way. This is not philosophy. This is physics".'

I start to laugh as Will glares at the large photo of Einstein who is clearly lying perfectly still.

'Let me ask y'all a question. Why do you want to be in love? Give me your reasons. Yes, let's start with you.'

A man in his twenties runs his hand through his blonde quiff and clears his throat.

'I just want someone to share my life with,' he replies.

'Great. And you, gentleman with the glasses and the dark coat?'

'Companionship.'

'Uh-huh. Lady in the pink jumper?'

'Security... and romance, I guess.'

'Excellent, blonde woman with the ponytail at the back.'

Dammit. My heart jumps and hits my stomach with a thud. She's found me.

'Erm, I want to be in love because I...'

'Don't overthink it, sweetie. First thing that pops into your head.'

'Sex!' I blurt out. Oh, for goodness' sake, why didn't I just say companionship like the old fella? I hear a few giggles from the audience, Will included.

'Oh, hell yeah!' Anna responds. 'Probably the most honest answer yet. Be all about that intimacy, darlin', I know I am.'

'So, Anna's a pervert too. Good to know,' Will whispers, and I elbow him hard in his side.

'And you, sir?' She's looking right at Will. 'Why do you want to be in love?'

'I want a family,' he replies, in the most beta male voice he can muster. 'I want to have at least seven children and build a life with the woman I love.'

Typical. I get laughed at, but Will gets every single woman making 'aww' noises. He's basically just been granted permission to every vagina in the room, including Sally's.

'Oh, that's wonderful,' Anna remarks. 'You two are killing it with your honesty up there.'

Will and I glance at each other, determined not to laugh.

'And although everyone gave good answers, they're not the real reasons. You see, the reason we all want anything is to be happy. It's not getting *the thing*, it's the feeling it produces. And if you can feel that feeling first, the thing you want will have no choice but to follow. Sounds backwards, doesn't it? Y'all are thinking, "How can I feel happy before I have the thing that will make me feel happy?".'

Everyone chuckles, hanging off her every word. The air is thick in here from the rapid increase in devotion and fawning. If this is only day one, by day six she'll be arriving to a sea of people bowing and curtseying. I'm not denying that she's charismatic, but people seem ready to believe anything she says.

'It's really not that difficult. It doesn't matter what you're thinking about, just think about something that will give you that feeling. The easiest way to start this process is by thinking of what you're already grateful for. Things that you already have which make you happy. Open your books.'

The notebooks we've been given are surprisingly fancy. White hardbacks with velvety covers and lined inside.

Anna takes a long swig from a green, metal water bottle. 'I want you all to write down five things that you are grateful for – *really grateful for*. Close your eyes if it helps.'

The room goes deathly quiet. Will nudges me to look at his book, where he's already written:

I'm not grateful for anything. My life is a sham.

I turn to a page at the back of my own book and reply:

How about YOUR WIFE?

Dimples. He scribbles back:

She only married me for my nihilism. She'd reject my gratitude.

I turn to the front of my notebook and write THINGS I'M GRATEFUL FOR in capitals on the first page. This should be easy. I have a wonderful life.

1. *My daughter*
2. *My family and friends.*
3. *My business.*

I draw a blank. This can't be right. I can't only be grateful for three things? There must be something else, but what?

1. ~~*Olivia Colman?*~~

I look around and everyone else is happily scribbling away while Will and I seem to be contemplating how utterly ungrateful we are. I peer over to see what he's written, hoping for inspiration.

1. *Boobs*

I throw him my best *are you serious?* look which is hard to do behind my glasses but he obviously understands as he whispers, 'What? It's true. I am.'

'You can't write that!' I insist, embarrassed that I'm anywhere near him. 'It's offensive.'

'To who?'
'Me!'
He starts writing again.

1. *All boobs except Nora's boobs.*

He then covers his work with his hand and turns away from me. It's like dealing with an eight-year-old.

'All finished?' Anna asks. 'Good. Now I want you to do this daily, upon rising. Give your gratitude to the universe for the beautiful things and people and experiences that have brought you joy. That feeling you get when you sit and think about them, is the feeling which will attract the next good feeling, and the next. This is the bliss you will bring forth when you move on to step two in this process – scripting the next great love of your life.'

CHAPTER 14

We have a thirty-minute break before our final session of the day (another meditation) and although it's only 4pm, I'm exhausted already. I take some tea from the machine and step outside to get some air, moving past the smokers and out towards the gardens to the side of the house. I say 'garden', it's pretty much a private meadow because for some reason the rich need a lot of grass. To the right, I spy a small, iron bench near a ceramic bird bath and take a seat, sipping on my tea while my arse gets used to the freezing metal it's perched upon. I've only been away for one day, but it feels longer. Charlie will have barely noticed I'm gone, but she's in familiar surroundings. I'm miles away, surrounded by strangers and being followed around by a grizzly bear of a man. Honestly, doesn't he have work to be getting on with?

Will sits beside me and grimaces. 'I just had to speak to some woman called Briony from Essex. It was awful. She was about twelve and held my hands for no reason. Both of them.'

I can't help laughing. 'Maybe she thinks the universe sent you for hand-holding.'

'I don't care if she thinks FedEx sent me, I'm not into it.'

He sticks his violated hands into his pockets and leans back. 'Fancied a little time to yourself?' he asks, already knowing the answer. 'Some privacy to script your new boyfriend?'

'I don't want a new boyfriend,' I answer swiftly. 'I never did. It's my idiot friend and sister who think I do.'

'Nah, I see the way you look at your man Brad,' he replies. 'That's the look of a woman with a working libido.'

'Doesn't mean I want to date him!' I insist, which is a complete lie because if he asked me out, I'd be updating my Facebook relationship status before we even sat down to dinner.

Will isn't buying it, but thankfully he leaves it alone, instead telling me that it's time for meditation.

'One hour to go and then back to my beer,' he proclaims. 'You're welcome to join me.'

'I'm too tired,' I reply. 'Maybe another night.'

'You're not still weird about having a drink with me, are you? I really am disgustingly harmless.'

'No, I actually am tired!' I insist cheerfully. The truth is, I fully intend to have a large glass of wine, but I want to do it alone in the ugliest, comfiest clothes I own. I stand up and stroll back inside the house, stopping first at the bathroom. If she's going to play the meditation water sounds again, I need to be prepared.

Miranda is already sitting cross-legged in the meditation room as she welcomes us in for the second time today. I grab a large blue cushion and throw it down on top of the yoga mat. The rest of Group Two are also looking weary, especially Russell whose fedora is now long gone, revealing an impressive bald spot. Meg, however, looks as fresh as she did this morning. I'd ask what her secret is, but I have the feeling the answer is 'being born in 1996'.

Miranda waits patiently for us all to settle, reminding Will again that lying down during meditation is discouraged. I get the feeling she's going to have to remind him twice daily as he's determined.

'Our evening meditation will be slightly different. The process will begin as we practised earlier, but we're also going to add in some relationship affirmations. You've already briefly worked on self-affirmation during your cosmic ordering session but now we're going to focus on love and relationships specifically. Just listen to my voice and repeat the words either out loud or in your head, whichever you feel more comfortable with. Let's begin.'

I close my eyes as the water sounds start to trickle from the speakers and begin breathing to her count, waiting for the mention of the mysterious lavender light that is going to penetrate my head at any second. Once again, my mind is wandering and as much as I try to focus, all I can think of is Will's look of dismay at having his hand held and how I'm going to get the lid off my hot tub.

'Breathing deeply... allowing in love and breathing out the stress of the day.'

I am going to starfish my bed.

'Feeling calmer... going deeper.'

She held his hand, ha!

'I am unique... I am loveable... I am ready to feel and experience love to its fullest.'

I'm what now? OK. This is new.

'I am a loving person... I am ready for love... My past is not important, the right person for me is out there... Breathe deeply...'

I hear everyone *whoosh* in unison.

'I think positively about love... I am surrounded by people I love.'

I smile as I think of Charlie and my heart swells.

'I deserve love... I love the feeling of being in love.'

Flashbacks of meeting Charlie's dad appear in my mind. I knew from our second date that I loved him, and it was the best feeling in the world. I felt like anything was possible.

'The person I'm looking for is looking for me too... I love deeply and with passion.'

Damn right I do! Shit, did I just say that out loud?

'The universe is creating circumstances and events to ensure I find love.'

I can hear people gently repeating the affirmations, so softly it's almost like a collective whisper, and as I listen, for the first time, my mind becomes clear and my body light. Everything feels calm and relaxed. It's just me and my—

'And as I count back from five, you will awaken feeling alert and refreshed. Five... four... three... two... one... eyes open!'

Why did she finish so abruptly? My eyes open and dart around the room, to see everyone rising to their feet.

'Be well, everyone, and enjoy your evening. I'll see you in the morning.'

'That was odd,' I say to Will who yawns as he stands up.

'What was?'

'She was all "reeellaaxxx" and "you're a love magnet" and then suddenly ends it? Seemed much longer this morning, no?'

Will looks confused and checks his watch. 'Nope. One hour session, same as earlier. Did you space out?'

'I don't think so,' I reply. 'This stuff doesn't work on me. I was completely awake.'

He smirks. 'You did! You were totally in the zone! Are you a hippie now?'

'Shut up.' I stand and pick up my cushion. 'I don't believe you.'

'They got to you, Nora,' he mocks as I walk away. 'The universe has plans for you!'

I hear him laughing as I return my cushion to the pile at the back of the room. He's such a wind-up merchant.

'He's right, you know.'

Startled, I spin around to see Brad holding several yoga mats, which he places on the top shelf of a cupboard. His T-shirt rides up over his stomach and I give a little gasp – not loud enough for him to hear, but enough to make my vagina want to come out of involuntary retirement.

'Sorry?' I reply. His eyes are so green, it's distracting.

'The universe does have a plan for you, but I get the feeling that you're not entirely convinced yet.'

I see Will behind him making sly humping motions. I'm going to drown him later. No one will miss him.

'Me? No... why would you think that?'

He shrugs. 'I've been doing this a while. You get to know who's fully immersed in the experience and who needs some extra guidance. Come and see me in the main hall before meditation tomorrow. Say, eight thirty am?'

I nod as Brad places his hand on my arm and tells me, 'You'll be surprised how your life opens up once you start living it.' And with that, the sex god saunters off along with everyone else, leaving me in the room with the hairy man-child.

'Ooh, private session with Brad!' Will remarks. 'Whatever will you wear?'

'Oh, grow up,' I reply, rolling my eyes. 'He's just doing his job.'

'Nah, I think he secretly likes you. You know those nineties films where the hot guy transforms the dowdy, repressed girl into a sex kitten —'

'Dowdy! That's rude.'

'Well, she's never really dowdy, they just make her wear glasses and a ponytail.'

Without thinking, I reach back and touch my hair.

'All I'm saying is, you might end up Prom Queen.'

'I'm leaving.'

I quickly put on my shoes before Will has time to do his and dart out of the building.

At the bottom of the hill, I spot Kenneth and Patricia, obviously arguing. From their body language, it looks like he's on the defensive. With only one path back to my cabin, I'm forced to awkwardly manoeuvre past them.

'It doesn't matter who she is, Patricia. Anyway, she's just a friend.'

'Bullshit. I know all of your friends because they're *my* friends.'

They both stop arguing. I just smile and keep moving. They don't even wait until I'm fully out of earshot to continue.

'*You* might have spent the last year crying into our divorce papers, but I haven't. I've been meeting people. Going places.'

I hear her tell him that *brothels don't count* before I'm out of range. I'm dying to know what went on between them and also, would it kill them to provide a bit of backstory before they start insulting each other?

I scuttle down to the store inside reception, planning to load up on free wine, snacks and some more wood for the log burner. The cabin is warm but there's something about a real fire that calms my soul. *My soul?* Maybe Will is right. Maybe they did get to me.

No Persephone this evening, but I am served by someone called Felicity who has skin like glass and very delicate hands.

'If you access the homepage on your television, you'll find the menu for dinner this evening which you can order via your remote. Just allow about an hour for it to be delivered.'

They think of everything here. She also asks if I'd like my wood delivered and my urge to say, '*Doesn't every woman?*' is overwhelming but I restrain myself, telling her I'll manage. I don't want to have to hang around fully dressed until it arrives, I need to slob out.

Three minutes later I realise that this was a big mistake.

Between carrying my two bottles of white Zinfandel, a share bag of giant chocolate buttons, three bags of crisps and a pint of milk, my arms are less than capable of performing additional lumberjack duties. I make it a further ten steps before I need to stop for a rest.

'They have delivery vans for that sort of thing!' I hear Will yell. Why is he always just behind me, yelling crap?

'I'm fine,' I reply, picking everything up like I'm competing in *Britain's Strongest Man*. 'It's not far...' I begin waddling down the road but again, my weak arms fail me.

'Look, give me two seconds,' he insists. 'I'm going to grab some orange juice and then I'll help you.'

I want to martyr on, but my hands are already stinging from the weight of the bags digging into my palms. I nod and accept defeat, dropping everything where I stand. He returns quickly as promised and lifts the wood and wine bag with ease.

'Planning a big night?' he asks, peering in. 'You should leave room for dinner... unless chocolate and wine *is* dinner?'

'Would that be so terrible?'

'Not even a little bit,' he replies, 'but it'd be a shame to miss a free meal. I hear the lamb Wellington is good.'

'I think I just want to lock the door and not have to see another human until morning. Thanks for the help.' I unlock my door and he drops the bags in the small entrance hallway, obviously taking the hint that I want to be left alone.

'No worries, Nora. Have a good night! See you tomorrow.'

'Sure will,' I reply. 'Have a good one.'

I close the door behind me and lock up for the night, already looking forward to a long, hot shower and a quiet night. But first: the fire.

CHAPTER 15

By quarter past ten, I'm restless. I thought some wine might throw me into a mini coma until morning, but it seems to be having the opposite effect. I'm not tired at all, just tipsy.

I spoke to Charlie earlier and she's fine, telling me that she's making fruit salad in Home Economics on Monday. I panic slightly that she'll now think she's proficient in complex knife work and remind her to be careful like the overprotective nightmare I am. One day she'll sigh so hard at me, she'll pass out.

The fire is burning nicely, every crackle making me feel like I'm totally owning this wilderness shit. If I didn't have access to food via my television, running water and a hot tub, I'd practically be Bear Grylls.

The hot tub. I think I'm just tipsy enough to attempt it again. Mothers lift cars off their offspring, I'm pretty sure I can lift the lid off a goddamn fancy paddling pool.

I pull back the living room curtains and peer through the glass, but it's so dark outside, I struggle to see anything but my own reflection. I press every light switch near the window until I find the one that illuminates the deck. Bingo! Behold the outdoor bath.

Sliding open the doors, I step outside, marvelling once again at the stillness of the night and approach the large square box with the heavy brown lid. I can do this. I will gain access to chemically treated, bubbly water if it kills me. *But please don't kill me*, I think. *I don't want to end up in the Darwin Awards hall of fame.*

I grab the left-hand corner and pull it upwards. It creaks and moves with me but the other corner five feet away isn't budging. I release and crouch down, hoping to carefully examine the lever and find a button so it'll retract like a Transformer, but no such button exists. Annoyingly, I can hear Will's hot tub whirring away, taunting me. I try again in frustration, but to no avail, slipping slightly on the frosty decking.

'Oh, frickin' hell,' I exclaim.

'You alright over there?'

'I'm fine, Will.'

No reply. I turn and go back inside, wondering if I've maybe missed a manual or some helpful hint in the welcome pack. Surely not everyone who uses the hot tubs has upper body strength. I overheard one of the guests commenting on how lovely the hot tub was and she looked like a strong gust of wind would end her. I go to the kitchen table and begin searching through the literature I'd previously ignored. Oh, they have a red squirrel sanctuary nearby. Cute! Maybe I could drive—

Thud.

Click

Whirr.

I spring to my feet and look outside, just in time to see Will in his white robe, heading back down my patio steps. I open the doors and witness the glory of my fully functioning hot tub, complete with soft glowing lights and rising steam. I squeal and yell, 'Thank you!' to Will who replies, 'Happy to help,' like a Walmart employee.

It takes me approximately ninety-seven seconds to throw on

my swimming costume and tie back my hair before I'm decked out in robe and slippers and back at the hot tub. Even though I'm completely alone, I feel more than a little self-conscious as I disrobe. The cold air prickles my stubbly legs, my heavy boobs are not appreciating the lack of unwire and I don't even try to suck my stomach in, it's beyond assistance.

I step in and let the warm water envelope my legs, before sinking in deeper until I'm completely submerged to my shoulders and resting in one of the small bucket seats. The water feels delicious, but I feel vulnerable, and choose to sit with my back to the cabin to reduce the possibility of someone just appearing from nowhere and dunking me under. I hear faint music floating over from Will's cabin and it makes me feel a little calmer. I need some background noise to know I'm not entirely alone.

Eventually, I close my eyes and breathe, attempting to relax but it's not easy.

In for three... out for three... or was it four? I think it was four. *Oh, whatever, just do it, Nora, it worked earlier.*

My swimming costume rides up my arse and I fish it back out.

Nothing... just think of nothing... axe murder... stop it...

Am I the only person on the planet incapable of chilling out in a hot tub? I feel foolish: foolish that I couldn't open the hot tub, foolish that I'm doing this, foolish that I'm here in the first place but most of all, foolish that after being bombarded with positive energy and affirmations all day, I feel lonelier and more pathetic than I have in a long time.

I look up at the sky and gaze at the stars, which are bigger and brighter than I've ever seen. It's so beautiful and so humbling that all at once, I feel small. Insignificant. Hell, I feel *emotional*, what is wrong with me? Maybe this alone time isn't good for me – too much time to reflect. Too much time to wonder why exactly I'm forty and not even close to sharing the second half of my life with someone. Without warning, the tears begin to flow down my cheeks, and I wipe them away angrily. I don't do self-pity. I am where I am because that's the way my life has worked out and no amount of meditation or self-aggrandising can magically change that. There are so many people here, with so much hope that they will be able to undo or forget the pain they've known, with hope that somewhere someone will repair all the hurt, but I don't believe that. There is no love of my life. I will never be 'the one'. I am the one before they marry and even the one while they're married (Neil Sutton, 2017, huge mistake) but I'm never just 'the one'. I scowl at the sky like it's responsible, but it isn't. If I'm certain of one thing, it's that the universe does not give one solitary shit that I'm alone. And one day, hopefully, neither will I.

I attempt to dry my eyes with my wet hand and laugh at how preposterous I must look. I thought hot tubs were supposed to be fun. They should write *may cause tear-inducing rumination when mixed with wine* on the safety pamphlet. I think I'm done for this evening.

CHAPTER 16

BOOTCAMP: DAY 2

'And how are you this morning, Nora? You're looking a little tired.'

I walk around the chairs in the main hall, towards Brad who unsurprisingly doesn't look tired. Brad looks like he slept on a damn cloud.

'Must just have slept heavily,' I reply, ignoring the fact that I cried for at least an hour before bed and another hour in bed, resulting in red eyes and pillow face. 'I'm fine.'

'Come sit with me.'

I oblige, pulling across a chair. I feel like I'm being given a performance review by my really hot boss. I still feel a bit emotional this morning; I wonder if he'll hug me? I hope not, I might start crying again.

'The first night after bootcamp can be hard on a lot of people,' he says, placing his hands on his lap. 'You're alone, vulnerable and you've released a lot of emotion, even if it isn't evident at the time. The most important thing is that you don't suppress this; there's no right or wrong way to feel. If you need to cry—'

'No, it's just—'

'You won't be the only one, I assure you. There will be a lot of eyes just as red as yours this morning.'

My bottom lip starts to wobble, like Charlie's does when she thinks I'm mad with her; thinking about that makes mine wobble even more.

'I don't know where this is coming from,' I start to say, before the lump in my throat ensures that no additional words can be spoken without a sob in between each. 'I... just...'

'This is a positive response,' he assures me, his hand moving from his lap onto mine. 'Clearing negative blockages from your subconscious is the only way to allow in new and more positive desires. You're already vibrating at a high frequency.'

I shake my head. 'I'm just having a small meltdown, it'll pass, and I'll be back to—'

He squints at me. 'Why would you want to go back? So, you can continue to repeat the same behaviours and patterns? The ones that led you to your so-called "meltdown"?'

'Well, not exactly,' I reply but then pause. Something in what he's saying resonates with me.

'We feel things for a reason, Nora. Pain is an indicator that something isn't right, whether it's physical or emotional. You wouldn't ignore a physical pain in your heart, why are you choosing to disregard an emotional one?'

'I get what you're saying, but we can't just go around wallowing in self-pity, can we?' I reply. 'You have to move on.'

'But how can you truly move on if nothing has changed? Nora, when the universe—'

'I don't buy this *universe* stuff,' I say bluntly. 'I'm sorry, I just don't get it.'

'I know.' He smiles warmly at me. 'That's fine because whether you believe it or not, the universe, or God, or Source or whatever you want to call it, is working with you anyway. It will always respond to your vibration.'

I sigh. Brad may have perfectly shaped ears, but they're just not listening to me.

'Forget about the universe for a minute,' he continues. 'You will get what you want by believing and trusting in you. YOU, Nora. There is nothing in this world that you can't have. It already exists, you just have to align with it to bring it into your experience and alignment comes from truly believing that you already have it.'

'I don't know how to do that.'

His hand grips mine a little tighter. 'That's why you're here.'

I hear voices coming along the hallway as the rest of the bootcampers arrive for day two.

Brad moves his hand away and reaches for his notebook on the floor. 'Enjoy this week, Nora. I have no doubt that you're going to finally realise what an extraordinary woman you really are. Remember, the universe is always conspiring with you, not against you. I'll see you later.'

I can't help but blush as I return my chair to the front row and scurry towards the back where I'm more comfortable hiding out. Extraordinary? Me? What an odd thing to say, I'm the least extraordinary person I know, but I'll admit, it's flattering. Maybe he does like me?

Stop it, Nora. Get real. You might be self-sufficient and not entirely unattractive, but you are still the same woman whose skirt became entangled in the wheels of a Tesco trolley last week. Extraordinary people don't have to ask security guards to cut them free while other shoppers look on. This is how lonely older women get duped by younger foreign men looking for citizenship. He. Does. Not. Fancy. You.

I give myself a shake before spotting Will heading towards me, looking as tired as I am but minus the red eye.

'Alright, Nora! I was knocking on your door this morning

until I remembered you had a hot date with the love guru over there. You look tired... Nora, did you bang the teacher?'

'Keep your voice down!' I reply. 'People might think you're serious!'

He shrugs, placing his coat on the back of his seat. This morning's T-shirt is Metallica. He looks in better form this morning, almost like he's made half an effort, rather than none at all.

'Thanks again for helping with the tub. It was driving me crazy.'

'No problem. There's a safety catch on the right-hand side; you must have missed it.'

'I know, I'm an idiot.'

'Nah, you just didn't know there was a safety catch.'

His response reminds me of Victoria. Whenever I declare my stupidity, she's the first to remind me that not knowing something doesn't constitute being a failure. I wonder how she's getting on this week; I must text her later.

As I look around the room, I see that Brad was correct. There are a lot of wistful-looking faces this morning. I also notice that people are less fancy than they were yesterday. Perfectly curled dos are now thrown up in tight top knots, fully made-up faces are now highlight- and contour-free, false lashes are gone, but Russell is still clinging to his fedora for dear life.

Anna arrives just as we're all seated and apologises for being late.

'I had a small shower emergency,' she explains, 'I hope y'all will forgive my wet hair, but I didn't want to waste a single second of your second day.'

As she starts introducing our tasks for day two, Will leans in and whispers, 'Did you also feel like a bit of a plank, sitting alone in your hot tub?'

I nod. 'Kind of, yeah.'

'All I could think was, "I'm a grown man having a bubble bath outside". I've never felt so emasculated.'

I snort and then cough to try and cover it up. 'You men are so fragile.'

'We are.'

'So, after morning meditation, we're going to start the first of our speed dating workshops. This will be done within your groups of ten.'

A few awkward giggles can be heard through the audience.

'You're here to re-establish yourselves as worthwhile romantic partners, so I want to find out exactly how you all interact and connect when making a first impression with a potential mate.'

I see one woman put her head in her hands. I guarantee she's experienced speed dating before and it didn't go well. I feel her pain. I attended one session in 2009 where I met a man who'd written thirty-six novellas about Swedish pirate hookers and lived with his gran.

'Now, for this exercise, we're looking to examine how you come across in this situation, body language, flow of conversation, etc. I'll see you back here at ten am.'

Will reluctantly stands up again, informing me that 'this meditation shite is dull'. 'Want to skip it and go for a wander?' he suggests. 'We could drown ourselves in the loch. That might be more exciting.'

'I'm going to give it another go,' I reply assertively. 'Maybe there is something in quieting your mind. I could use a bit of quiet.'

'Wow, Brad must be one hell of a mentor,' he teases. 'Do you love him yet? A spring wedding is good for me, I look good in linen. *Mrs Brad...* what's his surname again? Begins with an H... Hoodwinker? No. Hood*wanker?*'

'Stop being ridiculous,' I insist as we walk into the red-

carpeted room. 'I'm allowed to change my mind about meditation, it doesn't mean I've been brainwashed.'

'You're right,' he agrees, kicking off his heavy boots. 'But if I
see you chanting at the moon, or performing any kind of sex
ritual... well, I'll be forced to join in, cos that sounds kind of
fun.'

I laugh loudly as I pick up my floor cushion, causing
everyone to turn and look. Anna gives me a smile which says
stop disrupting my beautiful Zen ambience, you moron so I make
an apologetic face and dash over to my yoga mat. Will follows.

It's only my third time meditating but I feel like I'm getting
the hang of it. I inhale and exhale correctly and the number of
obscure thoughts which race around my head are diminishing.
The water sounds are still a little pee-inducing but at several
points my mind is clear, and it feels wonderful. Like I'm not
even there. I don't completely zone out like last time but when
we're finished, I feel focused and more enthusiastic about my
day. That is until Will opens his trap.

'Ready to be chatted up by these clowns?' he asks. 'I wonder
what they'll write about you?'

Oh shit. It's speed dating time.

CHAPTER 17

As we return to the main hall, my stomach is in knots. I haven't been on any kind of date in years. I'm no good at self-promotion. If Faith was here, she'd be selling the shit out of herself, but me, I have no real bragging rights to speak of.

'This will be excellent material,' Will remarks quietly. I grab him back by the sleeve.

'You'd better not write about me!'

'Course, I won't. Anyway, I wouldn't mention names. I'm not here to shame anyone... well, not yet anyway.'

Before I can reply, we're in our groups with Brad who is positioning the chairs in two rows of five, facing each other. They're just far enough apart so we won't hear what the next person is saying, much to Will's disappointment. He hands us all a printed sheet with names listed down the left-hand side.

'OK, troops, boys one side, girls to the other. You'll have three minutes each and then the men will move to the right, girls stay where you are.'

Allison giggles, smoothing down her red hair nervously. The rest of us all look somewhat sombre. I notice that Will makes a beeline for Meg, beating sweet-faced Nish to the seat opposite her. I think Meg is probably everyone's type to be fair. Sixty-year-old Tim sits opposite me, I assume because I'm the least visually intimidating female in the group. I ponder whether this is a good thing or not.

Brad pulls over a spare chair and sits at the end of the rows. 'I'd like you all to take notes about the other person as you go and be honest. Whether they are rude, funny, arrogant, not attentive, annoying, sweet – whatever; write it down.'

'But isn't it all subjective?' middle-aged, bald Paul asks. 'What someone finds rude, someone else might find refreshing.' I notice that Paul has the thinnest, most pitiful moustache I've ever seen. It looks like it has been whispered onto his face.

Brad nods. 'Yes and no. We tend to find that appearance is far more subjective than personality. If you get five people saying you're rude, then it's something to work on; just like if five people find you funny or charming, it attests to the good qualities you have. Remember, we're not here to rate sexual attractiveness, we're here to rate character. You won't attract someone you really want until you are the best person you can be. Let's get started.'

Tim and I just look at each other, neither sure where to begin. His startled expression hasn't changed once since he arrived at bootcamp. He's at least twenty years older than me with a brow so furrowed he looks like he's been ploughed. I wonder how much courage he had to muster up to come here.

'So, tell me about yourself, Tim,' I say. 'Do you have any hobbies?'

Tim thinks for a second then nods. 'I do enjoy old movies. Chaplin, Laurel and Hardy, Bogart, James Cagney. I used to watch them with my wife.'

I don't want to ask about his wife. I presume she's dead, but who knows? She might have run off with the neighbour. It's not my business.

'Lovely,' I reply. '*Casablanca* is one of my favourite films.'

His eyes light up. 'It's a wonderful film. They don't make them like that anymore. Modern films can be so coarse.'

'And do you still work?' I'm not sure anyone has paid attention to Tim in quite some time.

'Oh no, dear, I retired a couple of years ago. My sons run the business now – Pinnock's needed some younger blood.'

'Pinnock's? The biscuit makers?'

He nods. 'Eighty years we've been going. It'll be here long after I'm gone.'

It's very strange sitting in front of the man who is partly responsible for your current weight problem.

'And you, dear?' he asks. 'I imagine your life is far more interesting than mine.'

I feel a bit sad for him. It appears even millionaires get lonely.

'Well, I have a daughter and I run a café, so it's really not that exciting, to be honest. I do like—'

'Single mum, then?'

'Yes, for a few years now.'

'Dad not in the picture?'

'Um, yes, he is, but I'd rather not discuss—'

'Well then, you're not a single parent, are you? If he sees her, he's involved.' Tim's startled look has changed to one of mild contempt.

'I'm not really looking to discuss my custody arrangements but—'

'He contributes financially, yes? Then you're not doing it alone, are you? By saying you're a single mum, you imply that the father doesn't care.'

Now my back is well and truly up. I cross my arms and glare at this rude old bastard. 'Yes, his seven pounds a day helps enormously, Tim. But he doesn't do doctors or dentists, or daily school runs or take time off work when she's sick or do homework or any of the important stuff. He cancels when he has something better to do, won't budge outside his routine if I need him to and will never, ever give me credit for the bright, happy girl she is and continues to be on my watch. But unlike you, she will never know any of this.'

He sits there, mouth open and face flushed. 'I didn't mean anything, I just—'

'Just what? Thought you'd campaign on behalf of Fathers for Justice? You don't know my life and you have no right to assume anything.'

As he glares at me, I notice his very weak chin. It's practically non-existent. I wonder how he folds towels.

'Time's up, everyone. Gentlemen, move to the right.'

Tim stands and shuffles to the front of the group while Russell with the fedora scooches over into his seat. I write 'misogynistic old git' beside Tim's name and take a deep breath.

'This is weird, innit?' Russell announces with a big grin. 'Like trying to impress people you don't even want to fire into. No offence.'

'None taken,' I reply. 'Though maybe if you're *trying* to impress, that wasn't the best opener?'

'Aw, shit, man! I didn't mean I wouldn't... cos I would; you're fit, innit? It's just, like, you're not my type.'

His London slang is bugging me already. 'Russell, it's fine. You're not my type either.'

'You go for the rough types, eh?' he replies, looking down towards Will. 'I've seen you guys... little looks, quiet chats. You got cosy quickly, girl.'

'What? Him? No! I have no idea what you mean. Anyway, shouldn't we be—'

'Honestly, man, we've all noticed it,' he continues. 'Like, you know when you just click with someone. You guys are clickin' hard!'

'Do you work, Russell?' I ask, determined to steer the conversation away from whatever this is.

'Yeah, man. I work in retail.'

'Nice! Anywhere interesting?'

'Radcliffe Menswear. You know it?'

'Sure,' I reply, thankful he's moved on from my non-existent clicking with Will. 'They have a big store in Edinburgh. Do you work on the shop floor or are you—'

'I own it. Russell Radcliffe.' He shakes my hand.

Is everyone here a business tycoon? I always imagined that wealthy, successful people would be like they are in movies, like *Wolf of Wall Street*, but this guy acts like he couldn't run a bath, never mind a clothing empire.

'So, you're going to write good things about me, then?' he asks, peering over at the folder sheet of paper on my lap.

'Well, you're friendly!' I reply. 'And honest. I guess those are plus points.'

He beams. 'Thanks. You too! Older women are better at this shit, though. You ain't got to impress anyone. Eyebrows over there straight up asked me what my house is worth.'

He motions over to Allison who is now sitting silently with Tim. I laugh. I think I underestimated Russell. He might be a fedora wanker, but I'm worse; I'm a judgemental wanker.

'So why are you here?' I ask him. 'You don't seem like you need the universe to help you with your life.'

'Between you and me, the Law of Attraction got me to where I am in business,' he replies. 'But my relationships, man, they're going nowhere. I'm twenty-nine, I don't want to be forty and end up...'

'Like me?'

'I didn't mean it like that. Look, women don't need men, but we need women. It's a fact that when a man reaches a certain age and he's never been married – well, women stay away from that shit, like we're serial killers or obsessed with our mothers or something.'

'I'm going to add *insightful* to your notes.'

Russell laughs. 'I like you, Nora. I see why wild boy Will got in there first.'

'Time, gentlemen! Move to the right.'

I don't have time to argue my case again before Russell is gone and I'm left facing Nish. Just him, Paul and *wild boy* Will to go before we can break for coffee. God, I need coffee.

Nish sits and scribbles on his paper before we begin, like he's taking notes for a big test. From what I can see, he's written a lot about the last two women, whereas I've mainly scrawled random words and an angry face after Tim's name.

'Tell me about yourself, Nora,' he says mechanically, clicking the lid back on to his pen.

'Well, I run a small business in Edinburgh,' I reply. 'I also have a daughter and—'

'Great. Good start. And do you have any hobbies?'

Has he made a list of questions? 'Um, just the usual. Cinema, reading, seeing friends. I work long hours and—'

'What's your biggest pet peeve?'

He's most definitely working from a list.

'Not being allowed to finish sentences.'

'Great. OK, so where do you see yourself in ten years?'

In prison for murdering Tim. And possibly you. Double murder stretch.

'Nish, slow down!' I plead. 'We're supposed to be chatting, not interviewing!'

He shakes his head. 'I think you'll find we're supposed to be collecting information from the other person, to assess compatibility and relationship potential.'

'Are you always this efficient?' I ask, trying to not laugh. 'It's a bit methodical. How about allowing me to ask questions too? I read somewhere that conversations require a back-and-forth element.'

He looks annoyed. 'We only have three minutes, being methodical saves time.'

What an absolute virgin.

'You have very nice eyes when they're not rolling back in frustration, you know.'

He stops looking down at his notes. 'What?'

'I'm just saying, you have lovely eyes. How old are you, Nish?'

'Twenty-four... am I allowed to ask how old—'

'Nope. Where do you live?'

'Manchester, but my mum is Nepalese and I was born there.'

'Very cool. And you work in...?'

'Quantitative analysis. Freelance. And you?'

'There you go! A conversation! We're rolling now. I own a café.'

He laughs and grins widely. 'That must be fun. You seem like a happy person.'

I make a mental note: *remove Nish from kill list.*

'Thank you, Nish! Look at us conversing. Isn't life grand?'

'I'm sorry,' he says embarrassedly. 'I guess I'm overthinking this whole thing. I just wanted this week to be... well, a game changer. I don't date very often. OK, ever. I've never dated.'

'And you thought the universe would help?'

'Well, I was raised Buddhist...'

'Ah! Gotcha.'

I notice that Nish isn't writing anything, instead he's just smiling. Maybe I've broken him.

'Time please. Gentlemen, move to the right.'

As he moves seats, I write, *Lovely man! Just be yourself.* God, I sound like his mother.

Next, I have Paul and as much as I try to stop being judgemental, I can't help but cringe at his gold chain and bracelet. I don't know why it bothers me so much. He clears his throat.

'How's it going?' he asks, without waiting for a reply. 'I'm Paul Barnes. Work in film. Live in Bearsden.'

Bearsden! I could hear Faith's 'suitable boyfriend' list being ticked as they spoke. To her, even Fred West would be a viable candidate if he came with a desirable postcode.

'Yeah, we met yesterday,' I reply. 'But OK. I'm Nora, I work—'

'Nice, look, I should probably tell you that I'm ready to get serious. Marriage, kids – the lot. I'm not interested in anything casual.'

'I don't even know how to respond to that, Paul.'

'Isn't that what women want?' he asks, fiddling with his bracelet. 'Someone who just lays their cards on the table. No bullshit, no bluffing?'

When did I become the spokesperson for womankind?

'I'm sure some do,' I reply. 'Some might find it off-putting. It's like me saying that I'm only into cheap, meaningless hook-ups and domination.'

He stops fiddling with his bracelet. 'Are you?'

'No, I'm just saying that it's an equally unusual thing to blurt out on a first date.'

'Ever been tethered?'

'Sorry?'

'Tethered.'

I pause, trying to work out what the hell he's talking about. 'Tethered. Like a horse?'

'Sure, whatever.'

'Do I look like a horse?'

'Well, you mentioned the domination, I just thought—'

'Stop speaking, please.'

He shrinks back into his seat and resumes bracelet fiddling while I open my notes and write WTF IS WRONG WITH YOU beside his name. There is no further conversation.

'Good work, everyone, last round. Guys to the right, please!'

Will plonks himself down and immediately notices my frown.

'Woah. That bad? You sort of look like Theresa May when you scowl.'

I nod, hoping that isn't true. 'I had a nightmare once where I was naked, and everyone was laughing, and a bird started pecking at my bare arse. This was worse.'

'What kind of bird?'

'No idea. I take it your dates were better than mine?'

He opens his sheets of paper. 'It hasn't been totally awful. I mean, people are just people, right? Everyone has their pros and cons. I try not to judge based on a three-minute chat.'

'Yeah, me neither.' I rub my nose to make sure it hasn't grown seven inches.

'Weirdest thing though,' he continues, 'three people mentioned you. Well, us. Apparently, we're either old friends, old flames or living proof that the Law of Attraction works. They've all been discussing how we click. I think they had a meeting.'

'I did hear something,' I reply. 'It's so ridiculous! Honestly, I think everyone is so bloody love-focused, they're seeing things. Like a group hallucination.'

'You don't think it's odd?' he asks.

'What, odd that we happen to get on?' I reply. 'Not really. I've been known to get on with other human beings.'

He sits quietly, mulling it over.

'Do you think it's odd?' I ask. 'Ha ha, have they gotten to you too?'

'God, no. I... I just feel like I've known you for ages. There was a definite gravitational pull when I saw you. Like, I was supposed to meet you or something.'

'I think we both just looked out of place. It's natural to seek comfort in similarity.'

'Perhaps,' he concludes. 'I'm glad it happened, regardless. I might have been stuck with Meg over there.'

'What's wrong with that?'

He clears his throat. '"Like, I've manifested everything in my life, like, one day I asked for more Instagram followers and James Franco liked a swimsuit picture I posted and then I had like fifty thousand more followers by the end of the month".'

'Pretty sure she doesn't speak with that accent,' I reply, laughing. 'I thought you weren't into judging people.'

'Pfft,' he replies, 'I was just trying to sound principled. I hate everyone. If there's anyone you like, I could put in a good word for you... you know, like how you brush your teeth twice a day, give to charity and that I'm almost certain you carry a gun in your underwear.'

'I'm fine, thanks. Let's just get on with this, shall we?'

'You're right. Enough of this tomfoolery. Let's fake date. Woo me, Nora.'

'Sure,' I reply, leaning in. 'So, tell me, Will... do you like being tethered?'

CHAPTER 18

Feedback from the speed dating was an eye-opener to say the least. Brad read our comments anonymously, forcing us all to sit there and smile as we were ripped new ones by the other members of our group.

Paul's comments were unanimously bad, ranging from 'a little intense' to 'would not want to relive that experience' while Nish's comments varied from 'needs to relax' to 'pleasant young man'. I was surprised that Biscuit-face Tim only got bad feedback from me, but perhaps I was the only one he decided to lecture.

'Now we move on to Will.'

I could see Will squirm as Brad began looking through our notes. I wouldn't be surprised if the other women found him a little standoffish, considering he'd rather be anywhere else but here.

'Attentive... charming... very easy to talk to... funny... we have some great comments here, Will, it seems you're quite adept at holding conversation.'

Of course, he is, I think, *he talks to people for a living.*

Will rubs the back of his head and smiles while the other men quietly size him up, like he's now the one to beat.

'Let's move on to the ladies.'

Oh God, here we go.

'Allison – hmm, we have a couple of comments here which mention your eagerness to find out how much people earn or have spent on various things. Maybe not appropriate for an initial conversation?'

Allison flicks her hair back and sniffs indignantly. 'I think it's perfectly appropriate, I wouldn't want to waste anyone's time.'

'Meg – lovely comments here, but perhaps taking a brief pause every now and again to let others speak might be something to consider?'

Meg looks hurt, but Brad isn't buying it. 'This is a bootcamp, Meg,' Brad reminds her. 'We're here for quick results and sometimes brutal truths are necessary. Take note but don't take it to heart.'

She nods but her expression doesn't change.

'Jillian – a couple of negatives here. Firstly, looking bored and secondly, fishing for compliments... but also seductive.'

Jillian giggles and fires a look at Tim who winks at her. Jillian and that old Jammy Dodger? Really?

Patricia's comments all centre around her slagging off her ex-husband, Kenneth, which doesn't surprise either me or her. She's obviously out for blood.

'And last but not least, Nora.'

My face is burning already. I'm perfectly aware of my own flaws but having them read out to me isn't an experience I'm relishing.

'So, firstly we have belligerent.'

Up yours, Tim.

'Dismissive.'

Definitely Paul. I brace myself for the rest of my public shaming.

Brad continues, 'But then we have – "easy to talk to" and "sound as a pound".'

Redemption!! God bless Nish and Russell!

'And finally, "strong and stable".'

Bloody Will. He snickers loudly.

Brad places our sheets on his chair. 'I know this hasn't been the easiest task for some of you, but you all did very well. By the time you leave, you'll be confident enough to charm everyone you come into contact with. But for now, take half an hour and grab a coffee.'

We all disperse, grateful that this part of the day is over. As I head towards the bathrooms, Nish sidles up beside me.

'Thanks for not being too harsh on me,' he says awkwardly. 'You're very easy to talk to, like I said in my notes.'

I laugh. 'I thought that was you. You're welcome, but no need to thank me! You just have to loosen up a little. You'll be great!'

He smiles. 'No one has ever said they like my eyes before.'

'Glad to be the first!' I push open the toilet door and walk in. He's still beside me, beaming.

'Nish, this is the ladies' room.'

'Oh, right. Sorry. See you when you come out.'

I close the door behind me and find a cubicle. See me when I come out? What the hell? Please no, I do not have time for a puppy.

I take my time in the bathroom, even chatting with a woman about her brand of fake tan in the hope that Nish will get bored and wander off. Unfortunately, when I get back into the hall-way, he's still there.

'I'm just going to grab a coffee and make some phone calls, Nish. I'll see you later.'

'You have really nice eyes too.'

Will walks over to us, cornering Nish, while I take my chance to get in line for some coffee. Eventually Will joins me.

'You're welcome,' he says, grabbing a plastic cup and holder. 'He's rubbing up against Meg now.'

'Nish is harmless!' I informed him. 'He just thinks he's found a friend, that doesn't mean anything salacious. I'm old enough to be his mum.'

'Nah, you've maybe got nine or ten years on him. It's a perfectly reasonable assumption – younger guy, older MILF.'

'Oh, get lost. You're making me uncomfortable now.'

'Probably not as uncomfortable as Nish is feeling in those tight trousers.'

'You're the worst.'

I fill up my coffee and take it outside, hoping that neither Nish nor Will follow me out. Instead, I am greeted by torrential rain and thunder, forcing me to either take shelter with the smokers or go back inside. I choose the latter, finding an empty room for a moment of 'me' time.

I sit at a round wooden table in the middle of the room, one which looks like it's being used to store materials for the boot-camp. Boxes are piled high beside empty cups and some scribbled-on notepads partially covered by jackets and sweatshirts. It's nice to find an area that doesn't reek of sandalwood or lilies. I sip my coffee and scroll through my phone, noticing that everyone has already texted me to save me from annoying them later. Part of me is glad that everything appears to be running smoothly and another part is annoyed that everything isn't falling to pieces without me. I know it's only been a couple of days, but no one seems to miss me.

I give myself ten minutes of peace and quiet, throw my cup into the already full wastepaper bin and wander back into the main hall, where Nish is nowhere to be seen and Will is chatting to Paul. I *knew* that the tethering story would make him investigate Paul further. I'll be curious to see Will's article when it's published; maybe he'll be able to make more sense of this whole affair than me because right now, it's just a bizarre mess.

The seats have all been arranged back into their original rows, so I take the left outside seat on the back row and pull out my itinerary.

Telling Tales

Storytime? I bet this is a load of made-up testimonials featuring folk who were once cat-owning hermits but now have six husbands and a house made entirely from vibrational brickwork. Or maybe we have to snitch on each other... oooh, I quite like that idea.

'Are we ready to begin?' Anna asks, appearing at the front of the room like a genie. Will sits beside me, surreptitiously messing with his phone which makes me think he's just recorded his conversation with Paul. Has he been recording me?

'Telling tales is something we're all very good at,' Anna says. 'The stories we tell ourselves, and other people, to justify why we are where we are.'

Will finally places his phone in his pocket and slouches. I grumpily nudge his leg away from mine.

'We all have tales of heartbreak, of how we've been the victim of some terrible scoundrel who used us up and threw us away. Tales of parents who didn't do enough, or parents who did too much or bullies who taunted us, the list goes on.'

My mind is suddenly swarming with the faces of everyone she's mentioned. My mother who failed at the most important role she had, Charlie's dad who crushed my heart under his size tens, that ginger kid in school who called me 'no tits Nora' because I developed later than everyone else and even the woman at the deli counter in the supermarket who looks at me like I murdered her entire family every time I go in. They have all made me who I am.

'These people do not define you.'

Oh.

'These people are purely a figment of your past and the only point in time that matters, is this one right now. So, for this task, I'm going to ask you to tell these tales for the last time. I want you to work in pairs for this exercise, preferably someone you feel comfortable with.'

There's a buzz of anticipation as people get themselves into pairs. Will and I just nod at each other without the need to ask. Usually, I feel anxious about these kinds of things, worrying that no one will want to pair up with me, like being picked last in gym class. I glance around, hoping that no one else is feeling this way and see Nish looking in my direction. I gesture that I'm pairing up with Will and he looks wounded, but thankfully he's sat beside Meg who can offer him distracting cleavage.

After a brief pause for seat switching, Anna asks us to tell our tales.

'Take turns getting everyone and everything out of your system but do not reply, question or attempt to comfort the other person – doing this will only legitimise their belief that they are the victim. There are no victims here. It's very hard to change something you feel you have no power over. Take back the power. Accept responsibility. By the end of this exercise, you will leave your sad stories at the door and start creating new ones.'

A sea of faces turn to each other and say... absolutely nothing. The only sounds are a few nervous giggles and stifled coughs. Anna stops striding and places her hands on her hips.

'Did y'all come on a bootcamp expecting it to be easy? I'm sorry, people, but you're going to have to dig deep here. Be brave. Bare your soul! Y'all came here for a reason, let's do this!'

For the first time, Anna sounds like a bootcamp drill

instructor instead of a salesperson and very slowly, people begin telling their tales. Will throws me some side-eyes as we both remain spectators at this event.

'You want to start?' I ask him, knowing that his answer will be no or an expletive to the same effect but I'm persistent. 'Go on. What made you the bundle of joy you are today?'

'I'm not doing this,' he replies. 'I don't get paid enough to tell strangers my innermost secrets.'

'But we're best friends now!' I tease. 'Remember? We are the poster couple for bootcamp. The clicking twins, the—'

'Still no.'

'Meh. Worth a try.'

He turns to face me, resting his arm on the back of the seat. 'Feel free to share with me, though. I am here for you, Nora.'

'Uh-uh. Nope. You think I'm going to tell a journo my secrets—'

'Shh!' He glances around nervously. 'I told you I wouldn't write about you.'

'Whatever. I'm not sharing anything intimate unless you do.' I cross my arms like a petulant child. 'Let's see how long it takes for Anna to yell at us. We might get asked to leave! You're already on thin ice for your meditation napping.'

'*Attempted* meditation napping, and fine – one thing each but no bullshit. You first.'

I agree, moving my chair around to face away from everyone in case they're all expert lip readers. Thankfully they're all knee deep in self-despair.

'My dad died when I was ten. Heart attack. That was the last time I had a positive male role model in my life.'

He frowns. 'Sorry to—'

'No comments or questions, remember?'

'OK. My dad died a few years back too. Mum still lives in Edinburgh.'

I wait for the rest of the admission. 'And?'

'Nothing. That's it.'

'Seriously?'

'Fine, OK. After my dad died, I found out he'd been cheating on my mum for years. She never knew... still doesn't. That really messed with my head. She's a kind woman, you know and now I'm left carrying his dirty little secret. He was careless with people, so I try very hard to be a good man but...'

'You don't think you are?'

'I do believe that's a question.'

Bah. My turn again.

'I have no relationship with my mother because she cannot survive without a man, even at the expense of her children's happiness. I'm the complete opposite, thankfully. My child comes before me.'

I pause as I realise that my need to ensure I'm nothing like my mother means that Charlie's happiness might have come at the expense of mine.

Will looks at me with a puzzled expression as it starts to sink in just how little consideration I give to my own needs. Charlie is everything, so I am nothing? Yikes, that wasn't my plan.

'Earth to Nora... you alright?'

'Sorry. Just having a think. Your turn.'

'Why does this feel like a competition?' he says, scratching his head. 'My life really isn't that complicated and—'

'But... my... my... my dog was like my child!'

The sudden outburst from the front row makes everyone jump. It seems Ashley from Group Four is really unravelling. Anna takes her to the side while we try not to gawp.

'Funny how no one ever says their child is like their dog,' Will remarks, still throwing glances over to Ashley, who is now blowing her nose. 'Anyway, you have another go while I think of something. What else do you want to never speak of again?'

I give him the benefit of the doubt. Maybe his life just isn't that complicated.

'Apart from this bootcamp? Hmm, my love life, one hundred percent. I'm sick of thinking about it, my family commenting on it, everything.'

He raises an eyebrow like I'm about to reveal something juicy.

'My first, proper long-term relationship was with a man called Luke who spent most of it high and my last was with a man called Stuart who spent most of it keeping me down.'

I haven't thought about Luke Young in a long time. A six-foot, skinny twenty-three-year-old who only stopped smoking weed when he was asleep. I don't even remember how we ended things, unlike my breakup with Stuart. I remember every word of that.

'Since my last relationship, I've coasted between unavailable men I can't have and men I know I don't want. If I already know it's not going anywhere, it won't hurt when it inevitably doesn't... yet, it still does. Isn't that pitiful? Being rejected by someone you didn't want in the first place, and it still stings. It's like, "I'm not even good enough for YOU?!" Anyway, all I know is I haven't met anyone worth disrupting my life or Charlie's for and I don't expect to. Why am I even telling you this?'

'Charlie is your son?'

'No, my daughter. Charlotte.'

'Ah. Nice name. I know I'm technically not supposed to comment but—'

'I don't need a response,' I say, cutting him off. 'Saying a lot of this out loud is actually making me realise that I've made a rod for my own back, but there's nothing I can do about it now. Just tell me something personal about your love life and make me feel less pathetic.'

He sighs. 'You're not pathetic. At least you're not separated from your wife and desperately hoping she'll change her mind. Now, *that's* pathetic.'

Wow, I wasn't expecting that! I try not to react but it's tricky as he's obviously struggling with it. Turns out he's far more complicated than he thinks.

'When we met, neither of us wanted kids,' he continues. 'But after eight years, clocks start kicking and things change. I mean, I know I'm forty-two, but I think I'd be a great dad.'

Bloody hell, he just keeps bringing the surprise revelations. I automatically assumed it was his wife who wanted kids, not him.

'Sabine won't even consider changing her mind and thinks I'll eventually resent her for denying me the chance to become a dad. What really kills me is that I'm not sure she's wrong... anyway, we split almost a year ago. I haven't spoken to her in six months.'

And he still keeps the ring in his pocket, I think. God, this is both sad as hell and remarkably romantic.

'And I also got dumped by a girl at university who said I was too thin and said it was like shagging *Hollow Man.* So, I'll see your heartbreak and raise you body shaming.'

The laugh that leaves my throat is a welcome release.

'Time's up, everyone.'

'Do you want to know something really annoying?' I ask, as everyone packs up. 'I do actually feel better after saying all this crap out loud. I don't feel so burdened.'

He bobs his head from side to side, like he's unsure. 'Hmm, I think you feel better hearing that someone else is also having a hard time.'

'Not at all! At least you've been married! I'm going to die without ever knowing that kind of monotony.'

Now Will's laughing. 'Maybe I feel a little better too, *maybe.* Man, I hate that they got this part right. Next, I'll be crying in my hot tub.'

I glare. 'It was a long day.'

'OK, everyone, it's time for lunch but I'm really impressed with how y'all threw yourselves into this task. I realise it wasn't an easy one, but you did it! Your stories are out there now. Leave them there. You have made space for more vibrationally worthy pursuits. Fill that space with joy. Now, if anyone feels they need additional support, please see your mentor.'

'Do you need additional Brad support?' Will asks, grinning. 'I wonder what that entails? Bicep therapy?'

'You're very dismissive of Brad,' I reply. 'He's good at his job. Are you jealous?'

'Yes,' he admits. 'You caught me. I too wish to be a real-life Ken doll. Remove my genitals and pull up my collar.'

'I think his genitals are very much intact,' I reply, glancing over. 'I think everything is right where it should be...'

'Um, he's not a piece of meat, Nora,' Will replies, tapping me on the shoulder. 'Men have feelings too, you know. Even the Brads of this world deserve respect!'

I roll my eyes and walk away but I don't get very far before I begin to titter. Brad does look like a Ken doll and now I'll never be able to unsee it. Dammit.

I'm still thinking about our workshop as I arrive back at the cabin. About how I've managed to become someone who is so crap at love and relationships. When I met Stuart, he'd just broken up with his ex and I convinced myself that my only job was to be better than her. To give him more than she'd given him. But nothing I could have done would have been enough because he just kept me around while he waited for her to come back and when she didn't, I became the target for his sadness. It's taken me ten years and one bootcamp to finally realise that he wasn't angry that I wasn't good enough for him, he was angry that *he* wasn't good enough for her. Even after he moved on to

Julia, I still hoped that he might suddenly wake up one morning and realise just what a fool he'd been and that I was the one all along. How pathetic.

I've spent years thinking I was somehow too broken to ever be properly loved. All that time just wasted. Years spent putting whatever love I had into Charlie because she was my chance to get something right and although I don't regret that for one second, I feel sad for me. I accepted my loneliness far too easily and now it feels normal. Now I don't know how to feel any other way.

I turn on the shower and throw my clothes into a pile by the door, hoping to wash away the lingering emptiness. I'm so tired of feeling empty. I'm better than this, I deserve more than just existing for my kid. I turn on some music and step into the shower, promising myself that things will change. Maybe I won't ever find true love with someone else, but I'll be damned if I'm spending the next forty years not loving myself enough to at least try.

CHAPTER 19

I dry my hair, throw on some comfy clothes and light the fire before looking at the dinner options on the TV menu.

Starters
Homemade vegetable broth with a crunchy warm, half baguette (vg) (v)
Filo-wrapped king prawn with a sweet chilli dipping sauce
Cured meats with toasted bread and chilli chutney

Mains
Asian-style stir-fried beef with broccoli
Chicken pot pie with sweet potato mash and baby carrots
Vegetarian quiche with chickpea couscous (v)

Desserts
Sticky toffee pudding (v)
Large chocolate Brownie (vg) (v)
Selection of cheeses (v)

I decide on the prawns, stir fry and toffee pudding and am informed that they will be with me within forty-five minutes which gives me plenty of time for a glass of wine and half an episode of *True Detective*. I'm already feeling brighter; it seems that a hot shower plus rage singing to Slipknot equals a better frame of mind. It's weird, in my late teens and twenties, I never understood Slipknot's appeal but recently I appear to have fallen under their curse. Pretty sure they'd be thrilled to know that they're finally appreciated by some forty-year-old single mother with sneeze incontinence and a fondness for squirrels. Regardless, I'm embracing my inner metalhead for as long as it lasts.

I snuggle up on the couch and give Charlie a call, who assures me that everything is great, and Faith is taking very good care of her. Faith yells that she'll call me later (which she won't) and to piss off and have fun. What she doesn't know is that I'm about to get my dinner delivered and I'm cosy as hell. This is the most fun I've had in years.

Next, I try Victoria.

'Nora! Are you good? How is everything?'

'I'm great,' I reply, giving the fire a wee stoke. 'It's pretty full on but the accommodation is great. How's the café?'

'Same old,' she informs me. 'You're not missing much. Tracey has been working her arse off, we should give her a few days' holiday when you're back.'

'I love that girl,' I reply. 'Definitely. And how are you? How's Benjamin?'

'Never mind about him, how's the man situation there? Are you bringing anyone back in your suitcase?'

'No one is here for *that*,' I reply. 'It's more about being a better person than hooking up. One of the mentors is hot but he's out-of-everyone's-league hot.'

'Hmm, not sure you're supposed to shag the staff anyway,' Victoria responds. 'But hooray for eye candy! Listen, I have to run, we're going to the theatre, but I'll see you when you're back! Love you!'

'Love you too.'

I hang up and smile. I am loved, even if it's not romantically. This kind of love lasts longer anyway.

When dinner arrives, I set it all out on the coffee table in front of me, so I can watch TV while I eat. I'm starting to feel like I'm on holiday. No interruptions, no rush to be anywhere; just me, a glass of white and a surprising amount of broccoli in my beef stir-fry. I might even have another hot tub later. If this is the way the rest of my evenings will play out, I'll consider this a successful trip. I press play and settle down for the night.

I'm halfway through my third glass of wine and second episode of *True Detective* when the power goes out. I shoot upright in my seat like a meerkat. The entire cabin has been plunged into darkness, bar the eerie glow from the log burner which has instantly changed the atmosphere from holiday home to *Hammer House*.

My heart is in my mouth as I scramble around for my phone to use as a torch and make my way to the patio doors, pulling back the heavy curtains. I nervously step outside. Not a single light from the cabins or the pathways. It's a complete blackout.

I wave my phone around in the air, hoping to get one bar of signal to call the emergency out-of-hours number but it's hopeless. I'm stuck here in the dark. Alone.

Of course, there would be a power cut, I think, *because no serial killer worth their salt would ever disembowel in a well-lit area.*

I look around to see if anyone else has come out of their cabin but it's only me, just standing there like a big wine-drenched, broccoli-and-crisp-filled target. I retreat inside with the *Halloween* theme tune playing softly in my head.

Stop panicking Nora. The staff won't just leave you to stumble blindly in the dark until morning. Someone will come and tell you what's happening.

It takes thirty-two minutes before I hear a knock at the front door. A hook-nosed man with a combover presents me with six tea lights and a huge, cooler-sized bottle of water.

'Toilets are electric, love, you'll need this,' he says, placing it near the kitchen door. 'There's a problem with the cables on the main road – the whole area is out. Power company says it should be fixed by morning.'

'Is this all I get?' I ask, staring at the tiny candles. 'These won't last long. Nothing bigger back there... like a floodlight?'

He shakes his head. 'All we have, love. Best just sleep through it. Happens a lot around here, you'll be fine. If you need more firewood, we've left a stack near reception.'

He wanders back to his little truck to continue with his tea light delivery while I close the door and move back beside the fire, pacing aimlessly. It's only 10.23pm. Maybe I could just watch the rest of my show on my phone? I let out a little whine when I realise that no power means no Wi-Fi. The underfloor heating cools rapidly beneath my feet. It's like a dystopian nightmare and my current survival skills are limited to fire stoking and crisp opening. What if they make us fish in the loch? I've never—

A loud knock on my living room window jolts me back to reality. I cautiously draw back the curtain to see nothing outside, before Will's face slowly appears at the window and I have a minor heart attack.

'Will!' I yelp, letting him in. 'Are you allergic to front doors?'

'Just thought I'd see if you were alright,' he states, grinning. 'Besides, I had to wait for you to invite me in. Vampire's code and all that. Thought we might combine our little tealights and have a séance or something?'

'Can you believe that's all they've given us?' I exclaim, pacing the floor. 'I mean, even a pillar candle would be more useful. Or a torch. Or you know, a backup generator!'

'Yeah, I had a feeling you might be freaking out,' he muses. 'Do you want me to stay over?'

'What, here? With me?'

'Well, some people don't like sleeping in the dark,' he replies. 'It's a thing.'

'I'm perfectly capable of sleeping in the dark, I've been doing it for years. I don't need anyone to babysit me.'

'It's fine, I don't mind,' he assures me. 'Unless you snore, that might be a problem. I'm a very light sleeper.'

'Yes, I snore like a dragon, now if you don't mind—'

'Or maybe you're a sleep-farter?' he considers. 'I dated one once. I couldn't sleep all night for laughing.'

'Ugh, you're ridiculous. Goodnight, Will, I'll see you tomorrow.'

He shrugs and slides open the patio door. 'Alright, just don't expect me to come running over at four am when you hear someone breathing under your bed. I'm happy to ward off any nutcases who might try and get in, not ones who are already inside.'

'Nice try, I'll take my chances.'

He leaves and I sharply draw the curtains behind him, now trying to shake off the image of someone hiding under my bed. What an arsehole.

I drag my pillow and duvet from the bedroom to the couch and decide to sleep there. Just in case. If the electricity isn't back on by morning, I'm going home.

CHAPTER 20

BOOTCAMP: DAY 3

I awaken to a jaunty door knock indicating that breakfast has been delivered to my cabin. I glance at my phone; it's 7.35am, which means I survived the night, as did my phone battery but only three percent remains. The fire has gone out, but the lights are all on again, as well as the heating, which pleases my feet as I stand up from the couch to plug my phone in to charge beside the television. It's funny how daylight makes everything far less threatening; at one point during the night I was convinced that someone was hiding in the bathroom, causing me to hold my bladder all night and dream about pissing myself. I dash off to the bathroom at top speed.

Teeth brushed and same jeans worn for the second day, I collect my breakfast basket from the front door where I spot Will leaving the cabin to the right. Meg's cabin. I feel my stomach plummet a little before quickly closing the door, so he doesn't see me. As I stand behind the door, I'm surprised that I feel somewhat miffed. He's obviously offered his blackout protection to every woman here, not just me, his bootcamp buddy. The voice in my head starts to mock me.

What, you thought you were special? Aw, that's adorable,

Nora. Yeah, I'm sure he was thinking of you while he shagged Miss Lifestyle Influencer over there.

I tell myself to *shut the hell up* and grab a croissant from the basket, jamming it into my face sideways. I'm doing it again. Feeling rejected by someone I wasn't even interested in, but this time I've caught myself doing it. That's progress. This isn't about him, it's none of my business what he does. This is about me.

When I arrive at the house for our morning session, we all gather in the main room and await the last few stragglers who arrive looking red-cheeked and sleepy. Will comes in a couple of minutes late, smelling of aftershave.

'Sleep alright?' I ask, trying to be as nonchalant as possible.

He places his jacket on the back of the chair. 'Not really,' he responds. 'I could do with another hour or two.'

'That's a shame,' I say, opening up my notebook as Anna walks down to the front of the room. 'Did Meg's snoring keep you up? Or maybe her farting? If she had the stir fry, there was a lot of broccoli.'

He looks at me in surprise. 'How did you—'

'I saw you leaving this morning. Quite the white knight, aren't you? Nice aftershave.'

He smirks. 'She called me over as I left yours last night. It seems she's not quite as brave in the dark as you are. Oh, and before you ask, I slept on her couch.'

Anna claps her hands together like a headmistress, causing us all to quieten down.

'Not my business,' I whisper back as she starts to speak.

'Then why mention it at all?'

'We all had an exciting night, didn't we?' Anna says, laughing. 'I don't know about you, but I was a little freaked out in the dark. Glad to hear that some of y'all found roommates, it warms my heart to know that you have that level of trust with each other already.'

I look around the room as people nod and wave at each other. Was I the only one who slept alone last night? I can tell Will has a smug look on his face but I'm not giving him the satisfaction of looking at it.

'I've been assured that everything is now running smoothly, and for the inconvenience, we're hosting dinner here this evening where you can all get together and continue to bond. Dress up! It'll be fun.'

People seem more excited about this than I am, probably because they have brought more than one fancy outfit. I only brought one dress for the end-of-bootcamp party and now I'll have to wear it twice. The shame.

'So, this morning, after meditation, we're going to look at redefining love, which I'm sure you will all find beneficial. A quick reminder that our first yoga session will be this afternoon, so please change into appropriate clothing at lunchtime.'

She dismisses us all for meditation and I skulk through behind Will, wondering how my very unfit body will cope with yoga. Victoria does yoga, but her body is made entirely from rubber. I can't even touch my toes. Maybe I'll snap something and be allowed to lie in bed for the rest of the week?

We gather our cushions for meditation and wait for Miranda to join us. Today the room smells of rose oil and patchouli as well as the aroma of someone's well-worn trainers. Will has assumed his lying-down position as usual, while everyone else chats among themselves. His left hand swipes out and taps me on the leg.

'She does tarot, you know,' he says in a low voice.

'Who does?'

'Meg.' He turns on his side to face me, whispering, 'She read my cards last night, it was weird.'

My eyes dart over to her, watching her unzip her hoodie.

'Really? Why doesn't that surprise me? Did she tell you anything interesting?'

He scratches his stubble. 'Hmm, she said I was going to have a torrid affair with a stubborn woman who wears glasses and can't open a hot tub.'

My eyes swiftly move from Meg to him. 'What? She did?'

'Of course not. It's all nonsense, but I played along.'

I look at his body stretched out beside me. I hadn't noticed just what good shape he's in. He hides it well under those ridiculous T-shirts. Not gym-ripped like Brad but wide and lean. *The kind of torso you could snuggle into after—*

'What did she actually say, then?' I ask, interrupting my own train of thought while my brain congratulates me on being the most undersexed woman in history.

'Stuff that applies to everyone,' he replies, unaware of my leering. 'Nothing specific – bad relationships in the past, a new one on the horizon, etc. People pay her forty quid a pop to turn over cards and make shit up. I'm in the wrong game.'

'My granny used to read the cards,' I reply. 'Wow, I haven't thought about that for years. And she read palms... and tea leaves. She was mental. My dad's side of the family were all a bit kooky. Well, except him. He was as straight-laced as they come.'

'Sorry, everyone, Miranda is feeling unwell today, so I'll be taking the meditation class.' Brad strides in like he owns the place and takes his position at the front of the room. Will grudgingly sits up.

'Your boyfriend's here,' he whispers.

'At least *my boyfriend* doesn't read tarot cards,' I mumble back.

I watch Brad settle into the lotus position. My thighs hurt just watching him.

'Now, if we're all ready, let's start with a deep breath in...'

Smirking, I close my eyes and let the world slip away.

. . .

At ten thirty, we all grab coffee before the next session. I've never wanted to get out of a room so quickly. I'm completely shaken by that last meditation for two reasons: 1. I still have Brad's dulcet breathy tones ringing in my ears and every time I closed my eyes 2. Will's torso was there, just looking annoyingly masculine. I couldn't get them out of my mind. It was the most awkward meditation session so far and now I feel like I've been involved in some bizarre mental three-way that was both horrifying and the most erotic thing to happen to me in years.

'You alright?' Will asks as he reaches across me for the milk. 'You look a bit flushed.'

Do you know what else feels flushed, Will? My vagina.

'I'm fine,' I respond. 'Just a bit warm in here. I'm taking my coffee outside.'

'OK, cool, I'll join you.'

I smile politely and walk towards the door, hoping that he drops dead before he has the chance to spend his break with me. It feels like that time I had a sex dream about my neighbour Mike and couldn't even say hi to him without my face bursting into flames.

I take a seat on my usual bench and blow into my coffee, while Will stops to chat to Harriet, a woman from Group One who wears the same pair of gold sandals every day, regardless of the weather. I'm so annoyed with myself. It's one thing to have secret lustful feelings towards a younger American who is out of my league, but it's unacceptable to drag the maddening, though admittedly funny, journalist that I've been sharing intimate life details with along for the ride. Will's even more messed up than I am, I don't need him in my head. I sit for a moment and try to clear my mind, reminding my lower regions that none of this shit is real.

He probably looks like a nightmare under that T-shirt. Just matted back hair and a plethora of badly spelled tattoos.

The entire group seems to be congregating outside today and as I watch them converse, I can't help thinking about how different everyone is on paper – but inside, they're essentially the same. Regardless of gold sandals or fedoras or wealth or age, everyone just wants to be loved.

I've almost finished my coffee by the time Will trundles down to sit with me and thankfully I'm calmer than I was when I left meditation class. It must be all that heavy breathing, I decide. It's only normal. I haven't had sex in three years; a firm handshake could set me off.

'I thought I'd been rumbled,' he begins, taking a swig of his half empty cup. 'That Harriet woman is convinced she knows me. Wouldn't stop throwing names and places at me, to see if one of them stuck.'

'And?' I ask, purposefully looking at him from the neck up. 'Have you met before?'

He nods. 'About twenty years ago. Her name used to be Harriet Ogilvie and she used to be blonde and ninety pounds heavier. She was married to my first editor, Marcus. I think they're still on good terms.'

'Well, even journalists come on retreats like this,' I reply. 'It's not that big a deal, surely?'

'My wife still works with Marcus,' he replies quietly. 'I don't want her to find out I'm here. I don't want—'

His voice trails off as he throws the remainder of his coffee into the grass.

'You don't want her to think you're moving on?'

He locks eyes with me but doesn't reply. He doesn't need to; I can see the answer on his face.

'Anyway, I gave her the *I'm a retired house builder* line, which is dull but lucrative enough to be believable that I could afford this place. Seemed to work.'

'Retired at your age?'

'That's just how lucrative it was... Besides, everyone's too interested in talking about themselves.'

I laugh. 'You have a point. You've never asked me anything about myself. Where I'm from... what I do for a living.'

He squirms. 'You're right, I haven't. Let me guess?'

'Go for it.'

He looks me up and down then stares like he's trying to extract clues from my very soul.

'You run a business. A restaurant... no... a coffee shop.'

I glare. 'That's cheating. Who told you?'

'Nish,' he replies. 'He was filling me in on your little dating chat last night at Meg's cabin. He's a tad smitten, I think. He said you were intriguing.'

'He did? Well, that's very... hang on, he was at Meg's cabin too?'

Will tuts. 'You think I just shacked up alone with some wee girl for the evening? I invited Nish over straight away.'

'She's a grown woman!' I insist. 'Besides, you were willing to shack up with me!'

He grins. 'Yeah, but you're my buddy. Buddies hang, they don't shack.'

Normally, a man describing me as his 'buddy' is a fate worse than death but this time, it doesn't feel like any kind of rejection. It feels right.

'Time to go,' I say, lifting my cup from the ground. 'You ready to define love?'

He sighs. 'Not particularly.'

'Great,' I reply. 'Me neither.'

We head back towards everyone else and make our way inside where Anna is already waiting to begin.

CHAPTER 21

'We're taught from an early age that true love equals a happy ever after. That we have a soulmate out there and that our romantic lives will only be truly complete when we meet them. I'm here to tell you that this is wrong.'

I notice a few confused people side-eye each other, while Anna projects a picture of two flames onto the screen behind her.

'You can have many, many soulmates in your many, many lifetimes. A soulmate is simply someone who is made from the same kind of energy as you. These do not just have to be lovers; they can be friends, family, anyone you have a deep connection with. Ever just click with someone? Feel like you've known them all your life? That's a very good indication that they are a soulmate. However, it's not uncommon for these people to come in and out of your life quickly, which of course can lead to confusion.'

I see Will scribbling on his notepad before nudging me.

I think you are my soulmate. Please have better dress sense in our next life.

My entire body shakes as I desperately try not to laugh, but now Will's shaking too, and people are tutting. Thankfully, Anna hasn't noticed.

'The only person who is meant for you, and only you in the spiritual sense, is your twin flame.' She points to the picture behind her. 'Your twin flame is far more powerful than your soulmate. It's literally the other half of your soul. Your soulmate will improve your life, but your twin flame will complete it.'

The confused faces now have a glow of excitement, because clearly a twin flame is better than some old soulmate.

'However, as with everything,' she continues, 'connecting with your twin flame, or even a soulmate, requires you to be vibrating on the same level as they are. You are here participating in the human experience, as is everyone else. If you're not vibrationally aligned, unfortunately you'll never connect. That's why it's so important to get into a place where you know and love and appreciate yourself because that's a kind of vibration which cannot fail to attract the same.'

'So, we might never meet our twin flame?' Meg shouts out. I can hear the desperation in her voice.

Anna smiles. 'You absolutely will, sugar; it just might not be in this lifetime.' She turns to the rest of us. 'This is why we need to redefine love. Y'all have this romantic ideal that must happen immediately or you've somehow failed. You cannot put life on hold. Fall in love with everyone you meet, take as many lovers as you desire, stop thinking that the next relationship should be the last one! There is no *last one* because nothing ever truly ends. Every experience teaches us about what we want and don't want, which in turn affects the choices we make going forward.'

She clicks on her slides again.

LOVE IS WHAT YOU DECIDE IT IS.

'You define it. You make the rules. Tell the universe what you want and live like you already have it until you do.'

'What if we did have it, but we messed it up? Can we get it back?'

As everyone turns to look at Kenneth, a couple of things become clear. Firstly, this is now just a shouty free-for-all and secondly, he's absolutely talking about Patricia.

'It depends on them,' Anna responds. 'You cannot make someone feel what you want them to feel. All you can do is *you* and hope that you are a vibrational match for them.'

'But what if that person refuses to change?' Patricia turns her entire body to glare at Kenneth. 'What if you let them back in and they're still exactly the same low-life scumbag who never appreciated what they had?'

Will scribbles:

THIS IS BRILLIANT.

If I were Anna, I'd be feeling so uncomfortable right now, but she's still smiling. God, she's good. I want to be her when I grow up.

'So often we think "this person would be perfect for me if they'd just change". Forget that! You have to get into a place where everything about them is accepted by *you*. If something doesn't feel right, look at why it bothers you, not why it doesn't bother them.'

Patricia shakes her head.

'I see what's happening here,' Anna remarks. 'We all do. Now – I don't normally do this, I'm no marriage counsellor, but since y'all seem eager to do this publicly, let's see where it goes.'

A hush comes over the group as Brad pulls two chairs to the front and requests that Patricia and Kenneth take a seat. I swear, if I had popcorn, I'd be truly happy right now.

Anna walks back and forth behind them while we all look on with bated breath.

'So, let's keep this simple,' she begins. 'And please only one at a time, this ain't *The Jerry Springer Show*. Who left who, and why?'

Anna has barely finished her sentence before Patricia announces that she left Kenneth because he cheated.

'I knew he would cheat,' she insists. 'There wasn't a day that went by where I wasn't thinking about it. It was a miserable existence.'

Anna places her hand on Patricia's shoulder. 'OK, and Kenneth. Is this true? Just so we're all on the same page.'

Kenneth nods. 'But I only cheated once, and it was months after she first started accusing me.'

Anna doesn't place her hand on Kenneth's shoulder, instead she turns to Patricia. 'So, let's see... you woke up every day and told yourself that Kenneth was screwing around... and then you were surprised that he did?'

Woah. Even Will gasps. Patricia looks both confused and hurt.

'We'll get to him in a minute, hon, but do you understand where I'm going with this? We get what we think about and all you could think about was your man screwing someone else.'

'So, it's my fault?'

'This isn't about fault, sugar, it's about vibration. Morality is subjective. When we don't feel worthy or good enough, we start to project that on to other people. If I feel like crap then other people must feel that way about me too, right? Why didn't you feel good enough?'

Patricia's voice starts to tremble. 'The older I got the less interested he became. He worked with women half my age and they loved him. He's a very handsome, charismatic man!'

Will and I glance at each other, wondering if we're looking at the same man as Patricia. Each to their own, I guess?

Anna then turns to Kenneth who by now looks terrified and is undoubtedly wishing he'd kept his mouth shut.

'Why did you choose to cheat?' she asks bluntly. 'Because it was a choice.'

Kenneth slinks down in his chair a little. 'I just thought, if she's accusing me of cheating, then—'

'Well, that's bullshit,' Anna replies. 'What was lacking in YOU that made you go elsewhere? Patricia's already owned her part, now it's your turn.'

'She changed,' he states. 'And the age part was never an issue, I've always been deeply attracted to Patricia. But over the years she became someone far more independent than the woman I married. She didn't need me and that was unsettling. Flirting with younger women made me feel powerful. It made me feel needed.'

'So, you spent your days thinking *my wife doesn't need me* and then you were surprised when she left?'

Honestly, I want to applaud. Everyone is on the edge of their seats.

Anna places a hand on each of their shoulders. Patricia is a blubbering mess and Kenneth just looks shell-shocked.

'In relationships, communication is vital,' she says. 'The cheating wasn't the problem; it was just the result of something that was already very broken. Work on yourselves first, my friends. No matter how close you are to your partner, they cannot read your mind. Be open and be willing to listen.'

I see Kenneth whisper something to Patricia before taking her hand in his and kissing it. There's an audible *aww* from everyone as she leans in for a hug. My heart skips a little. I can tell she's hesitant, but it's also a start. Even Will's dimples appear in approval.

'Now let's break for lunch,' Anna announces, visibly pleased by this result. 'Great work, everyone.'

The room is in high spirits as we march down towards

reception. We've all just witnessed two people start to heal and now it's our job to dissect every damn second of it. Will and I both get soup and a sandwich from the reception café before sitting by the loch to eat it.

'I'm actually really happy for them,' I say, dunking my bread crust into my soup. 'The way he kissed her hand... I didn't think stuff like that happened outside of Richard Curtis films. Ouch! This soup is like lava.'

'I'm not entirely convinced that wasn't staged,' Will remarks, stomping all over my optimism. 'For exactly that reason. People don't behave like that, outside of movies. Not in the UK anyway. I once heard a bride tut and sigh before she said, "I do". Generally, people just aren't that openly gushy over each other.' He bites into his sandwich as I stare in disbelief.

'You've never been that level of nuts over someone? Not even your wife?'

He shakes his head, still chewing. 'No... well, maybe I was a bit, but she's more restrained than me. I don't remember us ever publicly leaping on each other.'

'They hardly *leapt* on each other,' I reply. 'But maybe they should have. People should leap on each other more often.'

We sit in quiet contemplation for a moment. It's so peaceful. The loch is so still.

'So... when was the last time you leapt on anyone?' he asks.

'Never,' I reply, 'But I've wanted to! I've just never been with anyone I was one hundred percent sure wouldn't just dart out of the way mid-leap.'

Will pauses. 'You know, that's kind of pathetic. Sweet but, well...'

'Oh, screw you,' I yell, throwing the last of my sandwich crust at him. 'I am not pathetic, just cautious.'

'I'm only winding you up,' he assures me. 'You should be able to leap on as many men as you like without fear of face-planting. They would be lucky to catch you.'

'Damn right.' I reply. 'They should be lined up like—'

'AGH!'

I see Will drop his soup container and quickly pull at the wet stain on his trousers. 'This shit is scalding!'

'You've probably got a burn,' I inform him. 'Go and get those trousers off, I have some antiseptic cream in my cabin. I'll bring it over in a sec.'

He agrees and we go our separate ways, though I'm far slower as I'm still determined to hold on to my soup. It's deadly but delicious.

Five minutes later and I'm knocking at his door with a tub of Sudocrem and a half-eaten sandwich. He yells at me to come inside. His cabin is identical to mine, though it's already showing signs of disrepair, commonly known as 'lived in by boy'. Clothes are strewn around, empty mugs lie unwashed and it smells like testosterone mixed with feet.

'You should open some windows in here,' I mutter, not loud enough for him to hear but loud enough to appease my burning desire to say it out loud. I hear him walk from the bedroom.

'Any damage?' I ask. 'Your jeans might have— WOW, OK. You're in your underwear. Good. Right then.'

My neck nearly breaks as I whip my head around to face any other direction than Will's pants. His Prodigy T-shirt covers the main parts but I'm still very aware of what lurks beneath.

'Oh, for God's sake, you'd see more at the beach,' he mocks, pulling out a chair at the kitchen table. 'It's really freaking sore actually. You got that cream?'

Still not looking, I pass him the white tub.

'Why do you carry around nappy rash cream?' he asks. 'Do you chafe easily?'

'It's good for blemishes,' I reply, watching some birds land on his decking. 'And other stuff... listen, just rub it on.'

'They're only pants, Nora. Can you at least take a look at the burn? I might need to put a dressing over it or something.'

I purse my lips and turn around, pulling out the chair beside him where he's rolled up the bottom of his underwear to reveal a red mark at the top of his thigh. Hardly the third-degree trauma I was expecting, and his junk is still covered. I give a little sigh of relief.

'I think you'll survive,' I tell him, looking away as he applies the cream. 'I like your T-shirt by the way; I saw The Prodigy years ago – '97 or '98 maybe? On Glasgow Green.'

'The Event in the Tent?' he asks. 'I was there! I still lived in Edinburgh at the time.'

'Really?' I reply. 'That's so funny. We could have been standing side by side and never have known! How is it feeling?'

As I turn, my gaze inadvertently moves slightly to the left, landing upon the outline of his penis and I quietly gasp. My head whips back at record speed. That can't be real?

'Thanks for helping,' he says, clicking the lid back on the tub. 'It's like payback for the hot—'

'No problem! Fine! It's fine! See you for yoga,' I blurt out, grabbing the cream from his hand. I need to leave. I was bad enough with his torso, I cannot have THIS in my head too. Nope. Nooo. No way.

'Um... OK. I mean, if you hang on two mins, we can—'

Discuss the size of your penis?

'I need to make a phone call,' I reply, tripping over the chair leg as I head for the hills. 'Smell you later!'

Smell you later? For goodness' sake.

I rush back to my cabin, slamming the door behind me. Throwing down the cream, I lift my soup which I left to cool while I was busy trying not to look at Will's knob. I feel like such a creep. He's trusting me to help with a painful burn and I'm all *PENIS! YOU HAVE A PENIS! What are you? Twelve? Get a grip, Nora.*

Spooning some vegetables into my mouth, I grab my phone and dial the café.

'Café 12, Victoria speaking.'

'I'm losing it here, Victoria.'

'Nora? Nora, we're kind of busy. What's wrong?'

'This place has turned me into a pervert, that's what's wrong. I saw a penis and—'

'Whose penis?'

'Well, it was still inside his boxers, but I saw the outline. And his chest is wide. And *then* there's the American mentor who is just, ugghhh, and—'

'Hang on, I'm moving somewhere quieter.'

Ten seconds later, I hear her close the door. 'Nora, this is what happens when you don't have sex for a century and are then within smelling distance of the opposite sex. All those pheromones, they mess with you. It's science.'

'It's ridiculous, is what it is. I'm forty! I should be able to—'

'Bang him instead of calling me at work?'

'I was going to say deal with it in a responsible and grown-up fashion.'

She laughs. 'How dull. No chance of sleeping with him? I mean, get a proper look at it at least!'

'Victoria, I'm not going to get him to slap it down like a bad poker hand. Besides, he's married. Well, separated, but still in love with his wife and blah blah blah. He looks huge though.'

'How huge?'

'Remember when we went on holiday to Greece, and you hooked up with that German guy and he could only get the tip in?'

'Really? That big?'

'At least.'

She laughs. 'That wasn't fun. You've given birth though, you have room.'

I snort loudly. 'For God's sake, Victoria, it doesn't stay dilated. It's made of muscle, not cheap knicker elastic.'

'Look, I need to run, Tracey's on her own out there. You'll be fine. Just think unsexy thoughts. You'll be home and frigid again before you know it. Love you!'

'Frigid?'

She hangs up and I stare at my phone like it's going to reply on her behalf. Eventually I place it on the table and get back to my soup. I only have fifteen minutes left and I need to change for yoga with Brad... *Flexible Brad... Bendy Brad.*

Oh, piss off, me.

CHAPTER 22

Yoga takes place in the meditation room, but we're joined by Group Three, which means space is tighter than normal. Brad, wearing dark wide-legged yoga pants and a white vest, puts the twenty of us into four lines of five. I've thrown on some leggings and a clean T-shirt for yoga but most of the women in the room have come as the Kardashians: tight, bottom-hugging, wet-look leggings, cropped tops and one-piece catsuits. I've never felt like such a plain Jane in my entire life. The only other person unhappier to be here than me is Tim who is wearing a shell suit from 1988 and undoubtedly wishing he was back then. Will sits behind me in grey joggers, possibly the worst thing a man with a noticeable package can wear, but I keep my eyes front and centre, thankful that I don't have to stare at him for the next forty-five mins.

'I know many of you are experienced with yoga,' Brad says, folding his little origami legs. 'But today we're going to keep things simple. Yoga is another tool we can use to tune out the physical world and tune into it the spiritual one, through deep breathing and connecting with our bodies. So, everyone, legs crossed and spine nice and straight – this will help the blood circulate more easily. OK, palms facing up and take a deep breath in... and out... now when we breathe in, we want the stomach to expand and on breathing out the stomach should contract.'

Wait? What? Hang on a sec. For the first time in my life, the simple art of breathing has become complicated.

'And breathe in again, pushing the stomach out first—'

I try again and I end up pushing my pelvic floor into my yoga mat. That's not right. *What the hell, Brad? I know how to breathe. I'm an expert. You can't just change breathing.*

Brad stands and starts walking up and down the lines, observing everyone's attempts to reverse breathe. I can't see if anyone else is getting it wrong as they all have their backs to me. I peek behind me at Will and see him, eyes closed, legs crossed, nailing this.

Traitor. I turn back around to see Brad making his way towards me. I feel like I've been caught trying to cheat on a test.

'Problems?' He bends down behind me and takes my right hand, placing it over my belly with his on top, then leans in. I recognise the smell of the complimentary shower gel that hangs in the bathroom. I haven't been this close to a man since the last great disappointing shag of summer three years ago.

'Um, well, when I breathe in, my stomach follows.'

'Yes, some people breathe like that.'

All people, Brad. All people.

'This might help,' he says quietly. 'Focus on guiding your breath towards your hand.'

I nod and remain silently perplexed as he makes his way around the rest of the class. Perplexed and mildly aroused. My lack of intimacy curse strikes again.

After what seems like three hours of endeavouring to breathe incorrectly, Brad asks us to stretch our legs out, exhale deeply and reach for our toes. Oh, dear God, my toes might as well be in space as I'm not reaching them anytime soon. We repeat this a few times before we 'rock the baby', a move which involves cradling one of my legs like an infant while moving from side to side. My flexibility allows me about an inch of lift before I start to wobble like a Weeble. The rest of the class doesn't get any better. My downward-facing dog resembles a fat-arsed hunchback at the start of a race, I fall flat on my tits during planking and I almost boot Will in the face trying to do a sun salutation. I'm not the only one getting it badly wrong, however. Even those who appear experienced occasionally lose their balance, Jillian gets her earring caught in her hair and at least two people break wind, though no one owns up.

As we finish by giving thanks, I flop to the floor, feeling stretched to within an inch of my life. Is yoga supposed to make you sweat this much? I look at Will who's perfectly dry and not fazed by any of this.

'Did you even participate?' I ask, scanning his brow line for signs of perspiration. 'I'm a mess here! You just look like you've had a nap.'

'I do yoga,' he replies. 'Most days. Well, Pilates mainly. This was more like a light stretch.'

'Bullshit!' I reply. 'There's no way!'

He laughs. 'Why is it so hard to believe? I had back surgery a couple of years ago. Yoga was part of my rehab and I kept it up. My instructor is more physiotherapy-focused than spiritual. He doesn't give thanks to the cosmos afterwards.'

I'm unsure whether to believe him or not because he looks like the type of man who would bully fancy yoga types and steal their brunch money. I'm tempted to make him perform complicated Pilates manoeuvres in front of me but it's time for our last session of the day, so I put my shoes on and follow everyone back into the main room.

'For the last session today, I want you to go off and revise your cosmic love order. You can return to your cabin, sit in the garden or by the loch, wherever inspires you. See if your original thoughts on your ideal partner have changed. Sit quietly and reflect on whether the changes you feel within yourself have altered what you want from a potential partner. Thanks, everyone, we'll see y'all here at seven pm for dinner.'

I feel slightly guilty that I intend to use the last session to shower and eat chocolate, but I imagine I'm not the only one. Will mumbles something about having a nap while I observe Patricia and Kenneth scuttling off together like a pair of horny teenagers. I feel a pang of envy. It's been a long time since I've wanted to sneak off with anyone. I walk with Will back to the cabins, while everyone disperses in different directions.

'I think people are actually going to work on this,' I say, pointing towards Meg who's sitting on a bench near the loch. 'I feel like I'm bunking off school.'

'Me too,' Will replies. 'Fun, right?'

I laugh. 'A little. Though I could do without dressing up for dinner tonight. I just want to slob out in front of the telly.'

'I know what you mean,' Will replies, 'but if you think you're leaving me with that lot, you're wrong. I need some level of decent conversation. I'll pop over at six forty-five pm and we can walk up.'

I reluctantly agree and head into my cabin, desperate to get out of my sweaty yoga clothes and into the shower. I hang my one and only dress on the back of the bedroom door before heading into the bathroom. My mind might be on this evening but there's a nagging voice in my head, thinking about the task I should be doing. I turn on the shower and let it run while I grab my notebook from the kitchen table and flip back to the pages on cosmic ordering.

I laugh as I read through my notes.

Has siblings with ridiculous names like Beetroot and Windfarm.

Even my serious attempts were half-arsed.

Is funny.

Has full head of hair.

Really? I think. I've just described Ken Dodd. Am I so demoralised that I'll just settle for anything?

I throw my notepad on the table and return to the bathroom, stripping off. I've never properly thought about what I want from a partner because I've never considered it to be an option. Well, maybe once Charlie leaves home in her mid-twenties, but by then I'll be fifty. I can't imagine the dating pool is deep when you hit fifty. More of a murky puddle.

I step into the shower and vigorously wash off the day.

If I did get to order my ideal man, he'd be a lot more than hair and jokes. He'd be kind, honest, passionate, clever, tall, handsome... but not handsome enough to make me wonder what the hell he was doing with me. He'd know what I like without even having to ask... independent... great in bed... big, girthy—

Will in his grey joggers pop into my mind and I nearly drop my complimentary loofah. This is getting ridiculous.

It's just a knob, Nora. The knob of a man who has no interest in you and every interest in his wife.

I begin shaving my legs because hairs *poking through tights* is not the look I'm going for this evening.

And more importantly you have no interest in him! You're just confused from all the manly pheromones and the Brad arms and the heavy breathing you've been exposed to.

'Correct!' I say audibly, moving on to the other leg, surprised at my own level of awareness. I'm impressed. Maybe I have learned more than I thought? Maybe I really have left the old me at the door?

Though, maybe you should tidy up that overgrown pubic disaster... you know... just in case.

Oh, forget it.

By half past six, I'm ready. My uncomfortably constrictive control tights work miracles under my little black dress, leaving room only for liquids and lettuce. I admire my blonde hair in the mirror; it's shinier than usual and I've managed to straighten it without frying the ends. Contact lenses are in, smudge-proof lippy applied and after a quick spray of perfume, I slip my feet into my kitten heels and pour a glass of wine. For the first time in a long time, I don't feel like just a mum, or just that woman from the café. I feel like me. I manage four sips before I hear Will knocking at the patio window. He's early. I wanted to be one glass down before I had to deal with him.

'Good, you have wine. I've run out,' he says, bounding in. 'I thought I'd bought—'

He stops mid-sentence and stares at me.

'What? What is it?'

'Nothing. You just look different with your hair down... and a dress on.'

'Will, are you trying to tell me I look nice?'

'No... I mean yes. Yes, you look fine.'

I laugh. 'Great. I've always wanted to look *fine*.'

He grabs a coffee mug from the side of the sink and pour some wine, knocking it back in a oner. 'Shall we go? I'm starving.'

Before I've even replied, he's back outside waiting for me. I lift my phone and jacket and join him on the patio. Nish passes by and waits for us to catch up. I can see Meg, Russell and the woman who cried about her dog-child fifty feet in front.

'Hi, Nish, are you well?' I ask, buttoning my coat. 'Nice shirt.'

His black shirt has orange flames leaping around the bottom and I hate it.

'You look lovely, Nora,' he says quietly. 'I like your shoes.'

'Thanks, Nish,' I reply. 'That's very kind of you.' I see Will glance down at my shoes. If he says they're *fine*, I'll kick him. But he doesn't comment on them at all, he just keeps walking.

Before long we arrive at the main house, softly lit outside, with waiting staff ready to take coats and show us through to the dining room. It's ridiculously fancy and for once I feel like I fit in perfectly. My dress might be from TK Maxx, but it feels like Valentino couture.

The main hall has been transformed, with round tables dressed in white linen, sparkly lighting and not an incense stick in sight. As I take a seat between Will and Patricia, I spy Brad in a sharp black suit and skinny tie. Damn, that man can dress. Will on the other hand has thrown a suit jacket over his T-shirt and jeans and finished his look with a pair of trainers. I hate that he also looks good despite having made zero effort. Anna, dressed in red, is sitting at the top left table, chatting to Jillian, who has chosen a white trouser suit that's about thirty minutes away from being spilled on.

'Wine?' Russell asks, lifting one of the bottles from the middle of the table. We all nod. Nish, Meg and Allison join us while he pours the white and Will pours the red. I'm grateful that there are no seats left when creepy Paul attempts to sit with us. I can do without him imagining us all tethered while we're trying to eat.

'Can I just make a quick toast?' Allison asks, a cloud of vape escaping from her mouth. 'Since most of our little group is here, I just wanted to let you know how happy I am to have met you all. Well, most of you.' She throws a quick glare towards Tim, who is currently chatting with a woman half his age and twice his size. 'Old cheapskate,' she mutters under her breath.

'Anyway,' she continues, her daggers retreating, 'here's to us. May we find the love and financial security we all deserve.'

Will coughs on his wine while we all clink glasses and I make a mental note to find out what happened there. Three glasses of wine should do it.

A waiter appears at the table asking who requires the vegan and vegetarian options while Anna makes her way around the tables, ensuring we're all 'peachy'.

'I can see the growth in y'all already,' she gushes, placing her hand on Nish's arm. He smiles awkwardly. 'And you two. You're like magnets.'

She stares at Will and me. Wait, she's talking about Will and me?

'We are?' Will asks, a smile slowly creeping on to his face. 'But don't magnets repel each other?'

'They do,' she replies. 'But only if they're alike. Opposites attract, my sweet, it's as certain as gravity... enjoy your meal, everyone.'

She glides off to the next table while everyone giggles and makes *ooh*ing noises in Will's direction. I can tell it's making him uncomfortable, like the *ooh*ing might somehow reach his wife's ears and ruin any hope he still has of a reconciliation.

'Oh, relax, everyone,' I say quickly, deflecting the attention away from him. 'Will and I only get on so well because we both... erm... we both—'

'We met in rehab last year.'

I kick Will under the table. Rehab? What the hell is he saying?

'I know I can trust you all not to spread this around,' he continues. 'It was... it was a difficult time.'

'Drugs?' Allison asks, leaning in. 'Was it drugs? Booze?'

I glare at Will.

He shakes his head. 'No, nothing like that. Maybe I've

spoken out of turn. It's not my place to tell you what Nora was treated for.'

Aannnd it's all eyes on me. I purse my lips and try to look solemn. As much as I want to ram my kitten heel up Will's arse, there's a tiny part of me that is enjoying this. Besides, we're in too deep now.

'Shopping,' I say, cocking my head to the side, like Princess Diana. 'I had a shopping addiction.'

The women gasp while Will quietly snorts.

'Shopping?' Nish asks, sounding slightly disappointed that I wasn't a full-blown meth enthusiast. 'How much did you—'

'I spent thousands,' I confess. 'Designer clothes, custom-made underwear, imported shoes, anything. I even had Stella McCartney design my wedding dress.'

'You were married?'

'No. He left when he found out the extent of my addiction. He wasn't a wealthy man, you see.'

'Well, that was your first mistake,' Allison remarks bluntly.

'Perhaps,' I answer, stunned that they're believing this. 'Regardless, I went into rehab and, well, that's where I met Will.'

Meg suddenly chimes in. 'So, wait... is that why you're always dressed in cheap clothes? Because expensive stuff is a reminder of that awful time in your life?'

Will pretends to drop his knife so he can disappear under the table and laugh. I kick him again. 'You're so insightful, Meg,' I reply. 'That's exactly why. I've learned to be happy wearing high street rather than Bond Street. And now, I just need to find that special someone who will also love me, regardless of my label.'

Will finally finds his knife and reappears, his eyes teary from laughing, just as the waiters serve our dinner.

'You see, Will's getting emotional,' I say. 'It was a tough time for both of us. What with my overspending and Will's sex addiction...' I mouth the word sex like a repressed housewife. Now it's Will's turn to kick me.

We're served salmon parcels with pesto-dressed vegetables, but no one cares about the food. They're waiting for Will to tell his story, as am I. He stalls until the waiters have left before beginning.

'There isn't much to say,' he begins, clearing his throat. 'While Nora chose to spend money to get her kicks, I got comfort from shagging as much and as often as possible.'

'Porn!' Nish blurts out. No one is sure whether this is a question or a confession.

'Not quite,' Will replies. 'I prefer real women. But I cheated on girlfriends, I met women online, in bars, anywhere. It got to the point where it was all I could think about, all I wanted to do.'

He turns to Allison and leans in. 'Have you ever just had that urge... that craving for skin on skin, hot, sweaty grinding?'

She glazes over and quietly gulps. 'Uh-huh.'

'It's all consuming, isn't it?' he says, smiling seductively. I find myself staring at his dimples again. All Allison can do is nod. I think she's about to pass out.

He pulls back and shrugs. 'So, I sought help. I've been celibate for five years now.'

'FIVE YEARS?' says, well, everyone.

Will nods. 'That's why I'm here. I'm ready to be intimate again. To learn how to love again.'

'But five years, bruv?' Russell replies, looking genuinely shocked. 'I'm struggling at a week. That's crazy, man!'

'I think it's commendable,' Meg replies, cutting into her weird-looking vegan dish while Allison bobs her head in agreement. 'Like atoning for your sins or something.'

Of course. Will gets applauded for his fake recovery while I just get called a bad dresser. I start hacking into my salmon.

'Anyway, I'm sure you all will keep this to yourselves,' I say, moving the conversation on. 'We're not magnets or special soul-mates or whatever. We're just mates.'

Will and I do our best fake friendship smile at one another, and we all continue with dinner but there's a glint in his eye that makes me feel that it might not be entirely false.

As the evening progresses, I feel glad I decided to attend instead of lying on the couch eating chocolate like a podgy recluse. The company is good, the wine is great, and the highlight is the lemon cheesecake with raspberry coulis.

'I'll walk back with you,' Will states.

'You don't need to,' I assure him, scraping the last of my dessert from my plate. 'It's only nine fifteen. Pretty sure the maniacs don't come out until eleven pm. It's in the handbook.'

'I know,' he replies. 'It's more for my safety than yours. Allison's been giving me looks like she wants to deflower me. Besides, you have wine left. The shop closed at nine.'

I eventually agree as I'm a little tipsier than I intended. I'd appreciate the extra pair of hands when I inevitably trip up in these damn heels and fall flat on my face.

Anna thanks us all for coming and tells us she looks forward to seeing us bright and early in the morning. Anna shouldn't have plied us with booze if that was her endgame.

We collect our coats and merrily exit the main house, greeted by a cool breeze and a black sky full of stars. I stop to admire them.

'I think this is the only time I will ever admit to there being anything remotely magical about the universe,' I say to Will.

'Yeah, they're spectacular when they're not hidden by pollution, eh?'

We walk swiftly back towards my cabin, where we agree that Will should light the fire while I get the drinks. There's only half a bottle of wine left and two emergency cans of G&T

in the fridge. I turn on the lights and throw my jacket on the couch. I feel like I've had a proper night out. It's kind of pitiful.

'Put some music on,' Will requests as he lights the kindling. 'Nothing too middle-aged though. If I hear ABBA, I'll never forgive you.'

I press play and Slipknot blasts out. He raises an eyebrow.

'Slipknot? You're listening to Slipknot? You?

'What?' I reply, pouring the remainder of the bottle into equal measures. 'You don't know me. You don't know my struggle.'

He laughs. 'True. I mean I know you liked The Prodigy in your teens, I just wouldn't have pictured you as a Slipknot fan. Their music is dark. I'd have thought these days you'd be more... Ed Sheeran. Something inoffensive for the school run.'

'I'll listen to anything,' I reply. 'Including Ed Sheeran. I even know all the words to a Slipknot song. I'm full of surprises. I used to be wild, you know.'

'Doubt it.'

'I did!' I insist. 'I just never get the chance these days.'

'Prove it.'

'Prove what?'

'That you're full of surprises.'

'How? I'm not a Kinder egg, Will.'

'Skinny-dipping! Ever done it? We have a loch right there.'

I don't know if he's serious or not. I sip my wine and look at him suspiciously. 'It's about three degrees outside. Also, that massive "no swimming" sign makes me think – hmm, better not.'

He considers this for a second. 'Hot tub, then.'

'What?! This is crazy; I'm tipsy and more importantly, there's no way you're seeing me naked.'

He rolls his eyes. 'Yes, that would be awful. I might be forced to break my celibacy rule... Listen, I'm going in regardless. I'm a tad drunk, and it'll be fun. I guarantee every other person here is in their tub right now. Join me. Wear a swimsuit, wear everything you own, I'm not bothered.'

He takes his glass, opens the patio doors and lifts off the hot tub cover with one hand while I stand there, yelling that I'm not coming in as I watch him strip off and climb in. He's naked. In my hot tub. Naked! I edge out of the patio doors.

'You sure you're not coming in?' He rests his glass in the holder and lies back.

'Well, not now I'm not,' I reply petulantly. 'You're naked. You have sullied the water with your dangly bits.'

'Suit yourself.'

I walk out onto the deck and look over the lodges. Hot tubs glowing as far as the eye can see. Is everyone having fun except me? I hesitate, my heart beating rapidly as I find myself considering this.

'Life is short, Nora.'

Shut up, Will. I down the rest of my wine. I'm doing this.

I pull down my tights and kick them off, before slipping out of my dress, just as Will looks over to see me standing in my bra and humongous tummy shaper pants. I want to die.

'YAAASS!' he yells, encouragingly. 'Get those outrageous knickers in here.'

No human alive has ever entered a hot tub as quickly as I have, sinking underneath the water, hoping the bubbles will hide me from the neck down. Glancing at Will, I see that this clearly isn't the case. God, it's like bathing with a porn star.

If these pants weren't tight enough when dry, they're horrendously uncomfortable when wet. I squirm around, trying to pry them from my flesh.

'You don't look very relaxed.'

'I'm fine,' I lie, 'All good here. Just adjusting the undies.'

'Nora, I am aware that you have lady parts. I have seen many in my lifetime. Yes, you might get embarrassed for about six seconds until you remember that I also have my dick out and now we're even-stevens. I won't lay a hand on you, if that's what you're worried about.'

Worried? If only you knew the filth that rampaged around my head during meditation.

'Not worried,' I assure him. 'I'm just not confident. I don't even want to see me naked.'

I peel off my underwear and unhook my bra, throwing them both to the side of the tub. I'm naked in a hot tub with a man I only met three days ago. A man I'm not trying to impress. A man who doesn't appear to want anything from me except my company. I start to tentatively relax.

'So how is your article going? What's your angle going to be?'

He thinks. 'Hmm, hot tub housewife hotties perhaps? Shopping addicts gone wild?'

'Shut up!' I exclaim, splashing him.

'I'm kidding! There is no angle as such. I'm here to take it all in with an open mind – just like you.'

'And your thoughts so far?'

'It's strange,' he replies, lifting his glass from the side of the tub. 'Initially I was stunned by the level of bullshit and gullibility that goes on but...'

'But?'

'It's hard to explain. I think loneliness is universal but implying the universe is behind it all, is, well, *nuts*. BUT I don't think empowering people to like themselves more is ever a bad thing, nor is challenging them to let go of past bullshit. Let's just say, I've been pleasantly surprised by some aspects.'

'Yes, you got to see my fat ass. Worth the admission alone.'

'To be honest I was thinking that at yoga earlier.'

'What, that my ass is fat?'

'No, that it was worth the trip... Are you blushing?'

'No, I'm just warm,' I lie. I'm totally blushing.

He wipes stray water droplets from his face and grins. 'Let's play a game.'

'A game? What kind of game? I'm not spinning that bottle while there's still booze in it.'

'Tell me three facts about yourself, *but* only one of them can be the truth.'

'Hmm, OK.' I sit up straight and put on my thinking face, while he stares at me looking mildly amused. Three facts about me? Like what? I'm older than I once was? I tweeze my chin daily? Ugh, this is hard.

Before he dozes off, I pluck two lies out of the air and one fact from my brain. 'Right. Are you ready?'

'Ready.'

'Fact number one: I was once proposed to in the Bronx Zoo. Fact two: My favourite film is *Beaches*. Fact three: I have an irrational phobia of biting into fruit.'

He narrows his eyes at me and tries to read my poker face but I'm giving nothing away.

'Hmm... the fruit one could very well be true, as could the zoo. I'm not buying *Beaches* though.'

'No? Why?'

'Too sentimental. So, I'm calling bullshit on that.'

I laugh. 'Fine. You're right. So, which is the truth? Fruit or the zoo?'

'The zoo is too obscure to be fictional. I'm going with that one.'

I throw my arms in the air and delightedly tell him he's wrong. 'Nope, never even been to New York. I am in fact freaked out at the thought of biting into fruit, in case there's something living inside it.' I shudder but maintain my winner's stance.

'So where did you get proposed to?'

'Nowhere! I've never been proposed to!' I happily exclaim before grasping that this admission probably doesn't require winner's arms. I place them back beneath the water and purse my lips. I'm forty and no one has ever considered me marriage material. I suddenly don't feel like a winner.

He senses my melancholy and splashes me. 'No moping, fruit face. It's my turn now.'

I nod and smirk as he theatrically clears his throat. 'Fact one: I lost my virginity to my friend's mum. Fact two: I am good friends with Adele. Fact three: I studied piano at university for two years before deciding to become a journalist.'

'I'm not buying the first one, that's just a scene from *American Pie*.'

'OK...'

'And those hands look far too big and clumsy to play the piano. Guitar maybe, but not piano... so I'm going with Adele. For some reason that seems the most believable.'

'Wrong,' he declares. 'Because they are in fact, all true.'

My eyes double in size. 'No! Really? Are you bullshitting me?'

He beams proudly. 'Stephanie Hepburn, mother to John. New Year's Eve, 1994. He never found out. And I started playing piano when I was five. Studied at the Royal Academy. Met Adele through classmates.'

I'm stunned. 'Why did you give up?'

He shrugs. 'I decided that I wanted to write more than I wanted to play.'

I can't help but be impressed. This man is full of surprises. He can play the piano and knows Adele, and all I brought to the conversation was unbitten fruit and spinsterdom.

An hour later, we've finished the wine, my fingers are beginning to prune and I've laughed so much my sides hurt.

'If it makes you feel any better, I proposed to my wife three times before she said yes.'

'Not really. All that does is inform me that someone's been asked *three times* and I'm still at zero.'

He laughs. 'I think I should have read the signs after the second knockback. I just meant that it's made out to be a bigger deal than it actually is.'

'I'm learning that anything to do with love or romance is less of a deal than everyone makes out. Like this bootcamp. I can't think of anything less romantic than meticulously planning your next encounter.'

'So, this hasn't turned you into a hopeless romantic yet?' he asks. 'The universe will be disappointed.'

'Not really,' I reply, wishing I'd brought out the G&Ts. 'I mean, the thought of being with someone again isn't as alien as it once was, so maybe that's something.'

'Oh, really?'

'Yeah, but I'm in no rush. The idea of a relationship is always more exciting than the actual thing. It's a bit like Nando's – spicy at first but bloody boring underneath. My kid is my priority, I just need to remember that I'm important too. If I do get involved with someone, they'll need to have their shit together. I've had enough of being the before, the during and the after. I want to be the one.'

'The what now?'

'Ignore me. I know what I mean.'

'You should be with someone,' he says, catching my gaze. 'He'd be lucky to have you.'

I smile, but he doesn't break eye contact right away. Oh God, are we having a moment?

'I should get going,' Will says abruptly, indicating that the moment is over. 'It's been fun though... Ah shit, we didn't bring out any robes outside, did we? Bare-arse time.'

The look of horror on my face speaks volumes.

He laughs. 'It's fine. I'll grab them. Um, I'd look away now, if I were you.'

Before I even have time to avert my eyes, he stands to climb out.

'Will!'

'Nora, my dick has been in front of you for the past hour.'

'Yeah, underwater, not eye level! I mean, I can't *not* look at it when it's right there.'

'You're so weird. Back in a minute.'

He climbs out and I hear him soggily make his way inside. I internally squeal. His body! That torso! It's better than I thought it would be. He has a tattoo on his hip bone. Massive penis now confirmed. Ugh, why couldn't he have been as wobbly as I am? Why couldn't he have just been plain and uninteresting so that when he gets dressed, I won't be thinking about ripping his damn clothes off again? WHY IS THIS MY LIFE?

Will, oblivious to my inner turmoil, returns in a robe and hands me the spare. He turns his back as I climb out and cover myself.

'You good?' he asks.

If by good you mean stupidly aroused, then sure. Why not?

'Yep, I'm good!' I reply enthusiastically, trying to drown out the voice out of my head. 'All robed up. Nothing to see here!'

I'm so uncool I want to die.

We both move back inside where the fire is still going strong. I sink down onto the couch and sigh. 'It's been a fun night.'

'Definitely,' he replies, picking up his clothes. 'That was a blast. Give me two seconds and I'll be out of your hair.'

'Or you could stay?'

The words fall out of my mouth before I've even had a chance to consider their impact. *Shit.* He pauses, staring at me. He doesn't look impressed. *Oh shit, here we go with the inevitable awkward knockback. Nice work, Nora.*

'I'm sorry, I don't know what I was thinking. It's the wine! Forget I said anything.'

He still doesn't reply, but his trousers are on now.

'God, say something, Will! I feel like an idiot.'

'I was just thinking that I'm not sure which part of this evening was the bigger lie,' he replies, pulling on his T-shirt.

'What lie? What do you mean?'

He sits to put on his shoes. 'I mean, whether the bigger lie was the one we told to everyone at that table about rehab...'

'Or?'

'Or the lie we're telling ourselves, so we don't have to admit that we're completely drawn to each other for reasons neither of us can explain.'

As he locks eyes with me, my stomach tumbles into my feet.

'You looked really beautiful this evening,' he says quietly. 'And I think you're pretty damn incredible... but I can't stay because God help me, I won't want to leave.'

I'm not sure whether this is the most exciting thing that's ever happened to me, or the worst.

'So, what now?' I ask.

'Nothing,' he replies. 'I'll see you tomorrow, Nora.'

He leaves, closing the door behind him and I slump back down on the couch. I feel stunned. I feel annoyed. My head is spinning.

Do I even like Will? I feel like I really might like Will, but I didn't come here to like someone, especially not someone who likes someone else. This wasn't supposed to happen.

I feel like my heart might just explode. I need to call Victoria.

CHAPTER 23

BOOTCAMP: DAY 4

I'm feeling slightly hungover this morning, but that's not what's making me feel as peculiar as I do. My phone call to Victoria started with her telling me off for calling at midnight but quickly changed to her saying *ohmyGod* in between me also repeatedly saying *ohmyGod*.

'But it's only been three days!' she said. 'How on earth can he be all confused and besotted in three days? I mean, you're great and all but... I don't get it.'

I was briefly offended that she didn't think I was charming enough to bewitch a man in seventy-two hours. Then I looked down at my chipped nails and one hairy toe and concluded that she had a point.

'It's an intense set-up here,' I replied, 'Everything is very emotive and personal and things it would take a year to tell someone, you're confessing after four hours. A couple who were divorced and ready to murder each other are now madly in love again...'

'I thought you fancied the yoga teacher?'

'Everyone fancies the yoga teacher.'

'Are you going to sleep with him?'

'The yoga teacher?'

'No, this Will guy.'

'No!' I insisted. 'That's the problem. We want to and we can't and now we have three more days of ignoring how we feel.'

'Oh my God, you're so doing it. The tension will be too much. You'll be banging it out before the end of the week.'

'We won't! Look, he wants his wife, and I don't want to have yet another—'

'Yeah, the timing isn't ideal, but it doesn't change the fact that you seem to be disgustingly into each other AFTER THREE DAYS. Ugh, I wasn't even into Benjamin after three days – sorry, honey, I wasn't. Go back to sleep. Nora, this is a good thing. You haven't been interested in anyone for years!'

'But what if I'm only interested because he's not available?'

'Yes, but what if you're the reason he becomes available?'

That sentence hit me like a ton of bricks. If he was available, I'd need to consider having a relationship. Having feelings. Making room for him. Before now those things made me feel unnerved. But with Will... those things don't seem so scary. Only one thing does.

'What if he decides his wife is better than me?'

Those words are still ringing in my ears now as I brush my teeth. It's still the crux of my problem. How can I ever be 'the one' when I've already resigned myself to second best before they have? This isn't about Will or sex or anyone else, this is about me telling myself I'm not worthy and the universe saying, *'Cool. You're not worthy. Here's some second-rate shit to deal with. Have a nice ordinary life.'*

Anna was right. I get it.

I finally get it.

I scrape my hair back into a ponytail and throw on my clothes. I hear breakfast being dropped off, but I'm too psyched up to eat. I need to get out of here, I need to meditate, I need to get Brad to show me how to breathe from my damn perineum and most of all I need to put on my headphones, listen to music and walk until I feel ready to face Will later.

It's bitterly cold this morning but I'm layered up, complete with bobble hat and feeling more motivated than I have in a long time. I reach the side of the loch at 7.50am where I stand and admire the view. Everything is very still, very quiet and although I feel like the only person on earth, strangely I don't feel alone. I feel like the universe might just give a shit about me, because, for the first time in a long time, I'm giving a shit about me too.

Time to let go, I tell myself, watching the birds skim the loch. *No more waiting to be disappointed, no more waiting to fail because that's the only feeling that feels normal. No more proving that you're not your mother – you've already done it. Oh, and no more hating your body. Wear those bloody sexy pyjamas, get in that hot tub naked every night and remember that you're more than the sum of your parts. You have a great big arse and a great big heart, and you are enough. You are more than enough.*

I'm not sure when I started crying, but I can't stop. I'm crying for the wee girl who wanted her mum to love her more and for the grown woman who wanted someone to love her, full stop. Most of all I'm crying for the me that chose to live in the dark for so long, rather than fight to make sure her spark never went out.

'You alright, Nora?'

Startled, I turn to see Brad standing behind me, dressed in a warm jumper and jeans, holding a travel mug. I nod but the lump in my throat is making it impossible to currently speak.

'You're not, are you, you poor thing? Come, sit over here.'

I let Brad lead me over to a bench where we both sit. He hands me his mug. 'Camomile tea,' he informs me. 'Think you need it more than me.'

It takes me a minute to calm down but eventually I'm less visibly devastated.

'Sorry,' I say, sipping his tea. 'Just getting rid of some old ghosts.'

'I think this bootcamp has affected you the most out of everyone. No offence, but it's glorious to see.'

I laugh. 'My snivelling face is glorious?'

He nods. 'It is. It's the real you. Interesting that you chose to come to the water to unleash your emotions. Water is often used by witches; it's seen as a connection to the divine feminine. Spells for grief, or love or emotions in general involve water. You came here to be cleansed and it looks like it's working.'

'Um... witches?'

Brad smiles. 'I'm not implying you're a witch... though you do share the same alluring traits. I'm just pointing out that subconsciously you chose a very powerful place to cast out the old you. I'm impressed. Most would have just cried in bed.'

'In all honesty, I didn't want to come to the bootcamp,' I say, handing him back his mug. 'But everyone was so convinced that I was lonely. I came here to prove them wrong. I came here to show them that not everyone needs someone else to be fulfilled.'

'And now?'

'I've discovered that not being in love with yourself is a far bleaker future to face.'

Brad throws the remainder of his tea on to the ground and stands. 'I have to get up to the main house. You want to walk with me?'

'I'll see you up there,' I reply. 'Thanks for the chat.'

'No, thank you,' he says. 'You're doing so well, Nora. It's inspiring. See you later at meditation.'

As he walks away, I take a deep breath and compose myself. Then Will pops into my head and takes that breath away again. Whatever this thing is between us, we're both adults. I don't care what Victoria says, we're perfectly capable of moving past this.

.   .   .

I don't see Will on my walk up to the main house which gives my red, crying face time to go back to its normal pasty self. I get inside and say good morning to everyone, taking my usual seat near the back of the room. It isn't until I see Anna walk on stage that I notice Will is sitting in the second row.

'Day four, everyone,' Anna announces, 'And I hope y'all are noticing the changes that are occurring from within. I also hope you enjoyed last night's dinner as much as we did.'

Why isn't he sitting with me?

'After meditation this morning, we'll be delving into eye energy transfer with the lovely Brad, and this afternoon you'll have a visualisation workshop followed by yoga.'

Is he embarrassed about what he said? Is he just going to avoid me, like a child?

'Have a great day, everyone, I'll see you this afternoon.'

I get up and watch as Will rises from his chair and keeps his head down, focused on getting to the meditation room without having to make eye contact with me. This is so weird. I get that he's probably feeling awkward, but this is ridiculous. I walk behind everyone else and decide that if this is the way he wants to deal with it, it's no skin off my nose.

I sit beside Meg at meditation, while Will takes the solo mat at the front of the class, the one Meg usually occupies.

I can see her staring at Will, and then at me. Finally, it all becomes too much for her.

'I know it's none of my business, but what's going on with you and Will?'

'What do you mean?'

'You're usually joined at the hip and now he's there and you're here. You didn't sit together at the morning meeting either.'

Calm down, Sherlock.

I place my hands on my thighs and close my eyes as the meditation music begins.

'Will can sit where he likes,' I respond. 'There's nothing going on.'

I hear her mumble 'hmm' as the class begins. She waits a full fifteen minutes before she's unable to bite her tongue any longer.

'I'll read your cards at lunch,' she insists. 'Might shed some light.'

'I don't need—'

'*Quiet please. Focus.*'

I clamp my jaws shut and try to focus, but I can't. Not only is Will cutting me off but I'm also going to have to sit with Meg as she holds up the Three of Spoons or the Queen of Crabs and makes up a narrative to suit herself. Today is going to be a long one.

After an unsuccessful meditation, we arrive back at the main room to find Brad sitting on a chair at the front of the class with a video camera in front of him. Behind him, the words EYE ENERGY TRANSFER are displayed brightly on the screen. Before we can sit, Anna announces that she's placed name cards on the chairs, and we should sit accordingly. After a short search for my name, I soon discover that I'm sitting beside Will.

'From observing y'all over the past few days, we've paired you with the people we feel you're most at ease with. This is important for reasons we will explain shortly. I'll leave you with Brad now.'

I almost laugh. At ease with? Presently, I don't think Will has ever felt more uncomfortable with anyone in his entire life and I'm not far behind.

'You've heard the saying that the eyes are the windows to the soul? Well, this is true. They are a powerful energy source and an entry point for absorbing the energy around us. If we need to block out the outside world during meditation, we close our eyes. What we see will influence how we feel. For example, if we hear about a bad thing happening, we'll feel discomfort. However, if we witness it happening, the emotions are far more powerful. We also give out vast amounts of energy through our eyes and we can influence other people. Ever notice how catching someone's eye can make you feel a range of emotions. How seeing someone cry can make you do the same? In this way we can project, through the eyes, a huge amount of love and peace and calm. When one soul catches another, it's a hugely powerful experience. Now, it's just as easy to absorb any negative emotions, as it is positive, which is why I won't be doing this directly with you.'

Ha! He's scared of picking up our negativity germs. Quite right too; having to lock eyes with Tim would ruin Brad's jolly outlook forever.

'I'm going to look into the camera, which gives me the opportunity to make contact with you all at the same time. Afterwards, I want you to turn to your partner and do the same.'

Will glances at me and rubs his chin. This is going to be painful.

Brad switches on the camera and his big perfect face is projected onto the screen behind.

'Now, as we're here to focus on love, I'm going to vibrate from that place. Let's begin.'

Soft music plays as Brad places his hands in a prayer pose and looks at us all through the lens of his camera. We look at the screen and focus on him as he just contently gazes. If it wasn't for the fact that he's so visually delightful, this would be far more boring than it is. With the occasional blink, he never loses focus. Is there nothing Brad can't do? Yoga guru, meditation expert, professional starer. However, around the minute mark, something changes in me. It almost feels like my heart swells, and I can't take my eyes off him. Part of me wants to yell that it's working but I sit there, staring back, revelling in the delight that

I'm currently experiencing. At three minutes he smiles and ends the session.

'Well done, everyone. I hope that you felt the love I sent to you all,' he says, looking pleased with himself. 'Now it's your turn. I should warn you that this will be trickier than what we've just completed. This will feel more personal and more uncomfortable. Around thirty seconds in, you'll want to look away, but please stay with it for the full three minutes. Feeling awkward is natural, but once that passes and you connect – truly connect – with another human being, it's worth the discomfort. Please turn your chairs to face each other and begin.'

Will and I comply. I can tell he's annoyed that his plan to avoid me has been scuppered, but to his credit, he doesn't scowl too much. Instead, he visibly steels himself before he stares at me.

The uneasiness is real. We both look away several times before eventually holding our gaze and once we do, his eyes soften. Then his gaze wanders slightly towards my mouth, and my neck and mine mirrors it. My heart, once swollen from Brad's joy stare, is now beating out of my chest as my own eyes leave joy and trace their way down his torso. Eye energy has now become eye undressing, and my entire body responds. I shift position in my seat and try to regain composure, but I'm soon biting my lip and breathing like a pervert.

'Time, everyone!' Brad yells, breaking the spell. 'I hope you all managed to connect and raise your vibration to a higher level. Remember, if you feel the need, you can practise this with your partner in your free time. It's worth the effort.'

Will and I both stand and collect our belongings. He's about to speak to me when Meg bounds up.

'Ready for lunch, Nora?'

I look at Will. 'Um, well—'

'Sorry, Will, girls only!' she insists, grabbing me by the hand. 'See you after lunch!'

I don't argue, instead I allow myself to be dragged back to her lodge where I'm offered some weird couscous salad and plonked down in front of a deck of blue tarot cards.

'Does it matter that I don't really believe in any of this?' I ask, hoping to find some hidden bacon in this vegan lunch bowl.

'Not really,' she replies. 'Tarot is simply a tool and my intuition, along with your subconscious energy, will let me look at where you are right now and the possibilities of what the future may hold. Since we don't have a whole lot of time, we'll do a quick three-card cluster. Now ask a question you would like the answer to. Don't tell me, just ask it in your mind.'

I figure that with all the weirdness I've had to endure this week, another few minutes won't make any difference. I take a breath.

Is there someone out there for me?

I nod to indicate that I've asked before regretting my question and wishing I'd asked something less selfish. Like, will Charlie have a good life, or will my business continue to thrive? Not like it matters, I get the feeling this is going to be so vague it could apply to any question ever asked.

Meg takes a spoonful of her salad, then shuffles the deck, hands it to me to shuffle too and spreads the cards in semi-circle over the table.

I wonder what Will's doing right now.

'Choose three cards.'

I touch three and she gathers them up, placing the rest to one side. She's like a croupier in a tie-dye pantaloons.

'So, the first card represents the issue at hand, the second card tells you what not to do and the third is your guide to the correct path.'

She turns over the first card. 'Interesting. There is definitely someone out there for you,' she begins, and I nearly fall off my chair. 'The Lovers card represents not only relationships but choices and decisions that have to be made regarding them.'

She turns over the second. 'The Tower card. You've been shaken to your core recently. You've had an awakening. Don't ignore this. You must rebuild from your stronger foundation, not remain in the ashes wondering how you got there. The advice here is not to take refuge in something unstable.'

What the hell does that mean? Is Will unstable? Am I? She's right about the awakening though, I have a bucket-load of tears to prove it.

The third card makes her smile. 'Ah, the Death card. Don't look so concerned, this doesn't mean you're literally going to die, it means the end of a cycle. A dry spell, perhaps?'

I hope so, I'm pretty sure Laurence of Arabia has moved into my vajayjay. Laurence of my Labia... I try very hard not to smirk.

'Also, the fact that you've chosen this along with the Tower card and the Lovers makes me think that there is a big decision to be made. Things must end before they can begin. As this is the "what to do" card, my advice would be enjoy the moment while you can.'

She's kind of like the Riddler but still, part of me is impressed. She knew exactly what I asked. *Unless I inadvertently mouthed the words and didn't realise.* Regardless, I thank her for both the salad and the reading before returning to my cabin for the last twenty minutes of our lunch break. I know I should speak to Will, but I have the feeling we'll need more than twenty minutes to sort all this out.

You must rebuild from your stronger foundation, not remain in the ashes wondering how you got there.

I quite like that, I think, drinking my leftover breakfast juice. Onwards and upwards.

CHAPTER 24

I make it back up to the main house just in time for the afternoon session – Anna's visualisation workshop – but my mind is already distracted by the way Will looked at me during our eye-banging session. He arrives seconds after me and sits beside me, keeping his gaze firmly on Anna but his thigh dangerously close to mine.

'So far, you've made your order to the universe, you've written in detail about the type of relationship or person you want to meet, and you've worked hard on releasing your negative thoughts about yourself and your past. Now it's time to put yourself into that relationship. Visualisation is more than just daydreaming. I want you to immerse yourself in this parallel reality.'

Anna clicks her clicker and the screen behind her displays VISUALISING A NEW LOVE.

'Number one,' she barks. 'Put yourself in their shoes. Imagine how happy they are that they get to be with you. What better way to raise your vibration than to sit and think about just how awesome you are, right?'

We all laugh, but already I'm thinking about my Hobbit toes and the fact I need to chin pluck twice a day. What a catch.

'Number two,' she continues. 'Think about where you are. If you're in bed, feel the sheets beneath you and the softness of the pillows. At home? Reach down and take off your shoes. Touch your feet—'

Hairy toe, hairy toe.

'—and feel the floor you're walking on. Hard wood? Smooth tile? Thick carpet? Or maybe you're outside. Is it warm, is it winter? Take a breath of air.'

Everyone scribbles furiously but Will and I remain steadfast, staring ahead, making no sudden movements.

'And finally, feel thankful. Radiate excitement and gratitude that this is your life. Not only is this person crazy about you, but you feel the same connection. Enjoy it.'

She starts the music and tells everyone to close their eyes.

'Take your time. Relax. Breathe into your new reality. There is no hurry, just find yourself alone with your new partner. Take your time.

My eyes are closed but my brain is going at a million miles an hour. All I want to visualise is Will on top of me, but this is supposed to be about true love, not disgustingly hot sex. As I try to concentrate, I hear Meg's voice:

'Enjoy the moment while you can.'

Oh, piss off, Meg. This isn't enjoyable. This is torture. Sweet, loin-inflaming, sexy torture. *Oh for God's sake. Focus, Nora.*

'Where are you?' I hear Anna ask.

I'm in a room... the floor is dirty. I put my shoes back on. Why does no one ever clean this bastard— No. Wait. The floor is carpeted so I can squish my toes into it. Better.

'You hear a voice in the distance. Who is it? It's your lover.'

I was going to say window cleaner, but OK.

'Go to them and embrace them.'

But what if he's on the toilet? OK, fine. *He's in the kitchen. Making me a sandwich.*

I make my way into my imaginary kitchen and wrap my arms around the man standing at the worktop. Not Will. Not Will. Yep, it's Will. Abort embrace! It's too late. Will turns around and lifts me up onto the worktop because apparently in this reality I weigh ninety pounds. He firmly moves my thighs apart with his hand and...

I open my eyes and sit upright in my chair. There's no way I can sit here and porn it up, while everyone else is skipping through poppy fields on their way to church. I glance at Will, whose eyes are still closed. I bet he's imagining his wife. Probably also his future kids and his future dog and they're all wearing the same awful T-shirts. I close my eyes again and inhale slowly. I can do this. Seconds later I feel Will's hand gently brush against my thigh. Initially I'm not sure whether this is accidental, but when it remains there, I know I have two decisions: I can remove his hand or I can reach down and place my hand over his, stroking his fingers with mine. I choose the latter, every nerve in my body sparking like little fireworks. We stay like this for what seems like forever before Anna ruins it all by asking us to open our eyes. He quickly removes his hand from my thigh, and we separate.

'Great job, everyone. Twenty-minute recess before yoga. Have a great day.'

While everyone around us stands, we remain seated. My heart is racing. HE TOUCHED MY THIGH.

'So... yoga, then?' he asks.

He still wants to do yoga?

'Um, OK. Yoga.'

He strokes his stubble. 'Or not?' he replies. 'I mean, we could just not go.'

Yeah! To hell with yoga! Back to my thighs.

'Nora, I want you to come to the front of the class today, so I can help with your posture.'

For once, Brad's beautiful voice is not welcome and now he's standing in the doorway waiting for my reply. I give Will a *help me* look but there's nothing he can do. I nod at Brad and begin gathering up my belongings.

'You could say no, you know,' Will whispers. 'Just skip class.'

I furrow my brow. 'I can't skip class. He's seen me.'

'Why? What do you think will happen? You'll get into trouble?'

'Well, yes.'

The hall has almost cleared now, but I see Jillian and another woman looking our way and whispering. It's like high school. I pick up my handbag and throw it over my shoulder, ready to follow the others.

'Look, if we both don't go to yoga, people will notice that we are not at yoga, and I want to be gossiped about less than I want to do frickin' yoga.'

'So, yoga, then?'

'Correct.'

I leave first and march my stubborn arse into the yoga room, followed by Will. Obviously, I'd prefer to be alone with him than in here, perspiring profusely from something as simple as stretching, but maybe it's for the best. We're both being impulsive. It's all fun and games until you stick your dick into someone who's not your estranged wife.

Brad is his usual smiling self as we enter the room, welcoming everyone, while adjusting the blinds to diminish the afternoon sun glare.

'Please take your positions,' he asks politely, returning to his mat at the front. 'We'll begin shortly.'

I take the mat in front of Brad while Will takes the mat to my left, so thankfully he won't be staring directly at my arse the entire time. At least he isn't wearing his joggers, so I won't be distracted by his... I look again; *so*, his bulge is evident in any trousers he wears.

I do my best to make it through the class. Eyes straight ahead, wobbly poses attempted and not one glance at Will to throw me off course. Brad works hard to help with even the most basic of poses, but I think he eventually realises it will take a back brace and a mediaeval rack to help with my perpetual slouching.

'You'll get there!' he lies. 'Just keep practising.'

Finally, the class is over and muscles I didn't even know I had ache. I started this class in a state of arousal and now I'm in a state of sweaty discomfort. I need to get back to my cabin.

'You ready to go?' Will asks

I nod. 'But I think we should go separately. I need to shower and—'

'Nora, we need to talk.'

'I know. Just not now. I'll see you later, OK?'

He sighs, but accepts my decision, walking back on his own, while I do the same. If we're going to be alone, I need to feel prepared. I need to feel confident. Dammit, I need to feel dry.

CHAPTER 25

I give Charlie a call before I even sit down. I need to hear her voice. I'm only on day four but it feels like I haven't seen her for weeks.

'Hey, Mum!'

'Charlie! How are you, my sweet? God, I'm missing you, are you well? Is everything alright?'

'I'm good,' she replies. 'I got ninety-eight percent on my history test.'

'Oh, well done, you! That's brilliant, you're so clever. Is Aunt Faith alright? She's ignoring my texts.'

Charlie giggles. 'I know. She says it's for your own good.'

I laugh too. 'She's probably right. You're not allowed to ignore me though.'

'I need to go though, Mum; we're going to a Mexican restaurant for dinner, and I need to change.'

'Oh, is it that place near Rose Street? I love that place. They do the best tostadas.'

'I think so. Got to run, Mum, will see you on Friday! Bye!'

'Bye, darling, have fun!'

It's obvious that Victoria hasn't told Faith about my Will

problem because Faith would have been bombarding me with questions by now. I'm grateful. I can do without her going all FBI on his ass and googling him so hard she ends up on his nursery-school teacher's Facebook page.

I throw my phone on the couch and head for the shower, feeling better after my little Charlotte fix but desperately needing to wash the day away and sort my head out. It's one thing to intellectually understand that I need to refrain from getting involved with unavailable men but physically, my body doesn't understand this reasoning at all. I bet he's in his cabin wishing he hadn't touched my leg while I'm here wishing that this shower head was removable.

It takes me an hour to shower, dry my hair and order dinner, after which I pace around the kitchen waiting for my tomato and chilli pasta to arrive at my door. I'm wearing my new pyjamas, albeit hidden under my robe, but I have to admit, I feel feminine as hell. It seems my arse looks incredible in pink satin.

When the knock finally comes, I sprint to the door like Usain Bolt.

'Thanks very mu— Brad? What are you doing here?' I pull my dressing down around me tightly.

He holds up the bag. 'Dinner. Thought I'd help out and drop it off. The guys are busy tonight.'

'Oh, right,' I reply, 'Well, thanks, I—'

'I also thought I'd check in and see how you were feeling. You know, after this morning.'

'I'm fine!' I reply, preparing to tackle him for my food bag. 'Right as rain! Just going to eat and—'

'I ordered the pasta too. Thought we could eat together?'

He brought his dinner too? Confused, I step aside, and he struts in, places the bag on the kitchen worktop and goes straight for the plates.

'I picked up some red as well,' he informs me, busying

himself with dinner prep, while I stand there wondering whether to go with this or call the police.

'Brad, are you allowed to be here?' I ask, watching him set the table. 'Isn't this breaking some rule?'

He pauses and looks a little alarmed, clutching his chest. 'Oh no. You're right. I'm pretty sure this is against the rules... maybe even the law. Oh, look, here is the constable to take me away.'

I laugh, feeling entirely foolish. 'I just meant, is this normal bootcamp protocol? Dinner with the middle-aged crybabies?'

'You're hardly middle-aged, Nora. And yes, it's allowed. We're a full-service team here. Anna is currently dining with another guest who has been having an emotional breakthrough. We find the intimate setting far less intimidating than the class environment.'

He stops taking the lid off the pasta and turns to me. 'If this makes you uncomfortable, I'm happy to leave. My husband always says I can be a little overbearing when I see someone I can help. I don't mean to be.'

Wow. I really have no gaydar whatsoever. I feel stupid. My talent for lusting after unsuitable men has just reached a new level. Who's next? The Pope?

I can't help but laugh. 'No, stay,' I reply. 'I could use the distraction. Red wine would be lovely. I should probably throw some clothes on, though.'

'Nah,' he replies. 'If I was at home, I'd be in my robe too. Just relax!'

After this afternoon, this is not how I saw my evening panning out, but Brad is good company once he strays from the universe repartee. Turns out red wine can transform anyone into a gossipmonger and also a stoner.

'I cannot believe you smoke weed,' I say, as he lights his joint. 'You come across as so clean-cut!'

'Nora, I do yoga, I'm not a priest. Besides, it's legal where I live. You Brits are so uptight. I would smoke outside, but the smell... well, I don't want to get arrested. Where was I? Oh yeah, we actually sent Sally, the personal assistant, down to their cabin to remind them that due to numbers, their participation was actually required in sessions. She said the entire place smelled like sex and ass.' He flicks his joint into a makeshift ashtray.

'I wondered why I hadn't seen Patricia or Kenneth since their little breakthrough!' I cackle loudly. 'It's sort of sweet though and kudos to you lot. You brought them back together!'

He takes a swig of wine. 'True. Though the universe obviously had plans for them anyway. We only facilitated the reconnection.'

'So, you wouldn't call it a coincidence that they were both here?' I ask. 'Or that maybe one of them knew the other was attending and bought a ticket to be near them?'

'Does that matter?' he asks. 'Remember, the universe is always conspiring. To call it a coincidence means you have no control. You always have control. But call it what you want – conspiracy, synchronicity, being on the same frequency, it doesn't matter. Just take responsibility. You can't control anything unless you own it first.'

I pour some more wine. 'I mean, I'm getting that. Sort of. I'm struggling with changing my past patterns of behaviour, and I know only I can control that. But it's hard.'

'Past intimacy behaviours?' he asks. 'Don't think we didn't see that lil' hand touch in visualisation, girl. We see everything.'

I cringe. 'Oh God. It's so silly! In the past, I've been known to get involved with men I know I have no future with... and then I'm devastated when they don't suddenly discover they can't live without me. Even if I don't want them to!'

'But you like Will?'

'That doesn't matter.' I reply. 'Yes, we're weirdly drawn to each other, but he has a whole ex-wife thing going on that I can't and won't compete with.'

Brad grins. 'Good for you. You let that woman you've never met come between you and hot sex. What's that saying? Fortune favours the spineless?'

'What? No, I just—'

He takes my hand. 'Nora, stop wasting time. This is your life. If you're convinced that it's going to be a freaking disaster it will be. If you approach it with hope and love, if you tell the universe that you're ready and grateful to receive what you've asked for, that's exactly what you'll get. Now I'm going to go call my husband and then get tomorrow's schedule in order.'

I walk Brad to the door, the effects of the red wine becoming apparent when the fresh air hits me. Even though Brad's smoked a full joint and had wine too, he seems completely sober.

'Just think about what I said,' he asks, pulling on his coat. How is any human in such great shape?

'I will.' I reply, 'And thanks for the arms— the, er, chat! Thanks for the chat.'

He chuckles and legs it towards his cabin, while I cringe yet again and close the door. What does Brad know anyway? He probably has seven million men ready to marry him tomorrow.

I return to the kitchen and open the patio doors to let the smell of cannabis out before stacking our dinner plates in the dishwasher, ranting to myself.

'Sure, it's easy for Brad to say just go for it because Brad is someone's "the one". I bet he's never had his heart stomped on. I bet he's just like, "Ooh, I have arms, let me just—"'

'Let me just what?'

I spin around so fast I almost get whiplash.

'*OhmyGod*, will you stop doing that! I'm going to have a heart attack.'

Will squints and sniffs the air. 'Did you have a joint and not give me any?'

It's like Woodstock in here. Am I the only one who doesn't get high these days?

'No, it wasn't me. Do I look like a stoner? It was Brad.'

He looks surprised. 'GI Joe smokes weed? Never saw that coming... hang on, why was Brad here?'

'I think the question is, why are *you* here?' I close the dishwasher and turn it on.

Will pulls a chair out and sits down. 'Because I was having some beers and I got bored and... my TV is playing up and... fine, I wanted to see you.'

I begin tidying things that are already tidy.

'Will, I don't think this is doing either of us any good,' I inform him, wiping the perfectly clean toaster. 'It's messing with my head.'

'And mine,' he replies. 'How do you think I feel?'

'I know how you feel! You *told* me how you feel!' I fold the dish towel neatly before unfolding it, so I have something to wave around while I talk. 'You *told* me you want to try again with your wife, then you *told* me that nothing could happen, but then you're touching my leg and you're coming over here and—'

'Can you put down the towel?'

'No! Look, this whole thing is ridiculous! We hardly know each other! This whole bloody *sharing is caring* environment has made us think we're closer than we are. But we're not. I mean, even Brad was telling me to go for it but—'

'You discussed us with Brad?'

'That's irrelevant,' I inform him. 'Look, on Friday we'll both go home, and this will all be forgotten.'

Will takes his jacket off and places it on the back of the chair. He reaches over and takes my wine glass, finishing what's left.

'You're probably right,' he admits, staring at the empty glass. 'Although I'm stunned that Brad said that. Totally thought he would have ulterior motives—'

'Brad's gay, Will.'

He raises an eyebrow. 'Wow. That boy is full of surprises.'

I throw the towel on the worktop and slump down in the chair across from him.

'I hate that I can't stop thinking about you,' he says, rubbing his forehead.

'Yeah? Well, I hate that you finished my wine.'

'I'm serious!' he exclaims. 'You're just *there*... in my head... all the bloody time!'

'Why are you yelling at me?'

'Because none of this is fair!' Now he's flailing *his* arms around. I'm tempted to pass him the dish towel.

'Who said life was fair?!' I ask, now yelling back. I move from the table and take sanctuary again in the kitchen. 'Is it fair that I finally met someone really great at the wrong time? Is it fair that I'm now closer to death than to living happily ever after? Is it fair that I'm about to completely undermine everything I've just said for the past twenty minutes?'

As Will locks eyes with me, it becomes clear what's about to happen. He stands and makes his way to the kitchen, pushing me up against the worktop.

'I can't stop thinking about you either,' I say softly. 'How is that fair?'

We pause for a moment, each waiting for the other to see sense, to call it off, but that doesn't happen. Seconds later, Will's mouth is on mine, his hands pulling open my robe while I grapple with his T-shirt. He kisses with such intensity that my knees buckle and the faster he breathes, the weaker I get.

'Here?' he asks, almost in a whisper. 'Or in the bedroom?'

I want to say bedroom – better lighting, more space, doesn't smell of pasta – but I don't want to move.

'Here,' I reply, 'or both. I don't care, just do it.'

As my robe hits the floor, he spins me around and kisses my neck before stepping back while undoing his jeans.

'Oh, for God's sake,' I hear him say. 'Those shorts... are you kidding me? As if I wasn't hard enough.' He grabs my hips and pulls me into him. I feel what he's talking about through his underwear. As much as I want him to pound me into oblivion, if he does, it's going to be awful. I wish they made tiny airbags for the cervix; I'd be a lot calmer about the impending collision.

'Wait,' I begin, reaching back to pause him. 'It's just...'

'I'll go slow,' he reassures me as his fingers creep inside my satin shorts. God, I feel like some virginal sixteen-year-old. My vagina isn't unchartered territory, I've had a kid! I've had dicks of all shapes and sizes. Still, there's nothing like a particularly large knob to both excite and terrify even the most seasoned shagger. But I need this. I need him.

Damn, even his fingers are thick.

He removes my top before his weight presses me down on to the kitchen counter, his breath on my neck as he moves my legs apart. When he does push inside me a little, I gasp and grab the edge of the worktop.

'You OK?'

'Hell yes. Keep going.'

He works himself in slowly, one hand on my hip, the other on my shoulder and although I appreciate that he's holding back, I need more. When I push back on him until he's fully inside, we both moan like a couple of sex-deprived fiends. He grabs my breasts and swears loudly as we take turns being in control. Eventually I submit and allow him to slam me and although it doesn't last long, I finish first with Will seconds behind.

We both stand there for a second, sticky and squashed against each other until my legs admit defeat and I need to sit down. I quietly pick up my robe and move into the living room.

Will puts his pants back on and sits in the kitchen, watching me deal with the wet patch that's now forming in my robe.

'Shit, we should have used something. Sorry, I got carried away.'

'Don't worry,' I reassure him. 'I have an implant. I'm covered. The last thing I need is another rug rat, draining my bank balance... oh, that was really insensitive, I'm sorry.'

He smiles. 'It's fine. Yeah, I want kids but not just with any old rando... shit, I didn't mean... you're not just any —'

I giggle as he starts to go red. 'I know what you meant.'

He slumps down on a chair and sighs, pulling on his T-shirt. 'That was...'

'Yeah. I know.'

'And I don't feel too weird about it,' he continues. 'Do you?'

'A little, maybe,' I admit. 'But at least that's it out of our systems, right?'

'Right,' he replies. 'Job done. No big deal.'

'Exactly.'

We sit in silence for a moment, the occasional smile passing between us.

'You want to grab a shower?' I ask. 'There's plenty of towels.'

'After,' he replies, getting to his feet.

'After what?'

He stands up and holds out his hand. 'After we do that again.'

He leads me to the bedroom, and I happily follow, but a sinking feeling pulls on my stomach.

You're going home in three days, Nora.
Do not fall for him.

CHAPTER 26

BOOTCAMP: DAY 5

'Good morning, everyone,' Anna chirps. 'I hope you're all as excited about today as we are! Tonight, we have our little soiree, so y'all better have brought your glad rags. Sally will be coming around with the menu; if you can let her know your choices and any dietary requirements before the end of the morning meeting, that would be great.'

Excited? I'm exhausted. I'd forgotten about the party tonight. I've had about four hours of sleep, but I'm grinning like a fool. Will left at 4am and there isn't a part of me that wasn't explored with his—

'Firstly, this morning we're going to look at how to keep your identity within a new relationship,' Anna continues, interrupting my filthy train of thought. 'How not to become a "we". I see you smiling there, Nora, and looking around, I think this resonates with everyone.'

I laugh but I have no idea what she's just said. Could have been anything. I'm too busy thinking about just how incredible last night was to care. Whoever said that men in their forties aren't in their sexual prime has clearly never met Will. I glance at him beside me, looking even more dishevelled than ever. He doesn't look back, but I see the dimples slowly appear on his cheeks, implying he's thinking the same thing.

'So, let's begin. Take out your notepads please.' Behind her the screen changes and the words IDENTITY SHIFT appear in bold black letters.

'When you meet someone, you are two very separate people. You may share interests, political affiliations, sense of humour, but fundamentally you are not them and they are not you. Even in terms of twin flames – they may be the other half of your soul but you've both developed separate personalities and personas. Now as wonderful and fulfilling as romantic relationships are, they are notorious for changing us into someone we don't recognise anymore.

'They make us people pleasers. They make us put someone else first. They make us forget who we are. Romantic relationships turn the *I* into a W*e*. The *me* becomes *us*.'

I nod without even realising. With Will, I feel like an I. Does that mean there's nothing romantic going on between us?

'Think about it; what other kind of relationship does this happen? Would you start referring to your best friend in these terms? Would you have a joint Facebook or bank account with them? Do you check with them before making plans that don't involve them? Of course not, so why do we surrender our identity in romantic relationships?'

'Sex,' Will says under his breath. 'What else?'

I feel myself tingle at the mere mention of the word.

'Having a clear, strong sense of self is vital. Yes, we want to be liked and accepted but being able to maintain boundaries and stay on our own path is important too. How many of you have felt lost after a breakup? Let me tell you something; you felt lost because you strayed from your own path and forgot your way home. Never forget your way home. It's entirely possible to build a life *with* someone, side by side, but do not build your life around them because all you're left with are the walls you built up and an empty space inside.'

Will looks pensive as he turns to a blank page. I wonder what he's thinking.

'Now, obviously there are compromises in relationships but taking someone's needs into consideration doesn't mean forgetting your own.'

Anna smiles at her audience. 'Yes, by all means, go to that boring art gallery you hate with your partner but don't start saying "we love art galleries" when that simply isn't true. If he hates that dress you love, tough shit; wear it anyway. If she hates your taste in music, tough shit; play it anyway. Never sacrifice your joy to placate others and never expect someone to stop being themselves to appease you.'

I notice when Anna speaks, she doesn't just command the room; she owns it. Every word flows effortlessly but sounds like it has been carefully chosen, just for you. The entire room hangs off every sentence like it's being said by some mystical entity and not just a normal woman with an engaging accent and expensive shoes.

'I want y'all to write down five things you'll do differently in your new relationship,' she requests. 'For example, in the past, maybe you didn't speak up enough. Maybe you didn't ask for what you wanted in bed. Maybe you didn't see your friends enough, you get the idea. BUT, as we're manifesting, write them like they're happening now. I see my friends regularly... I'm able to have open and honest discussions with my partner... I'm having the best, freakiest sex of my life!'

Everyone starts to giggle because now everyone is thinking about sex, and I don't feel like the biggest pervert in the room anymore. *Freakiest? Really, Anna?*

'Remember, do not write about what you won't do! Positive statements only!'

I open my notepad and consider my own list. What would I do differently, apart from everything? Where even to begin?

As I think over the myriad mistakes I've made in past relationships, I wait for the soul-crushing burn that normally accompanies them, but it doesn't come. The truth is, for a while I was happy with Charlie's dad. I loved him with every inch of my being, and I don't consider that to be a mistake. I didn't know what was ahead, I just knew what was in front of me at that moment. There's a difference between mistakes and regret, and I have to acknowledge that. It was not a mistake to love him. I just regret not knowing that I was worth more.

I find myself wanting to cuddle the girl who thought that settling for the worst was the best she could do. I want to tell the teenager who fought to be loved that she was picking the wrong battle and most of all, I want to forgive the woman who let her light go out. The familiar feeling of failure has been replaced by one of anticipation. I can't change the past, but I can sure as hell ensure I don't repeat it.

I smile and begin to write.

My Relationship.

1. *I ~~want to be~~ AM loved by someone who is lucky to have me.*
2. *I ~~can~~ always speak my mind without fear of rejection or abandonment.*
3. *I have room in my heart for more than my child. She will never be loved any less.*
4. *My needs are just as important as anyone else's.*
5. *I like who I am. ~~when I am in love.~~*

Pleased with my list, I sit patiently, swinging my leg, waiting for everyone else to finish. I try to sneak a peek at whatever Will is scribbling but he's hiding it behind one arm like it's a bloody school test. Does he think I'm going to copy him? I'm impressed that he's doing the work instead of writing me silly notes or attempting to sleep with his eyes open. I hope he isn't going to get all broody over his ex and announce that last night was a huge mistake. I mean, it probably was a huge mistake, I just don't need to hear it.

I'm starting to wonder if meeting Will is just a way for me to experience a positive, purely physical relationship for the first time in my life. Maybe our spark isn't anything other than sexual attraction and I'm overcomplicating things as usual?

Finally, Anna instructs us all to take our lists and venture outside, choosing a place to read them aloud to the universe while we take our coffee break.

'You have set your intentions,' she says. 'Speak them, feel them and tune into their vibration.'

'Ready for coffee?' I ask Will, and he nods enthusiastically. 'God yes, I'm running on empty.'

Five minutes later we sit at the back of the garden, far from everyone else and cursing Anna because it's about five degrees and the temperature is still dropping. The coffee helps a little but we're decidedly Baltic.

'Want to head back in?' Will asks, stamping his feet on the crunchy grass. 'I didn't sign up for hypothermia.'

'You mean you don't want to tell the universe about your list?' I laugh as he makes a face, as I have no intention of reading mine out either. 'I feel good about mine. It's all empowering and positive. I'm like Beyoncé, if Beyoncé was Scottish and talentless.'

'To be honest, there isn't much to read,' he admits. 'I did take a stab at it, but I don't know what I'd do differently.'

'Oh, come on, no one's perfect! Nothing you'd do differently to be happier?'

'I was happy with Sabine. We didn't split because there was anything wrong, we split because we wanted different things...

oh, hang on, this is weird, isn't it? Me talking about my wife after we just…'

What kind of name is Sabine anyway? French? German? I bet she's beautiful. He acts like she's beautiful.

'It's fine,' I assure him. 'Well, maybe a little weird but to be honest, there's nothing about this week that's normal.'

He smiles in agreement, sitting beside me on the bench, unaware that in my head, he's currently yearning after some seven-foot French model with an adorable gap between both her front teeth and thighs. 'I just don't want you to get hurt,' he confesses. 'Maybe if we'd met in a different life, then…'

As his voice trails off, I place my hand on his knee and squeeze it gently. 'Then we'd both be different people, Will. You are where you are, and I have no desire to be the person who makes your situation any more confusing. Look, we both want to be happy and neither of us are in a position to offer that.'

I sip my coffee as he slouches back, taking in what I've just said. 'You're right, of course,' he replies eventually, placing his coffee cup on the ground. 'But I'm still confused about one thing.'

'What's that?'

He places his hand on the back of my neck and pulls me into him.

'If all of that is true,' he asks, his lips almost touching mine, 'then what the fuck are we doing?'

As he kisses me, I melt from the inside out. I have no idea what we're doing but at that moment, all I know is that I'm not sure I want it to end.

CHAPTER 27

The cold weather ensured our kiss outside was brief, yet long enough for us both to return to the main house with a sense of sexual urgency that was hard to shake off. We've already had sex four times since last night, but my body is virtually screaming for him to touch me again.

We sit side by side in our next workshop, our legs brushing against each other purposefully and I can tell by the look on Will's face that he's feeling just as hot and bothered as I am.

'This will be our final affirmation session,' Anna explains, smoothing down her red jumper, 'but of course, we encourage you to affirm daily, on whatever you're manifesting because although we've been concentrating on love, these skills are applicable to everything else – money, success, health, abundance; everything has a vibration.'

We open our notebooks at the previous affirmations we've written. As I look at Will's page, he appears to have written nothing but drawn what looks like a cat with a human face.

'If the previous affirmations still ring true, I want you to say these to yourself and really feel it,' Anna says, bringing her hands up to her heart. 'I attract love. I am love. I love and get love in return... truly believe it... and if you think you can improve or continue the momentum you already have in flow, then feel free to adjust as needed. I want you to leave here today, knowing that you are all of the things you have written.'

Will is already scrawling on the page.

I know I am hard.

I bite my lip and try not to grin like a maniac. He sighs and continues writing.

Stop biting your lip. That isn't helping.

I want to laugh but the room is too quiet. Instead, I take my own notepad and reply:

Would it help if I told you I wasn't wearing any underwear?

He raises his brow as his eyes automatically dart towards my crotch area. Unless he has X-ray vision, he's going to have to take my word for it. I nod, letting him know I'm not lying.

He runs his hand through his hair before scrawling

I hate you.

My need to giggle is almost as overwhelming as my need to jump Will's bones. I'm forced to face the window and pretend to contemplate the universe, while I hear him take a deep breath. We have thirty minutes before lunch, plenty of time to calm down and behave like grown-ups.

I go back to my affirmation notes, but they don't resonate.

I am loved.

I am in a happy, fulfilling relationship.

I draw love to me.

Truth be told, at this moment in time, love and relationship pronouncements aren't my focus. Something is changing in me. Finally, it feels like something has begun to spark.

I draw two lines under my love affirmations and start a new list:

I am desirable.

I am shameless.

I am filthy.

I am seductive and I deserve this.

Unexpectedly Anna's words pop into my head.

'By the end of this bootcamp y'all are going to love yourselves so much that anyone else loving you is just gravy.'

Is this what she meant, because right now, I'm feeling invincible. I feel seen. I feel wanted.

Oh, sure, Nora. You get a little attention from a guy and suddenly you're Wonder Woman? Is your self-worth so dependent on—

'OH, SHUT UP, ME!'

This time I don't need to wonder if I said that out loud because Anna and Brad are staring at me, along with the rest of the room who have stopped writing and now looking at me like I've lost my mind.

'Are you alright?' Will whispers.

I laugh – properly laugh, like a hyena.

'Everything OK, Nora?' Brad enquires. He looks so cute

when he's puzzled. I nod through my laughter. A smile creeps over Anna's face before she claps her hands in delight.

'I love it when this happens!' she announces. 'I do believe that Miss Nora over there just kicked her old, unhelpful vibration to the curb.'

Nish *whoops*, which makes Will snort-giggle and I lose it again. Now everyone is sniggering.

'Stand and share with us, Nora,' Anna requests as I attempt to compose myself. 'What are you feeling?'

'It's hard to explain,' I say, rising to my feet. 'I'm just done.'

'Done? Done with what?'

'With myself,' I reply, wiping my tears of laughter with the sleeve of my shirt. The room goes quiet, but the empathy is palpable. Jillian nods, smiling warmly at me.

'I'm done with keeping myself in my place,' I explain. 'I'm forty years old. My place is wherever the hell I decide it is.'

Nish doesn't whoop again, but Patricia's yell of agreement is bolstering.

'I'm done feeling weak when I need help and I'm done being so bloody tolerant of my middling, uneventful, passionless life! I need more!'

'Go, girl!' Meg roars. 'You do you, boo!'

'But most of all, I am so, *so* done with my sad heart.' I laugh again, tickled by Meg's enthusiasm. 'God, I spent so long shielding my heart from false hope that I ended up giving it no hope at all! But being here has shown me that sometimes, no matter how hard you resist, there are people that you are just fated to adore. There's no rhyme nor reason, you just feel it in your bones... even if it's just for the briefest of moments.'

'Yes, Nora!' Brad yells, and begins to clap, quickly followed by others. I take a deep breath. For someone who doesn't like drawing attention to myself, I've failed miserably. Maybe this is the new me?

'Amazing!' Anna, exclaims. 'Thank you, Nora! Maybe this is a good time for anyone else who wants to share?'

'I'm done stressing over my male pattern baldness!' All eyes are off me and on to Russell, who stands up in the row in front and takes off his fedora. 'I am a good-lookin' dude. I can rock a shaved head.'

He leans back and high-fives me. I feel like I've started a Spartacus movement.

'Well, I think you're all fabulous!' Meg declares. 'And I'm done comparing myself to everyone else on Instagram. No one else looks like me, I should embrace that.'

I see Will raise his eyebrows and I just know he's thinking EVERYONE ON INSTAGRAM LOOKS LIKE YOU. I wonder what he's done with, if anything. Maybe me, after my little outburst. Even though everyone else seems to be happy to share, there's no way he'll be expressing anything publicly. That much I do know.

After Nish tells us that he's done trying to please his parents, Allison announces that she's done being nice to everyone. I kind of like this, despite the fact I suspect she's rarely nice to anyone. Ashley from Group Four is crying again, Jillian decides that she's done getting bikini waxes when no one gives a shit either way, and Anna declares it's time for lunch.

'Great work, everyone. Yoga at two pm. See you then.'

Despite some revelations being less life-changing than others, there's a definite sense of camaraderie between the group; like we all just buried a body and swore to take the secret to the grave. Spirits are high and laughter fills the hall as we all exit the building.

Before I have a chance to grab Will, Jillian pulls me to one side.

'I have a dress for you,' she says, pouring some liquid into her vape. 'It doesn't suit me since I went red. but it'll look great on you. You're a size fourteen, right?'

'Yes... but why do I need a dress?'

'For the end-of-bootcamp party, silly,' she replies. 'I heard you say you only brought one dress and, well, you can't wear that again, can you? No offence but it's the kind of thing you'd wear to an office party... or a wake. I'll drop it in to you.'

I'm not given the option of saying no because she's already halfway down the path, disappearing in a cloud of vape smoke like an appallingly assertive magician.

Will is waiting for me by the door, yawning like a man who desperately needs his bed.

'Jillian is giving me a dress for tonight,' I inform him. 'I think I've become an outreach programme since my stint in shopping rehab.'

'What's it like?' he asks curiously. 'I only ask because she dresses a bit like Helena Bonham Carter.'

'What's wrong with that?' I ask, ready to defend my hero.

'Nothing,' he replies. 'But maybe "retro scarecrow" isn't for everyone?'

'Works OK for you.'

He stops in his tracks and takes out his phone. '999? Yes, I'd like to report a massive burn.'

I laugh as we continue walking but cannot help wondering if he has a point. Jillian is a little eccentric. And at least fifteen years older. Oh well, if the dress is hideous, I'll just tell her it doesn't fit.

'That was some speech in there,' he says, elbowing me. 'Did you mean what you said?'

'Which part? About being forty? Yes, I'm afraid it's true.'

He elbows me again. 'No... you know... the part about meeting people you *adore*?'

'I did. Nish is totally adorable. I must adopt him when I get home.'

'Oh, good,' he replies, dimples on display. 'I thought for a second you might have been talking about me. Phew! Huge relief.'

I elbow him back. 'Never, you're awful.'

'I really am.'

Without warning, Will pulls me into the undergrowth at the end of the path, pushing me against an oak tree. As he presses up against me, his breath on my neck, I hear voices passing by, obviously oblivious to us being here. I feel giddy.

'I seem to remember something about not wearing any underwear,' he says, his hand wandering inside my trousers.

'Will, I'm not shagging here, there are folk ten feet away!'

'Who said anything about shagging?'

I'm not sure which part is more exhilarating: being finger banged harder than I have been in twenty years, or when he covers my mouth with his hand to quieten me as I come.

Afterwards, we grab some lunch and walk back to our respective cabins to change for the afternoon yoga class. I'm barely inside for ten minutes when Will appears at my patio window.

'You're not changed?' I remark, opening the door. 'We only have twenty minutes left.'

He steps inside and closes the door behind him.

'Yoga is cancelled,' he says, taking a seat.

'Really? Who cancelled it?'

'Me. Just now. Take your clothes off.'

I tsk. 'Nice try. Hurry up and change!'

He doesn't move. 'Nora, it's Wednesday. We go home on Friday morning. Spend the afternoon in bed with me. We can sleep, eat, and you can do that thing with your tongue again because I've been thinking about that a lot and—'

'Brad told me that when Kenneth and Patricia didn't turn up, they came looking for them.'

'So? We won't answer. They'll think we're dead. I'm OK with that.'

I sit down to tie my trainers. 'And you don't want your boss, or that Harriet woman who's married to your wife's boss, to know that you hooked up with some woman you barely know.'

'Can you stop making very sensible points please, it's annoying.' He admits defeat and stands again.

'We could come back here after the soiree?' I suggest. 'My tongue will still be available then.'

'FINE,' he replies. 'But you have to get naked the instant that door closes.'

'OK.'

'Well, unless you want to slip on those pink shorts again, I mean that would be acceptab—'

'I'll meet you at yoga, Will.'

He leaves as quickly as he arrived and I saunter up to the main house, eating my roast beef sandwich. 'Stupid Girl' by Garbage begins playing on my phone and I immediately skip to the next track. I don't need that kind of sass from the universe right now.

———

'Jillian, this isn't a dress, this is a masterpiece.'

I hold the red fabric against me while she pulls other items from the bag. 'I know, and as much as I love Ralph Lauren, that shade of ruby with my skin tone is just a no-no. Don't get too excited though, it's like so 2015.'

Excited? I'm practically mounting it.

'Also, it can be quite unforgiving around the stomach, so I've chucked in some shaper shorts and tights. Oh, and a little shawl for your arms; better than that black cardigan you've been wearing.'

I'm offended. That cardigan happens to be my favourite out of the twelve cardigans I currently own.

She throws these on the table and smiles as I continue admiring the dress. Is that a thigh split?

'Are you sure about this?' I ask. I'm starting to feel like a charity case.

'Of course,' she replies, 'Someone should wear it, why not you? You have shoes?'

'Shoes?'

'You know, shoes. Those things that go on your feet?'

'Just those black kitten—'

'Nope, they won't work. Size?'

'Um, five and a half – can get away with a six.'

'Leave it with me.'

It takes Jillian forty-five minutes to return with a pair of size-six silver strappy sandals, courtesy of Meg. It's like having a personal shopper. I thank her again and take everything to my room, praying it fits because otherwise I'm going to be the office party/wake girl again and that's just depressing.

By six thirty, I'm showered, my contacts are in, my makeup done and I'm curling the ends of my hair with my straighteners. I'm excited for this evening, it feels like a befittingly glitzy end to a very unglamorous week. I can only dress down for so long before I feel like I should be living under a bridge.

After squeezing myself into Jillian's shaper shorts, I'm thrilled to discover that the dress fits like a glove. It's like someone gave the designer my very average proportions and told them to go forth and make a viscose miracle. Anyone within a twenty-foot radius would have heard me squeal in delight as I tried it on, admiring myself in the mirror at every angle.

I smile and I realise that Will was right; I do get to be Prom Queen.

CHAPTER 28

'Nora. I'm begging you. Wear something else.'

I step aside as Will walks into the cabin, almost tripping over his own feet as he stares at Jillian's dress.

'You wear something else! I'm wearing this,' I assert, smoothing it against my skin. I feel overdressed and downright fabulous. The side split shows just enough leg and the V-neckline gives me amazing cleavage.

'I have to get through this evening without publicly humping you and that dress isn't helping.'

'I'm never taking this off,' I tell him. 'Ever. You'll just have to deal with it.'

He unbuttons his jacket and sits on the couch, rubbing the back of his neck, while I turn around to slip on Meg's shoes. I literally own no part of this outfit, except the earrings.

'It's even worse from behind,' I hear him say. 'Could you be any curvier? And what are those little sexy ankle, strappy heels... oh, come on; you're killing me here.'

'Die quickly then, I'm hungry,' I reply, sitting to fasten my sandals. 'You look great in that suit by the way. I didn't know you'd brought one with you.'

'Pah, there's a lot you don't know about me, Nora. I am a man of mystery and intrigue.'

'I know you like red dresses.'

'Not particularly,' he responds. 'I do like you in a red dress, however.'

'Well, I like you in a black suit.' I say, standing. 'You look dignified... respectable.'

'Respectable?' He raises an eyebrow. 'You sure about that?'

My mind flashes back to earlier at my kitchen table; him inside me, grabbing my hair at the base of my neck. 'Point taken,' I respond, my cheeks quickly turning the same shade as my dress. 'I take it back.'

He smiles and fastens his jacket. 'As much as I want to stay here, we should go. That dress deserves an audience.'

We arrive at the main house fifteen minutes later, having resisted the urge to repeat the kitchen table scene. Thankfully, we met up with Nish, Meg and Russell on the way there, which quashes any *oh, look, they arrived together again* gossip before it can begin. My toes are frozen but damn, these shoes are pretty. Meg also wore red, but her dress is shorter and made from a handkerchief and some shoelaces. She really does have the most beautiful figure. I'd be lying if I said there wasn't a smidgen of envy there, but even if I could drop fifty pounds, tan myself olive and grow six inches, I'd still just be a forty-year-old in a hanky. All the men are in suits, except for Brad. Brad has come as an honorary Scotsman in a kilt and the women are swooning in their Spanx.

'Ladies and gentlemen, the ballroom is now open.'

'Think he's gone traditional under that kilt?' Will whispers as we make our way upstairs. 'Not sure I want to see Brad's wang when someone inevitably gets drunk and pulls it up.'

'Kilt wheeching is inevitable,' I reply. 'And the fact you're not entirely sure leads me to believe there's a small part of you that wants to see his wang?'

'If only to prove my Ken doll theory.'

We continue to the top of the stairs where two servers in bow ties stand at either side of the ballroom doors, holding trays of champagne flutes. The cost of this bootcamp is beginning to make sense.

The first thing I notice when we enter the ballroom is the gold. Everything is gold, from the intricate leafy designs on the high ceiling, to the cornice walls and even the chandelier. Combined with the soft glow from the candles, I don't think I've ever seen a more beautiful room. The next thing I notice is the dancefloor, slap bang in the middle of the room. My feet perk up. I haven't hit a dancefloor properly since Faith dragged Victoria and me along to a wrap party in 2013, where she disappeared with some actor from *Game of Thrones* and left us alone with a table full of white-powdered noses, all bragging about their various accolades. We ditched them and danced for three hours straight, while poor Faith ended up with a cold sore and stubble rash.

There are nine tables around the dancefloor, each place set with a name card and what looks like some kind of gift bag in the middle of each plate.

'I bet there's a cyanide pill in there,' Will quips, looking for his name. 'I'll take yours if you don't want it.'

For once, Will and I aren't sitting directly beside each other, instead we're sat at opposite ends of the table, joined by Meg, Jillian and Nish

I'm both annoyed and relieved because a) I won't be able to feel him up under the table and b) I won't be able to feel him up under the table. We take our seats and smirk at each other while Anna attempts to get everyone's attention. She clinks her glass with a knife.

'Well, don't y'all clean up good!' she declares from the top table. I like her strapless pink dress. She looks like she's about to burst out of a cake. I want to open the little gift on my starter plate but no one else seems to be opening theirs. Do we need permission?

'I just wanted to thank each and every one of you for making this bootcamp one of the best we've ever had,' she says. 'I've seen such boldness and joy from y'all, and such commitment to become the people we know you can be.'

Everyone claps, congratulating themselves on being themselves. I do too. I'm splendid. I'm also opening that damn bag.

'Now, tomorrow is your last day but it's a day of reflection... or rehydration, depending on how much champagne we get through this evening, so there will be no workshops. Instead, we will offer yoga as usual, as well as massage and Reiki. If you're interested, the appointment sheets are on the table just outside the door. We'll also finish with a loch-side bonfire in the evening with music and meditation.'

'Oh, I'm so getting Reiki,' Meg says enthusiastically. 'My energy has been all over the place.' She sees me opening my giftbag and dives into hers.

It's a Holistically Yours bootcamp fountain pen, a small leather-bound notebook, a patchouli candle and some handmade chocolate. I'm pleased. I sniff the candle, while everyone else follows my lead.

'I'm not a fan of massages,' Nish says, taking the lid off his pen. 'Paying someone to touch me? It just feels wrong.'

Will chuckles. 'Pretty certain it's not *that* kind of massage, Nish. I'm going to get one though; my body's a little tender.'

I stop messing with my gift bag and look up. His focus shifts to me while he drinks his champagne. 'Must be all that yoga.'

I remain composed. I know what he's up to.

'How have you been feeling, Nora?' he asks. 'I know beginners can sometimes feel like they've taken a pounding.'

'Yes,' Meg agrees. 'Yoga can be brutal if you're not used to it, Nora. It's best to take it slowly at first.'

I blink at Will before turning to Meg.

'Oh, you're so right,' I reply. 'I've been trying to take it slowly. Will actually advised me just to ease myself into it, you know, inch by inch.'

I see Will flinch. *Gotcha, shithead.*

'It's a good way to approach it, Nora,' Will remarks, 'because when you finally get into the right position, like really *deep* into it... you feel the effects everywhere.'

'Oh, totes!' Jillian interjects, swigging from her glass. 'It's an amazing stress reliever.'

Will coughs, holding his hand near his mouth to cover his smile.

'My problem is that I just want to hold that for as long as possible,' he says. 'You know, really push myself as far as I can. I could happily skip the rest of this bootcamp and just give yoga all of my attention. It's *that* incredible.'

The instant he catches my eye again, I visibly writhe in my chair. He's so dead.

Before anyone can respond we're SWAT-teamed by a group of waiters armed with our starters. I excuse myself and head to the bathroom. I don't need Parma ham. I need to cool down.

As I make my way downstairs, I realise this staircase is going to be harder to negotiate the drunker I get. I'm either going to have to drink sensibly or lose my heels at some point during the night. I reach the bathroom and find Patricia there, back-combing her hair.

'Flat hair is not what I need right now,' she comments, savagely shredding at her hair. 'Menopause has a lot to answer for.'

'I think Jillian has some hairspray in her handbag,' I mention, slipping into a cubicle. 'Might help?'

I hear the door slam behind her as she rushes out to find her hair saviour. I use the loo and then wash my hands, running cold water over my wrists in a vain attempt to extinguish my intensifying ardour. I stand for a moment, admiring myself in the mirror, as both Jillian and Patricia storm back in, hairspray in hand.

'You shouldn't have washed your hair first,' Jillian says. 'Dry shampoo adds volume.'

I make a mental note of this while I manoeuvre around them and out into the lobby. I meet Brad at the bottom of the stairs, checking his phone.

'Hey, Brad! Think the Wi-Fi is a bit sketchy here.'

'It's non-existent,' he replies. 'Felix asked for a kilt selfie but it ain't sending... I'll try again later.'

He pauses to look at me. 'Well, don't you look beautiful! Self-acceptance suits you, you're practically glowing.'

It's not self-acceptance, I have a raging horn, Brad. Raging.

'Thank you,' I reply. 'I feel good. Although I think Ralph Lauren may have to take some of the credit.'

'I don't think he's the only dude who's made you glow, sweetie.'

I laugh in surprise. 'Um, perhaps.'

'The universe has a plan for you, Nora Brown,' he says, walking towards the main doors. 'Alignment is a beautiful thing.'

Brad and his tanned legs disappear outside while I head back to the ballroom, smiling to myself. I catch sight of the massage appointment board and sign myself up before returning to the table. I'm excited for this evening and for once, I believe every word that Brad said.

CHAPTER 29

'Would you like to dance?'

Nish awkwardly holds out his hand, his face sombre yet hopeful. I just know his palm is clammy. The truth is, I do not want to dance; that's nothing to do with Nish but everything to do with the sixteen-ounce ribeye steak, lobster tails and bucket of truffle fries now pinning me to my chair. I might as well have stuck my head in a trough. Ralph Lauren didn't take surf and turf into account when designing this dress. But how can I say no to Nish? It would be like kicking a puppy.

'Love to,' I reply with as much enthusiasm as I can muster, knocking back the remainder of my champagne. I take his hand and he leads me to the dancefloor where absolutely NO ON ELSE IS DANCING. I'm not surprised though; Anna's been playing Ace of Base for the past thirty minutes. I think I might have finally discovered her flaw.

Brad spots us and leaps to his feet, sprinting to the laptop. *Please let him have better taste in music*, I think, smiling awkwardly at Nish. If he puts on anything by Runrig or The Proclaimers, I'm bowing out. Ugh, I feel like a twat. I wish everyone would stop looking.

When the music starts, I feel a wave of relief wash over me. It's 'Can't Feel My Face' by The Weeknd. I love this song. I start to move. Nish watches me, his eyes wide like saucers.

Hang on, this is a sexy song... oh dear God, I'm dancing to a sexy song with a twenty-four-year-old like a dirty old cougar. I'm on the verge of patting him on the head and retreating slowly but then the beat drops and Nish starts to dance.

My jaw drops.

I look around the room and everyone has the same expression because we've all just discovered that Nish is cool as hell. The shy, awkward guy we've been seeing all week has been replaced by someone who has serious swag. Within seconds, the beautiful Meg has made a beeline straight for Nish and I happily step aside. Good for him.

It doesn't take long for everyone else to pile on to the dancefloor, drinks in hand, shoes kicked off. Everyone except Will, who either hates dancing or isn't drunk enough yet.

Three songs later, I boogie back to my table and unbuckle the straps on my sandals, letting my 'trodden upon by Tim' toes rest for a while. I slide into the seat beside Will.

'Not dancing?' I ask, pouring myself some champagne.

'I will,' he replies. 'I'm just waiting for a song I like.'

'I don't think Brad will have any Westlife.'

Panic! at the Disco's 'Girls/Girls/Boys' begins playing. I instantly think of Charlie. She's obsessed with them.

'This will do,' he says, 'Let's go.'

'You like Panic?'

'No but I like this song. C'mon.'

This time Will leads me by the hand to the dancefloor but unlike Nish, his hand isn't clammy, and his grip isn't weak. However, also *unlike Nish*, Will isn't the greatest dancer, but it doesn't matter. He has this cheeky dynamism which seems to draw everyone to him. Before I know it, he's swamped by women wanting to dance with him or even just near him. Even

Brad is making his presence known. I step aside and dance with some of the guys from the other groups, but my eyes are on Will.

He's like Andrew Morrison from high school – that one guy who was just badass regardless of what he did.

The more I watch Will, the more it sinks in that in two days we'll go our separate ways, and just like Andrew Morrison, one day he'll fleetingly pop into my head, and I'll wonder what happened to him. It feels strange to think that in two days he'll just be a guy I met once at bootcamp.

'Having fun, Nora?'

Anna's voice pulls me back into the present. 'I am, thanks,' I reply. 'Dinner was delicious.'

'Pleased to hear it,' she says. 'I thought you looked a little pensive just now.'

'I'm just lost in the music,' I lie. 'I'm good.'

She looks at me like I'm full of shit. Both her and Brad have this look down to an art form.

She looks at Will, who's twirling Meg around. 'The briefest of moments,' she muses, watching him dance. 'I liked that. That's really all life is – a collection of brief moments... but some moments last a lifetime.'

She shimmies her way through the dancefloor like an enlightened John Travolta and I decide that the best way to deal with the whole Will situation is to get drunk.

There's no champagne left at table two, so I steal a bottle from table six, grab my wrap and head outside from some fresh air. Thankfully the smokers are going back in as I go out, so it's just me, my bottle and my bare feet. I perch on a bollard and take a mouthful of Moet.

I'm feeling confused. I came here to escape Faith and Victoria telling me what I should do with my love life, only for them to be replaced with Anna and Brad.

In another life, I'd be seizing the bloody moment and

turning it into a future, but that isn't reality. I could pull love affirmations out of my arse and manifest my ideal partner down to the dimples on his cheeks, but that won't make Will feel any less for his wife. It doesn't matter that Will's wife *has* moved on from him because *he* still hasn't moved on from her. I cannot give my heart to someone who's given his to someone else. All I can do is be happy right now.

I'm making good progress on my Moet when Will appears, looking puzzled.

'I wondered where you'd gone,' he says. 'I thought I was going to have to ambush the ladies' toilets.'

'I'm a secret champagne drinker,' I respond. 'Got any cigs?'

'Do you smoke?'

'No. But I thought it might be fun to start.'

'I think you're drunk,' he says, perching beside me. 'Give me that.'

He takes a huge guzzle and passes it back. Everything he does is sexy now. I'm doomed.

'Want to ditch everyone and go hot-tubbing?' he asks, wiping his lips with the back of his hand. 'We could steal another bottle?'

'Hell, yes,' I reply. 'I'll grab my shoes, you grab the booze.'

The champagne heist goes as planned, with Will snatching two bottles plus some petite savoury pastries which had been placed on the tables while we were out. We giggle and stumble all the way back to my cabin, eager to get out of the cold and into the hot tub.

'I'll get the cover, you get the glasses,' Will orders, as I kick my half-buckled sandals off again. I oblige, eating an asparagus pastry as I go. I hate asparagus but I'm too drunk to care; food is food. Next, I scoot off to the bedroom to remove my tights and tummy-control shorts, revealing wobbly belly under dress but I still don't care. Grabbing the bathrobes from the wardrobe, I hear Will yell:

'DO NOT TAKE OFF THAT DRESS YET.'

Seconds later he appears behind me. 'I have been wanting to do this all night.'

I feel him slide the zip down slowly then gently pull the straps of my dress on to my arms. It slips down and falls around my feet. He unhooks my bra then kisses my neck as he moves his hands around to my breasts.

'We're not making it to the hot tub, are we?' I ask, as his hands move lower. He pushes me onto the bed and begins to undress, while I watch.

I guess the answer is no.

CHAPTER 30

BOOTCAMP: DAY 6

'Good morning, everyone, we're so pleased to welcome you to your Farewell Brunch! I hope you're all hungry!'

Anna looks like she's had twenty hours' uninterrupted sleep, unlike the rest of us who look like we've all slept inside a tornado. Clothes and hair askew, we shuffle towards the tables, some people looking for their name cards but most just grabbing whatever seat is closest before they throw up.

'Thank goodness we're not actually leaving until tomorrow morning,' Patricia groans, resting her head in her hands. 'There's no way I can drive. Or eat. Why am I even awake at eleven am?'

Russell and Kenneth grunt in agreement while Meg rubs her back supportively, but her teetotal, vegan face is judging Patricia hard. I'm secretly a little envious; to never have a hangover again might actually be worth never drinking again... but then I remember how fun it is to be drunk and the envy passes.

'Please, everyone, help yourselves,' Anna announces. 'Pastries, juice and cold food on the left, hot breakfast items on the right. We'll be bringing round tea and coffee shortly.'

Will looks surprisingly chipper, considering we didn't fall

asleep until after three this morning. He's made me promise to have dinner with him this evening. A last supper if you will, before we leave tomorrow. Even though I know it's our last full day together, it doesn't feel real yet. None of this does. It feels like a very lovely dream, one which I know I'll be gutted to awaken from. He sits next to me, chatting away to everyone while periodically squeezing my knee under the table to let me know that his mind is very much on me.

I manage to devour a fry-up and two cups of coffee before Anna tells us that today is a 'free roaming' day, culminating with our final meditation session by the loch at 9pm.

'As we said last night, use your last day as you wish. Take a nature walk, climb a hill, laugh with each other, have a winter picnic, visualise, script, whatever makes you happy, but most importantly, whatever makes you grateful.'

Climb a hill? I'm unlikely to be found up a hill unless chased there by bears. I think I'll pass.

'Massages will be in cabin three, please check the board to confirm your time; as our final meditation will be outdoors this evening, please wrap up well.'

'Meditating outside at night? In December?' Patricia questions, looking horrified. 'No, thank you.'

Meg daintily sips her herbal tea. 'I've read about how cold temperatures can actually help focus you... supposed to be therapeutic.'

Patricia bites into her croissant. 'Leeches are supposed to be therapeutic, doesn't mean I want to subject my body to them.'

'They've built a bonfire,' Nish interjects. 'By the water. I saw it yesterday before dinner. That might be fun.'

'I love bonfires!' Meg exclaims. 'Like, I once went to an exclusive festival where my boyfriend at the time, Jackson, played his handcrafted ukulele by the bonfire and then—'

'He was justifiably pushed in?'

She glares at Kenneth while we all snigger. 'He was

extremely talented. My point is that it was a very cosy and intimate occasion… romantic even. Honestly, Kenneth, your generation can be so old-fashioned.'

I finish the last of my breakfast, with my mind wandering to Charlotte as it often does. This time tomorrow I'll be on my way home and it can't come quickly enough. Despite my chaotic week, I've missed her terribly. I just hope she hasn't felt the same. She might be my everything, but I shouldn't be hers. Being here has reminded me that there's so much more outside my little insular universe and I want Charlie to experience it all, even if that involves heartbreak and handmade ukuleles.

Predictably, no one at our table intends to go on a nature hike or a winter picnic, choosing instead to go back to bed, get massages or relax in their hot tubs. I'm booked in for three o'clock. Will lets me borrow his gloves as we trudge back to our cabins, our bodies full of nitrates and buttered toast.

'I am going to sleep like the dead until my massage,' I say, shivering, seemingly unable to keep warm. 'What are you up to?'

'I need to get some notes down for the article,' Will informs me, smirking at my teeth chattering. 'Unless you need a warm body to heat you up?'

I shake my head. 'No way. It's your fault I'm so tired. I need the entire bed to myself. You'll get all handsy and then I'll need to zombie my way around this bonfire.'

'Fair enough,' he replies. 'I'll bring over dinner before the Wicker Man ceremony.'

'Sounds like a plan. Good luck with the article! Be kind.'

'The sex lives of the drunk and lonely,' I hear him yell as I drag myself towards the front door. 'Or maybe Jacuzzi Floozies?'

I'm too tired to laugh. I assume he'll write something favourable yet unsentimental, but I secretly hope his time here with me will be imprinted on his memory forever.

. . .

I sleep for three hours, and then I drag myself up to cabin three where one of the other life coaches, Lewis, has set up his massage table in the living room. Dressed all in white linen, he looks like a member of a boyband from 1994. It seems that in order to work with Anna, you must have biceps of steel as Lewis is also bursting out of his T-shirt sleeves.

'You can change in the bedroom,' he informs me. 'Underwear on is fine, if it makes you more comfortable.'

I decide it does, having already shown more of my body this week than I have in the past few years. I'll go bra-less but my knickers stay on. I slip on a robe and return to the living room, where what sounds like Gregorian chants are being played. If he's standing there, full monk, I'm leaving.

Thankfully Brother Lewis is still dressed in linen and holds up a modesty towel while I disrobe and clamber unceremoniously onto the table. He heats up some oil on his hands and begins with my back, pressing and kneading out knots which have probably been there since Charlie was born. It hurts. Why do people find this part relaxing? After my third yelp, he asks if I'd like less pressure and moves away down my body, towards the most middle-aged pants I own.

I'm sure he's seen worse than my M&S full cotton briefs, I think while his hands carefully work around the waistband. Maybe Meg will have her tiny, tanned derrière under a thong, but I need everything contained and chafe-free.

By the time Lewis has worked my legs and begins on my arms, I've forgotten all about my pants and I'm practically dozing off again. This is one part of getting older that annoys me. In my twenties, I could easily run on four hours of sleep and a can of Red Bull but now I'm planning early nights before I've even gotten up in the morning. Still, any worries I had have been rubbed into oblivion and I feel happy. Oily but happy.

. . .

I have time to shower before Will arrives with two pizzas. I feel a million times better and eighty percent softer.

He places the boxes on the table and kisses my neck.

'Damn, you smell of coconut. I'm suddenly not hungry for pizza.'

'I know,' I reply, sitting at the table. 'I smell like cake. I could eat myself. How did you get on with your work?'

He opens the boxes as he starts jabbering on about his article, picking the mushrooms off his pizza and placing them onto mine.

'It's a little tongue in cheek but I've highlighted all the major selling—'

'Why are you giving me your mushrooms?'

He pauses. 'Because you love mushrooms and I don't?'

'Since when did I love mushrooms?'

He squints at me suspiciously. 'You must have mentioned it. Did you eat them at breakfast?'

'Nope. I haven't eaten or mentioned mushrooms this week. It's really weird that you would assume I love them.'

'Sorry!' He reaches over to remove them, but I push his hand away.

'You weren't wrong,' I say, biting into my pizza. 'Just odd that you knew that.'

He laughs. 'Spooky... though pretty impractical info to be fair; your PIN number would have been more useful.'

I smile, but inside I'm a little freaked out. In the shower I said I wanted someone who knew what I liked without having to ask. Do fungi count as some sort of sign? It might be a silly coincidence to him but to me, it feels like more. It feels like he knows me – really knows me. Is this a soulmate thing? Twin flames? Did the universe conspire to bring me mushrooms?

'We should probably head down to the loch,' he states,

unaware that I'm silently questioning the esoteric significance of a pizza topping. 'I think this is the part where they do the human sacrifice. Might be fun.'

'Can you believe this is our last meeting?' I say, taking my pizza with me. 'Tomorrow we'll never see any of these people again.'

'Hmm, I dunno,' he replies, holding the door for me. 'I get the feeling we'll see Paul on *Crimewatch* at some point.'

I laugh. 'Wanted in connection to a tethering incident?'

'Exactly.'

We shuffle off to the loch-side, munching on pizza while speculating what will become of everyone after we leave. We decide that Nish will marry someone totally unsuitable, Meg will get lost in the rainforest and resurface twenty years later without having aged a day, Allison will have a least two husbands who will die in mysterious accidents, Russell will get hair plugs and Jillian will hopefully continue to donate her dresses to me.

'What about me?' I ask as we approach the water. Everyone has already begun to gather. 'What will become of me?'

'At fifty, you'll marry a twenty-six-year-old Tunisian waiter who definitely loves you for more than a UK passport.'

'Sounds reasonable,' I reply, 'although your future doesn't look much brighter.'

'Why not?'

'Because you'll marry Allison.'

His dimples accompany us towards the loch.

CHAPTER 31

The bonfire is burning brightly behind us as we line the bank of the loch, sitting side by side. Anna instructs us to close our eyes and take a deep breath in. Holding Will's hand in my right and Meg's in my left, I comply, feeling the cold air rush in through my nostrils before warm air escapes slowly past my lips. I smirk as I imagine how ridiculous we must look – forty adults in hats and scarves, sitting cross-legged in the dark with our eyes closed – but it doesn't feel ridiculous. It feels like an appropriately unusual end to a very unusual week. I came here expecting the worst and now here I am, expecting the best. Tunisian waiter aside, I'm eager to see what my future holds. In only six days I've been a lover, an inspiration, a friend and a Prom Queen. I've laughed until my face hurt, cried until my heart hurt and I wouldn't change a single thing.

By nine thirty, music is playing, we're all sipping hot chocolate and enjoying the bonfire, which is providing much-needed warmth. Will is deep in conversation with Anna and Kenneth, while I chat with Brad. There's a real upbeat revelry and I get the feeling everyone will be a little sad to leave.

'I know it's probably nothing, but Will just sat there, giving me his mushrooms like it's something we've always done.'

Brad laughs at the confused expression on my face. 'It's not nothing, far from it! You're connected, plain and simple. Jeez, Nora, we could see it from day one, I'm not sure how you keep missing it.'

'I'm not very in tune,' I reply. 'I mean, for a brief time I thought you were into me! I cannot read any signals correctly, I'm hopeless!'

'Oh, Nora, I *am* into you! I was drawn to you like bees to honey. You read the signals correctly, but you assumed it was a sexual thing because why else would a man be interested, right?'

'Ha ha, my self-esteem precedes me,' I reply, embarrassed but impressed by his insight. 'I guess I'm more used to attracting flies than bees.'

He gestures to Will. 'Not anymore.'

Shame he's already found his bloody queen, I think, but I give Brad a hug anyway and thank him for all his support this week.

'Go have fun,' he says, squeezing me back. 'And you have my email; I expect progress updates.'

I say cheerio and make my way over to Will, who's surrounded by people but quickly focuses on me, his eyes like amatory laser beams. I love the way he does that and it's absurd how quickly my body responds.

'You want to go back to mine?' he asks quietly.

'Yes... but shouldn't we stay and do goodbyes, though?'

He tilts his head to the side and considers this.

'No.'

'Good enough for me.'

We inconspicuously slip away, though to be fair, no one is paying us much attention. Half the crowd have already dispersed, and the rest are having a singalong around the bonfire. I could be piggy-backing Will naked, and I doubt it would distract them from 'The Greatest Love of All', which is being slowly murdered by the remaining few.

Once out of sight, he grabs my hand and rushes me back to his cabin but instead of ripping my clothes off he takes off my glasses, strokes my face and then kisses me so softly, it's like a tiptoe across my lips.

'I don't want to rush this,' he says, his hands moving down to mine. 'I want to... well, you know what I mean, right?'

He can't say 'make love' because a) it's creepy and b) it turns what we're doing into something much bigger than either of us are willing to acknowledge. I smile, indicating that I understand what he means. However, previous experience with Will has shown that desire is a far greater force than whatever willpower we foolishly think we have control of.

Three hours later, we've collapsed in bed, having shagged ourselves into a ridiculous, sweaty mess. In our defence, we did start slowly and there now isn't an inch of me he can't identify from touch alone, but as anticipated, sheer unadulterated lust won. I'm not sure we're capable of having sex again, even if we wanted to. It was perfect.

We lie together, inches apart, kicking off the covers for air. I'm aware that my mascara is probably halfway down my cheeks but it's not my main concern. My main concern is how he'll react to what I'm about to say.

'You've gone quiet,' he remarks, shifting uncomfortably away from one of several wet patches. 'Something on your mind?'

'I think we should say our goodbyes tonight,' I reply. 'Like, now.'

'Now?'

I nod, staring at the ceiling. 'I just don't want any difficult farewells tomorrow morning.'

'Why would it be difficult?' he asks, turning on his side. His hair is a disaster. It's adorable.

'Do I need to spell it out?' I sigh, my gaze still fixed on the ceiling light. 'What I said in class about meeting people you adore? I meant it.'

'Oh.'

'I adore you.'

I feel his hand rest on my arm. 'Nora—'

'It's not a big deal,' I insist. 'I'm not *madly in love with you* or anything. I'm just *into* you... it'll pass. These things always do, otherwise I'd still be pining over Neil Fletcher from primary school.'

He chuckles. 'Kimberly Spencer for me. She played the guitar horribly, but she was a goddess.'

'Well, I played the recorder. It doesn't get much cooler than that.'

'The recorder? Wow, now I'll never get over you.' He laughs again before pulling me into him. We lie quietly, holding each other for our last few moments. He kisses the top of my head then sighs.

'I wish we had longer.'

'Me too.'

'I wish I could say what you need to hear but...' His voice trails off, causing a lump in my throat. I don't want to cry. I came to this camp resigned to the fact that love was not in my future, I don't want to leave thinking the same.

'See! This is the last thing we need tomorrow,' I reply, trying to sound upbeat. 'I don't want to leave feeling sad. We shouldn't feel sad! This was exactly as it should have been. And I should go.'

'So, this is it?' he asks as I rise and head to the bathroom. 'You go back to your cabin, leave tomorrow and we pretend like it never happened?'

'God, no!' I reply, putting on one of his robes. The more I

try not to cry, the higher my voice gets. 'I won't pretend it never happened, I just won't dwell on it, I suppose. Life goes on.'

I'm smiling as I return to the bedroom, but he isn't even trying to feign happiness.

'But what if I dwell?' he asks. 'What if you never leave my head?'

'Hmm... lobotomy?'

'I'm serious. It took me months to feel this comfortable with my wife, but a few days with you and—'

'No, don't do that,' I interrupt. 'That's not fair. I won't be compared. It's not a competition.'

'I didn't mean it like that,' he responds, pulling the duvet over him. 'What *is* unfair is you telling me how you feel.'

'Why?'

'Because what's the point of admitting something I can't do a damn thing about?'

I grab my clothes from the floor and check the time on his phone – 3.33am. 'I should go.'

'Wait!' he says, grabbing my hand. 'Stay. Sleep here.'

'Better not,' I reply, swallowing hard. 'Difficult? Remember?'

He nods in defeat as I quickly kiss him and say goodbye, cradling my clothes in my arms.

'See ya, Nora,' I hear him say as the front door closes behind me. A tiny sob escapes from my throat as I make my way in the dark back to my own cabin, crawling into my own bed. Holding back my tears is pointless, so I don't even try but after a brief sob, I realise something important. Even though Will couldn't tell me how he felt, it doesn't matter because whatever I'm feeling is enough. For once what I feel isn't inextricably linked to someone else's validation or rejection. There is no mess to clean up, no promises broken and no hurt feelings to mend.

I realise that I was forty years old when I finally put myself first.

CHAPTER 32

'Leaving already, Nora?'

I'm going to miss Brad's morning smile, almost as much as I've missed Charlie's.

'I am!' I reply, handing my cabin key to Persephone as she prepares the coffee and breakfast sandwich I've ordered. 'Well, soon. Just thought I'd check out while I was grabbing breakfast. Multitasking and all that.'

'Good thinking,' he replies. 'We're here for another night, then on to London for the next bootcamp.'

'Well, good luck and thanks, Brad for... well, everything!' I say. 'It's been quite the week.'

I take my breakfast and thank Persephone. She doesn't care, she's too busy beaming at Brad.

'My pleasure,' Brad replies. 'You have my email, you better keep in touch, lady! I mean that. You've quickly become my new favourite.' He leans in and hugs me while Persephone's confused glare burns a hole in my back.

'You know it,' I reply. 'Take care.'

He holds open the door for me as I saunter back to my lodgings, soaking up the view before I return to Edinburgh. As much as I love my city, the beautiful clear, black night skies here have given me a sense of calm that I've never experienced before. This is where I found myself again. Where I found Will.

As I reach my cabin, I can't help but look for Will's car. It's still there. He hasn't left yet. I know we said our goodbyes last night, but it doesn't stop me wishing for five more minutes. I don't regret telling him how I felt, I only wish he could have said it back. Or written it in on his stupid bloody notebook. Something. Anything.

At half past ten, I text Faith and Charlie to let them know I'm leaving, while throwing my breakfast rubbish in the outside bin. One last check that I haven't forgotten anything, then I lift the handle on my suitcase and wheel it out behind me. Despite my reluctance to come here in the first place, I'm so very glad I did. This might have been the place I fell for Will, but this was also the place I finally fell for *me*. I smile to myself, closing the door behind me.

'Morning.'

'Jesus, Will!' I drop my car keys on the doormat. 'You scared me. Again!'

'Last one for old times' sake. Promise.'

He remains standing by my car as I pick up my keys and walk towards him, my suitcase grinding like an armoured tank as it scrapes across the gravel. His own car is parked beside mine, the engine already running. He's obviously not planning on staying long.

'I thought we weren't doing this,' I say. 'Last night—'

'I know,' he replies sheepishly. 'But, well, here I am... Steal anything good?'

'Huh?'

He gestures towards my case.

'Oh. Only Nish,' I reply. 'He's heavier than he looks.'

Will takes my case and loads it into the boot of my car. He's smiling, but I can tell he's trying as hard as I am not to make this any more difficult than it needs to be.

'So, you're heading back to Edinburgh now?' he asks, leaning on the car. 'All checked out?' He seems as reluctant to say goodbye as I am.

I nod. 'Yeah. I want to get back for Charlie. I've really missed her. You?'

'Not really, I've never met her.'

The burst of laughter is a welcome relief but dissolves any barriers or hope we had of keeping our feelings in check. I lean against the car beside him.

'Yeah, back to Brighton for me,' he says. 'Back to the real world.'

His voice trails off. I know what he's inferring but I don't respond. He kicks the gravel near my feet and sighs.

'Fuck, Nora. I mean...'

'I know,' I respond as he struggles to find the words. I feel my bottom lip begin to tremble. I stare at the ground, gripping my car keys in my pocket to steady myself. 'It's fine. Just bad timing.'

'Horrible timing,' he mumbles. 'Fucking horrible.'

I rest my head against his shoulder, quietly seething. The universe can piss off. If this was its plan, it's a cruel one.

Will senses my wrath and nudges me lightly. 'In another life, then?'

I smirk reluctantly. 'Yep, another life.' I let go of my keys and place my hand beside his. 'One where I'm better dressed.'

As he quietly laughs, I feel his fingers brush against mine before they finally interlock. I don't want to let him go. But it's time.

'Be happy, Nora.'

'You too, Will.'

He gives my hand a squeeze before he pulls away. I briskly

wipe the tears from my eyes while he walks over to his own car. I am not going to lose it.

Heart in my throat, I watch him get into the driver's seat and fasten his belt. I open my door and pause, trying to catch my breath.

Chin up, Nora. Get in the car, turn on the engine and drive. If Will can do this, so can you.

But Will isn't coping any better than I am. I see him press his head against the steering wheel before shouting the word 'Fuck!' so loudly I can hear it through the glass. He sits for a second before unbuckling his seat belt.

He's getting out of his car.

I drop my bag and rush towards him, meeting him halfway. He holds my face with both hands and kisses me for the longest time. For the last time. It's a kiss that both gently warms yet viciously blisters my heart.

'I do adore you, Nora' he admits, his head resting against mine. 'God, I adored you from the moment I saw you. You deserve to know that. I *need* you to know that.'

I nod in acknowledgement, my hands still holding his waist.

'I'm sorry,' he utters, 'I'm so sorry that—'

'Don't be sorry,' I interject, ignoring the tear that's escaping down my cheek. 'I'm not sorry. Even if this is all we get, I'm grateful we met. No regrets.'

I remove my hands from his waist and step back. Thirty seconds later, he drives back to his old life, and I do the same.

CHAPTER 33

'Will you stop texting Charlie! She knows what time you'll be home tonight, she knows you love her, give the girl some space.'

'How do you know it's Charlie?'

'Because the only other people you text are right here,' Faith replies. I hear Victoria giggle. 'Nora, just give me a yes or a no, it's really not that difficult.'

'Fine, I'll do it,' I exclaim, putting my phone away. 'But he'd better not be like the last one. Still can't believe he whipped *that* out over lunch!'

'I apologised for that,' Faith replies, a slight smirk beginning to form. 'I had no idea he wore top dentures. Listen, this one is far better; I think you'll have a lot in common and... ugh, this glass is dirty. Whose idea was it to come here, anyway?'

Victoria and I lock eyes for a moment. Reminding Faith that it was in fact her idea to come to Edinburgh's third-worst Italian restaurant on TripAdvisor seems futile. I watch her eyes dart around looking for a waiter as she pushes the offending glass into the middle of the table.

'You *always* think I'll have lots in common,' I respond, trying to pull her crosshairs away from the overworked waiting staff. 'But you also thought I'd have a lot in common with that mildly racist barber, so I'm not overly trusting.'

'Trust me, he's a definite contender,' Faith insists. 'Tell me, how do you feel about anaesthetists?'

'Numb,' I reply, laughing at my own joke. Faith isn't amused.

From the corner of my eye, I see Victoria's fork stealthily appear and spear my pasta like a silverware Shinobi. I frown. 'Something wrong with your salad?'

'Yes,' she replies, shovelling my tagliatelle into her mouth. 'It's salad.'

'Then why the hell—'

'Your problem is you're still holding a candle for that *man*,' Faith interrupts forcefully. 'Which, quite frankly, is a little ridiculous – sorry, can I have a glass that isn't filthy, thanks so much – a weeklong fling with a man does not merit this amount of pining, Nora. It's been weeks!'

'Pining?' I ask as the waiter speedily places another glass in front of Faith. 'Who's pining? I am fully committed to finding someone, honestly. I barely even think of Will anymore.'

This is mostly true. Since bootcamp, I have been far more open to meeting someone, though it has been trickier than I anticipated. Two months ago, I came back from Cairn Castle a different woman, an improved woman – stronger and far more optimistic about the future, but as hard as I try, my longing for Will has not passed quite as quickly as I'd hoped. And good God, I've tried.

Victoria cocks her head to one side with the *really* look she likes to throw in my direction when she suspects I'm talking nonsense. Which I am. I think of him frequently. I sigh as I suspect this *quiet dinner with the girls* I've agreed to is just another intervention.

'How many times have you looked at his Facebook profile?' Victoria asks. 'Or his Twitter account?'

'None,' I reply, 'And I don't even know if he has a Twitter acc—'

'All writers are on Twitter,' Faith insists. 'They can't help themselves. They think everything they write or think or eat warrants an audience.'

'Well, regardless, I'm not falling down that bloody rabbit hole!' I reply. 'I need to get over him, not stalk him on social media!'

'Ha! So, you're not over him!' Faith yelps victoriously. 'I knew it!'

I slump back into my seat and sigh while Columbo takes a triumphant bite of her steak.

'I want to look him up,' I concede, pushing my pasta around my plate. 'I just don't trust myself. What if his photos are public and I spend three weeks looking at pictures of him and his wife and then one day my finger slips, and I accidentally like a post? What if I tag myself in their old honeymoon photos?'

'Wow, you have thought this through, haven't you?' Vic says. 'Look, if you're really missing him, you should just contact him. I mean, what's the worst that can happen?'

'Um, literally everything I've just said.'

'So, you're too afraid to even find out?'

'What if I message him and he doesn't reply?' I feel my throat tighten. 'It obviously meant nothing to him, otherwise he would have been in touch. He probably hasn't even given me a second thought.'

Victoria sighs. 'Oh, Nora, of course he'll think of you, he's—'

'—AND now after all this Law of Attraction shit, I'm wary that even thinking this negative shit will make it come true!'

Faith rolls her eyes. 'That's absurd. If any of that nonsense was true, I'd be married to Leonardo DiCaprio by now. I spent most of my teenage years planning our wedding. Last time I checked, my surname was still Brown.'

'Still hung up on DiCaprio, huh?' I reply, smirking. Her

bedroom walls were covered in posters of him. 'I mean, he's single. You still might have a shot if the universe can make you twenty-five again. And a swimwear model.'

'My point exactly,' Faith responds. 'You cannot just magic something into existence by thinking about it.'

My head shoots back with a groan. 'Ugh, I know.'

'It's a little ridiculous,' Victoria adds.

'I KNOW!' I exclaim. 'It is ridiculous, *I am ridiculous*. Look at me. I used to mock women like me – someone pays them the tiniest amount of attention and they turn into grateful, lovesick morons who think the universe somehow brought them together.'

'People meet every day for no reason at all,' Faith insists. 'To imply that there's some higher power behind it... you got on well with someone for a week, Nora. There's nothing mystical about that.'

I take a gulp of wine and wallow in her bluntness. 'I know, but... it's so hard to explain... the connection we had... maybe it is all in my head.'

Victoria steals more of my pasta and chuckles. 'Nah, I know exactly what you mean.'

I raise an eyebrow. 'Really? You and Benjamin?'

She laughs. 'God, no. He was a slow burner. Remember the first day that we met? Mrs Ahmed's science class. I was the new kid, and you were made to come and sit with me.'

I smile, remembering her noticeably anxious face peering over at me from the front of the class. 'Of course. We had to share those really grotty safety glasses.'

'Well, after hanging out with you for two days, I just knew you were going to be my friend forever,' she says, smiling. 'We just gelled. It was instantaneous. I met loads of other kids but that only happened with you. I thought about you that day and well, every day since for the last, oh, twenty-five years.'

God, now I'm tearing up again, and for the first time this evening, Faith is quiet.

'Finding someone you just "know" before you even know them doesn't happen often. So, it's not weird or hard to explain. At least not to me, because that's exactly how I feel about us. We were meant to be. Just like me and this pasta.'

I laugh and push my plate closer to her. 'Maybe I will send him a message. Just something casual. What have I got to lose, right?'

Victoria nods. 'Unless the universe can use social media on your behalf, I think that's at least a start.'

'Just go for it.' My eyebrows shoot up in surprise as I see Faith raise her glass to me. 'I've never had that kind of connection with anyone. You both make me sick. Now go and be happy.'

Victoria laughs and we both join Faith in her toast. We continue with dinner as my stomach bubbles in anticipation.

'It's unsettling, you know?' I say, eating what's left of my pasta. 'I'm not used to having this.'

'Having what?' Vic asks.

'Hope,' I reply.

CHAPTER 34

'Do you know how many men called Will or William Thomson there are on Facebook?' I yell at my phone. 'Thirty billion.'

'I'm fairly certain there's only seven billion people in the world,' Victoria replies on speaker. 'But OK. Have you tried narrowing it down by location? Where does he live?'

'Brighton,' I reply. 'I think. Oh God, maybe it was Birmingham... or Bristol? Definitely a B word.'

I hear Vic tapping on her keyboard. I have already been skimming through Facebook profiles for thirty minutes, a sea of Will Thomsons all blissfully unaware that I've been deep-diving their information. She sighs. 'Nah, nothing in Brighton, though a lot of people hide their location or use variations on their name. I do.'

'Why? In case someone falls in love with you after a week and stalks you?'

I hear her chuckle. 'Pretty much. I'll try Birmingham next. You go through the rest of the Bs.'

An hour later, we still haven't found my Will Thomson, but I did find a different Will Thomson who owns a sausage dog called Thor and sells a suspicious amount of used car parts from his home in Newport Beach.

'This is useless,' I grumble, squinting at a fuzzy picture of Thor. 'He might not even be on here. I think this dog might have his own bedroom—'

'Oh, wait, didn't you say he was writing an article for some magazine?' Victoria asks.

'Yes,' I reply, '*FMQ*. But he said it would be under 'staff writer' or something, It's probably not even out yet.'

'But maybe he's written for them before? Sometimes journalists add their Twitter handle to their bio on publication sites.'

'I tried Twitter,' I inform her. 'Again, lots of Will Thomsons but none of them are him... it might be worth a shot though, I'm willing to try anything.'

We both google *FMQ* and start trawling through the articles. Apparently, sherry, Bitcoin and resistance training are very important to the menfolk of the UK. I click on the culture section and freeze at the first article.

Bootcamp for Broken Hearts

'Oh shit. I've found him. I've found the bootcamp article.'

'Where?' Vic squeals. 'What section? Does it have a byline photo? I really want to see this guy.'

'Culture section. It just says staff writer – no photo,' I reply, my eyes scanning the page as I begin to read aloud.

'*Bootcamp was an eye-opening look at how the 'new thought' movement sees the world and ultimately how we see ourselves. I saw myself leaving as soon as possible.*'

'Oh God, I can't keep reading. You do it.'

'You're such a pussy,' Vic responds. 'OK, I've found it.'

'*Ever wondered why you're still single? Well, wonder no more, my romantically challenged friends, Holistically Yours claims to have the answer. For the not-so-insignificant sum of five thousand pounds, this elite retreat will encourage you to challenge your existing beliefs, promote self-love, and help you manifest the person of your dreams into reality with a little assistance from the universe.*

'*In the interest of full disclosure, during my stay I was an unhappily separated-but-married man and therefore not their target audience. I was not looking to attract someone new, nor figure out why I was currently single. To be clear, I did not approach any of this with the intention of becoming a better man; I am not sure that's possible, even with the universe on side. I approached this purely as an undercover feature writer, assigned to give an honest account of what it's like to attend the exclusive romance bootcamps which have taken America by storm. Nothing more, nothing less.*'

'He's funny,' Vic compliments. 'And at least he's honest.'

'I guess. Keep going.'

'*The ideas presented are relatively simple (once you suspend all critical thinking and common sense) – what you think about, you attract, both positive and negative. Feeling is the key here – if you feel like you already have it, the universe has no choice but to deliver it to you. If you simply feel like you are dating the greatest woman alive, the universe will provide. Likewise, if you feel like a worthless turd, the universe will provide you with everything a worthless turd could want.*'

I can picture Will's face as he recounts his time there and I'm literally holding my breath as Victoria reads on.

'*It attracted a surprisingly diverse group of people, from young, wealthy millennials, to the more desperate, middle-aged last-chance salooners who, quite honestly, should have enough life experience to know better. All very nice people but the only common denominator among the group was loneliness. I have never seen so many lonely people in one room, and I've been to a Radiohead concert.*'

I smile to myself as she continues reading about the tasks,

the activities, facilities, and the workshops, but then she suddenly stops.

'Oh. Erm...'

'What?'

'Nothing? It's just really boring, isn't it? I mean, there isn't—'

My stomach drops. 'What did he say?'

'He didn't say anything exactly, it's—'

'Just read it.'

She takes a second to clear her throat and continues.

'I'd like to say it was a complete waste of time but having spent the week imagining reconciling with my wife whom I haven't spoken to for six months, she's just asked me to dinner. Maybe there is something in this after all?'

There is a silence as I process her words. *His words.* I feel like I've been punched.

'Nora, I'm sorry,' Vic finally says. 'Look, that doesn't mean that—'

'That I'm an idiot?' I reply. 'Of course, it does. I mean, I knew he wanted to get back with her. He never said otherwise. I just thought...'

'What?'

I don't reply. I just close my laptop and try to ignore the ever-growing lump in my throat.

'Want me to come over?' Vic asks.

'Nah,' I say quietly. 'I'm OK. I'll see you in the morning.'

We say goodnight and I climb into bed, the words *'lonely middle-aged, last-chance salooners'* creeping around in my head. Is that how he saw me? Some pathetic desperado? I thought at the very least we were friends. Actually, that's a lie. I thought we were more. I thought that meeting me would have changed everything for him. I thought that maybe, for once in my stupid life, I might just be the one.

———

Victoria is already wiping down tables when I arrive at the café the following day. Before I can even say good morning, she drops her cloth and makes her way over to me.

'Oh, Nora!' she exclaims, coming in for a hug. 'You look like you haven't slept a wink.'

'I got a few hours,' I reply, hugging her back. 'Couldn't get that article out of my head. Not quite the happy ending I was hoping for.'

'Yubi-hokay,' she mumbles, her voice muffled by my hair.

'I will be OK,' I reply, trying to convince us both. 'I just need to move on. I need something else to occupy my mind.'

'Good. OK, any ideas?'

'Yep.' I sniff, wiping off my tear-stained glasses. 'Not sleeping gave me a lot of time to think. I spent half the night chastising myself for behaving like a teenager and the other half thinking about something Brad from bootcamp said.'

'Was it "Woah, dude"?' she mocks in a Californian drawl.

'Very funny, no, he said, "The universe has a plan for you, Nora Brown".'

'Oh... right.'

'And I thought, does the universe have a plan for me? I don't even have a plan for me!'

'I thought you'd moved past all that stuff?' Victoria says, her brow furrowing. 'I mean, you don't actually believe that—'

'The way I see it – if the universe does have a plan for me, so far, that plan has been terrible: heartbreak, stagnation, loneliness, apathy. If the universe's plan is just for me to exist like this until I die, I'm going to have to intervene.'

'Ah! And?'

'Well, first we're rebranding this bloody café,' I inform her, my eyes scanning the room. 'New name, new décor, new floor, new everything. We should not settle for mediocre. We can do better. I can do better.'

She nods. 'Of course. I always say, the best way to get over a man is to take a wrecking ball to your business.'

'Oh, it's not just because of Will, it's—'

She places her hand on my arm. 'Nora, I know. I think it's a brilliant idea. I'm in.'

'Oh, thank God,' I reply, 'because that was my only idea and that took hours to come up with. I feel good about this.'

'Me too,' she agrees. 'How exciting! A new chapter for Café Shite.'

I smile as she instantly begins spitballing ideas for the café, while I take my bag and place it in the backroom. A new chapter is exactly what I need. No more ruminating over the past, no more wishing things had gone differently. Charlie's dad was a huge mistake, but making that mistake gave me Charlie. How can I ever regret that? But Will... Will and I might have been in the same place at the same time, but we were never in the *right* place at the right time and that's alright. Maybe that's the way it was always meant to be.

CHAPTER 35

FOUR MONTHS LATER

'Mum, that smells like you've dug something up. I know you're going through a whole Tina Turner phase, but can you burn something else when you're doing your woo-woo stuff?'

Charlie's snarky dislike of my Bootcamp patchouli oil candle rudely interrupts my evening meditation. My once sad and messy bedroom is now my happy place. My calm place. A place free from the bank loans, the builders, and the planning permission red tape I'm currently wading through at work. It's been four months since we started the café revamp and it's as exciting as it is stressful with one more week until opening.

It was the lovely Brad who convinced me to start meditating again. We reconnected a few weeks ago, after a rambling email from me found its way into his inbox, filling him in on my life since bootcamp. I didn't mention Will's article or that he was a bootcamp traitor. I might be a lot of things, but I'm not a grass:

So, yes, I'm still single but right now I'm having some sort of mid-life adventure where I've just remortgaged my soul to pay for wood panelling, new signage and checkerboard floors. This revamp is either going to be delightfully retro or a tacky mess. I

*also decided that the universe's plan wasn't working for me, so
have devised my own strategy, mainly involving an endless
cycle of anxiety, power naps and mango smoothies from the
new juice bar next door. It's been fun, if a little stressful. Still
somewhat bummed that the whole Will thing didn't go
anywhere, but that's life, right? You win some, you lose some.
My new chapter is looking promising, and I hope wherever he
is, he's happy.*

As usual Brad was his delightfully transcendent self. Like a
handsome, ripped Buddha.

*You can't lose, Nora, because nothing is ever lost – it's just not
in your vibration at that particular moment. Meditation is key
here; breathe, clear your mind and open your heart. You'll be
surprised what you find there.*

*Unless I find an electrician that turns up on time, Brad, I'm
not interested.* Still, we've agreed to meet for smoothies when
he's next back in Scotland.

I tell Charlie that I'll look for new oils that don't offend her
delicate nose holes and close my eyes again, my back pressed
against the head of my new, king-size, blue velvet bed.

When I first started meditating again, I was all over the
place, battling thoughts of the café revamp, life in general,
Charlie and, of course, Will. I tried so hard not to think about
him, at first unsuccessfully but over the past few weeks my
longing for him has diminished. Now he's becoming just a tran-
sitory affection which never fails to make me smile. I meant
what I said to Brad; I genuinely hope he's happy.

I look back on bootcamp now with a great deal of fondness
as well as a newfound respect for this whole reality-creation
lark. The mantra *imagination creates reality* isn't as 'woo-woo' as
Charlie puts it or as mystical as bootcamp would have me

believe because it's fundamentally true. I realise that I stopped imagining that my life could be better. I stopped believing that I even wanted it to, and my reality reflected that. I was lonely, I was stuck, and I was reliving the same day over and over again. So determined not to let past mistakes define me that I couldn't move forward. It's hard to create a future when you're stuck in the past.

While there are circumstances that I cannot dictate or control, I do have complete autonomy over where I am right now and the power to make it as magnificent as my imagination will allow. Faith said that people meet every day for no reason, but I believe there was a reason I met Will. I believe it was to show me what is possible. He reminds me that I'm capable of falling in love again and if nothing else, bootcamp has helped me view my life through very different eyes. Despite the niggling doubts that surface every now again, I know that there is someone out there for me and I know that I can be happy regardless. Best five thousand pounds I never spent.

I manage a further seven minutes before my phone rings and ruins my blissful meditative state. I bet Tina Turner remembers to turn her ringer off.

'Electrician's coming in tomorrow morning,' Victoria informs me. 'Sends his apologies.'

Like me, Victoria is equally anxious about the café opening next week but dealing with the pressure far better than I am. She's also superior at dealing with tradesmen who don't show up when they say they will. I tend to rage while she diplomatically charms the overalls off them.

'Thank goodness,' I say. 'No one else can fit us in.'

'I have the cash and carry tomorrow, can you be there, or shall I ask Tracey?'

'I'll do it,' I reply. 'Though I might murder him for not turning up last week.'

'Understandable,' she answers. 'No reasonable jury would

convict, but can you wait until he finishes putting the sockets in?'

'Sockets before slaying. Got it.'

'Thanks, will see you in the afternoon! Bye!'

She hangs up and before I can settle down again, I hear Charlie sniff then make a gagging noise.

'Fine, I get it!' I yell. Admitting defeat, I blow out the candle and open the window. I'll try another meditation session when Charlie's at her dad's. Or suffering from anosmia, whichever comes first.

CHAPTER 36

'All done.'

I pop my head out of the back room, to see Tommy the electrician's stubby finger flick a switch behind the coffee machine, which begins to autofill.

'Brilliant,' I reply. 'And the sockets behind the fridge?'

'All done,' he repeats. 'Inspection certificate is on the counter, with the rest of the paperwork. You're good to go.'

I make my way into the kitchen and do a quick check before he leaves. 'Thanks,' I say, happy with the result. 'Victoria will bank transfer whatever's outstanding.'

He nods and lifts his things, whistling a tune that vaguely sounds like a death march. 'Any probs, give me a bell. Good luck, hen!'

I wait for the door to close behind him before I give a loud squeal. We're ready. I can't believe we're ready. The cleaners will be here at two, then tomorrow we prep for opening on Saturday. To say I feel proud of myself would be an understatement and I haven't felt proud of myself in the longest time.

Twenty minutes later, Vic arrives, armed with bags from the

cash and carry. She also squeals, flicking the now working sockets on and off.

'It's really happening!' she chirps. 'This place is going to be awesome and it's all down to you, girl.'

I beam. 'Us,' I tell her. 'We did this. Oh, his paperwork is on the counter,' I say, shifting a multipack of kitchen roll into the cupboard. 'Told him you'd sort him out.'

She *hmm*s and starts rifling through.

'If he thinks I'm paying for the fact he messed...' She pauses and purses her lips. 'Oh my.'

'What?'

She holds something up and grins. I move in to look more closely. She's holding up *FMQ*. The edition with Will's article.

'How the...?'

'Either Tommy left this here or that bloody universe is sending you a sign.'

'Maybe Tracey left it?' I suggest as I peer at it suspiciously. Tommy is at least sixty-five. There's no way he's reading in-depth interviews with Tom Hardy or features on the Best Grooming Boxes under £100 – last month he left a copy of the *Daily Star* in the toilet.

Vic shakes her head. 'Doubtful. She hasn't been here since Monday, and it wasn't here when I closed up last night.'

I shrug and toss it on to a nearby table, but I am shaken. I thought about Will before I fell asleep last night. I thought about the last time I saw him. The way he kissed me as we said goodbye.

'Nora, nothing is ever lost – it's just not in your vibration at that particular moment.'

Oh, shut up, Brad. Yes, I might have been thinking about Will a little more than usual recently, but infrequent, margin-ally erotic thoughts about him don't mean anything. I give myself a shake and continue unpacking.

———

Faith pops round uninvited on Friday evening, catching me in the middle of dyeing my hair. We have the café launch tomorrow and I just want a relaxing evening alone. Faith knows this because I specifically told her not to come round and ruin my relaxing evening alone. Yet here she is.

'You can pay people to do that, you know?' she informs me, like I've just arrived on planet Earth. 'You've missed a huge bit at the back.'

Charlie usually spot checks my hair for me, but she's at her dad's house. I hand Faith the tinting brush.

'Help a sister out, then,' I say. 'I'm too poor for the salon this month.'

She throws her jacket over the chair and begins dabbing away at the back of my head. 'I wish you would just ask me for money, you know. I can't have you wandering around all patchy-haired and making your own clothes. You never know who you might meet at your relaunch.'

'Who I might... Oh no. No. No. Nope.'

'No what?'

'Please tell me you're not trying to set me up at my own relaunch.'

She stops painting my head. 'I didn't say anything about—'

'Faith!'

'Well, not set you up *exactly*... more an introduction of sorts.'

Allowing Faith to set me up again is something I'm beginning to regret even though I'm fully aware that dating is a numbers game, like *Countdown* but with more frequent conundrums. I've been on five dates since bootcamp, and they've all been less than successful. The third, Julian, was a real sweetheart but his need to text in the style of an eighteenth-century poet grew tedious rather quickly and the least said about the persistent scrotum-scratcher Matt who I dated last week, the better.

'Totally not appropriate!' I yelp. 'I'll have enough on my plate tomorrow, never mind being awkwardly congenial to... who is it this time? Your office security guard? Weird client? Desperate colleague? I'm so not up for this right now, Faith.'

She shrugs and whisks the brush around in the hair dye. 'Fine, I won't bother. Probably just as well, God knows how this dye job is going to turn out. It smells like there is a forty-percent developer in here. My eyes are burning.'

'Alright, Vidal, point made. Look, just promise me that your guest list for tomorrow isn't made up entirely of potential suitors.'

'I promise. Jeez.'

'Thank you.'

'I'd say it's closer to thirty percent – anyway, you're all done!'

She throws the bowl into the sink and darts out of the bathroom before I can inflict any serious bodily harm.

I clip my hair up on top of my head, pausing to hear Faith rummaging around in my kitchen. 'Bottom shelf, back cupboard,' I yell.

'Thanks.'

Faith rarely borrows anything from me, but when she does, it's always my juicer/blender. 'They sell them in supermarkets,' I remind her for the millionth time. 'You might as well just buy one instead of taking mine.'

'I only use it for margaritas,' she replies. 'Besides, you hardly use yours anymore. It deserves a more attentive home.'

Which is true. About three years ago I decided that juicing would be the answer to eternal youth but instead, I just got the runs. She knows one day I'll stop asking for it back, but it cost me a hundred quid and I'm not quite ready to let go, unlike my bowels.

'Got it, thanks. Get some rest!' she yells.

'Enjoy your pulverized booze,' I holler back as she heads towards the front door. 'I'll see you at twelve.'

I hear the door click and set a half hour timer on my phone before scrambling around in a bathroom drawer for one of Charlie's hydrating masks. I carefully unpeel it, placing the slimy tissue over my face. It's weirdly relaxing, almost like being at a spa, only I'm fairly certain that they don't issue monkey face masks as standard.

My (hopefully) punctual daughter will be back at ten tomorrow morning and then we'll head over to set up. I should get an early night, but I'm too nervous to get any meaningful rest. There are so many things that could go wrong and I'm considering all of them. What if no one shows up? What if everyone hates the café's new look? What if I turn up tomorrow with orange hair or a bald spot from overprocessing my greying roots?

Oh God, please let this go well.

CHAPTER 37

'Victoria and I would like to thank you all for coming, and a special thanks to our neighbours for putting up with all the noise and disruption that goes along with refurbishment. Hopefully, some free food and drink will go a little way to showing our appreciation. It's been a long time coming but today we say goodbye to Café 12 and welcome you all to Charlie Brown's!'

Applause rings out as Charlotte's scissors slice through the dark blue ribbon, and we finally open the doors to our revamped, American-style diner, complete with 1950s jukebox, cosy booths for kissing teenagers and the best handmade burgers in Edinburgh. My lovely daughter is of course thrilled that her name is above the door.

Faith's guest list was a nice touch. Local papers, bloggers, neighbouring businesses, and a couple of minor celebrities have all turned up (as well as some of Charlotte's school friends) to sample our menu of burgers, hotdogs, wings, ribs, mac and cheese, fries and shakes. I even invited café regular Jean along, much to Faith's disapproval.

'I'm not saying they can't eat here; I just don't think a group of elderly women is the right image for opening night.'

'Oh, come on,' I reply. 'Where's the harm? Jean and her little gang have been loyal customers since we first opened.'

'Maybe, but you're meant to be pushing your new vision, Nora,' she scorns. 'A fun, retro eating experience for a younger demographic with a high disposable income. I'm not sure moth-balls and dementia quite fall into this concept.'

'I'm going to tell Wilbur you said that.'

'Who?'

'Never mind.'

The café interior is now almost unrecognisable. Beige walls are now red, our grey floors now black-and-white checks with silver tables in the centre and dark red leather booths lining the walls.

'I can't quite believe we've done it,' Vic whispers to me as she waves at the owner of next door's juice bar. 'This place is now officially a blast.'

I nod, beaming from ear to ear. It couldn't have gone better; everyone came, everything works, and my hair is surprisingly on point. Even a normally stoic-faced Tracey is grinning as she runs the kitchen. We've hired additional staff to help out tonight and I like being on this side of the counter. Maybe one day we'll expand, anything is possible.

'Nora, there's someone I want you to meet.'

My current state of bliss dips for a moment when I see Faith gesture to a man in an expensive brown suit with a neat, salt-and-pepper beard to join us. Is this the man she wanted to set me up with? Oh God, he looks at least twenty years older than me.

'Larry Wilde, this is my sister, Nora.'

He holds out his hand while I try to place his name. It's very familiar.

'Lovely to meet you,' I say, 'Thanks so much for coming.'

He flashes me the most expensive smile I've ever seen on anyone over sixty. 'Pleasure,' he replies in a soft American accent. 'And I believe I should thank you for coming to our Scottish retreat. Faith says you had a ball.'

It takes me a second but suddenly it clicks. Larry Wilde. CEO of Holistically Yours. What the hell is he doing here?

'I did!' I reply. 'It was quite the week. In a roundabout way, it inspired all of this. A fresh start so to speak.'

He looks around and nods. 'My wife always tells me, when you change the way you look at things, the things you look at change. She's usually right.'

'Is your wife here?' I ask, looking around.

'Anna? No, she's running a retreat in Montreal right now.'

I nearly choke on my Buck's Fizz. 'Anna? You're married to Anna? The Anna who ran *my* retreat?'

'The very one.' There's a glint in Larry's eye that tells me he knows just how lucky he is. 'I'm here to do some business with my go-to girl. Seems we'll be making UK bootcamps a twice-yearly feature.'

Faith says something about exciting opportunities while I'm still stunned that Anna is married to the spiritual Kenny Rodgers. I was certain she'd be married to some kaftan wearing thirty-something with a man bun.

'Now if you'll excuse me,' Larry says, motioning to the buffet area, 'I have my eye on that mac and cheese. Pleasure to meet you. Nora.'

'Well, that was unexpected,' I say to Faith as we watch him make a beeline for the comfort food. 'He's not at all what I expected. His wife, Anna, can't be much older than me!'

She nods. 'He's quite the silver fox, isn't he? And richer than sin. Well done, Anna.'

'Indeed,' I reply. 'For a second there I thought—'

'That he was your blind date?' Faith laughs. 'Hardly. Besides, even if he wasn't married, he's one of my biggest clients. Conflict of interest. I don't need you breaking his heart and ruining my perfectly lucrative business relationship.'

'Faith, when have I ever broken someone's heart?'

She smiles. 'Oh, I dunno. I get the feeling that somewhere, out there, there's a man who's considerably heartbroken that you're no longer in his life.'

'Sweet of you to say,' I reply as Vic frantically waves over to me for help, 'but highly unlikely. Need to dash!'

Jean and Mary are the first to leave, Mary clutching a small doggy bag of beef rib bones that Tracey had left over, for her Great Dane. Seems like I'm not the only one with a soft spot for these women.

'I must say, I was a little apprehensive about this new look,' Jean proclaims. 'I was very fond of our old meeting place, you know.'

'Me too,' I reply, helping her with her coat. 'But I think it's all worked out, wouldn't you agree?'

She nods. 'It's marvellous. So bright and cheery!'

'Thank you, Jean, that's very kind of you to say.'

'Well, Dora,' she begins, 'I was saying to my son, Wilbur, that when you get to our age, you can feel a bit invisible. It's nice to find somewhere where you feel comfortable, and you've always made us feel welcome here.'

'You *are* always welcome here, both of you.'

She nods and picks up her bag. 'We'll be off, then. Bye, love.'

I get a little choked up as I watch them leave. I hope Wilbur is kind to his mother. She deserves it.

Three hours later, the last of the guests are leaving, including Larry who's given extra mac and cheese as a parting gift along with a promise that I'll join him and Anna for dinner when they're next in Scotland. I slip into a booth and kick off my shoes.

'Can I go to Joanne's house?' Charlotte asks, plonking down beside me. 'Her dad will run me home later.'

'Which one is Joanne?' I reply, looking over at the three teenage girls huddled by the door.

'Blue-streaked hair. Nose ring.'

'Hmm... and what do her parents do for a living?'

'MUM!'

'I'm kidding, I'm kidding. Yes, you can go but please text me her address, don't ride alone in the car with her dad and don't come back with anything pierced.'

'Ugh, you worry too much.'

'Always,' I reply.

She hugs me quickly and is off like the roadrunner before I can tell her what time to be home.

Finally, the diner is empty. The place looks like a bomb has gone off, but I've sent the staff home. We can deal with the mess in the morning. Faith joins me in the booth while Victoria locks the door and grabs a bottle of champagne from the fridge.

She returns with three glasses and proceeds to pop the cork.

'Well, ladies,' she toasts, rapidly filling each glass. 'Here's to a very successful launch.'

I raise my glass and laugh. 'I'm exhausted, but we nailed it.'

I'm certain that the entire street can hear us cheer as we toast.

An hour later we're still stuck to the booth.

'Thanks to both of you for all the hard work you've put in,' I say, picking at the remnants of some leftover nachos. 'In both business and in life, I'd be nothing without the pair of you.'

Faith laughs. 'What percentage is this wine? All I did was throw together a guest list, you two did all the work.'

'Hmm, I suggested the jukebox,' Victoria adds. 'You came

up with the rest. It's been all you, Nora. After seeing how it turned out, I'm kinda embarrassed I didn't do more.'

I shake my head. 'Vic, if you hadn't suggested going into business in the first place all those years ago, we wouldn't be here. And Faith, if you hadn't sent me off to that bootcamp, I'd still be stuck in the same, indifferent place I had been for years. I just want you to know how much I appreciate you both.'

'That bootcamp really got to you, huh?' Faith remarks. 'Maybe I'll sign you up for the next one. I think it's in—'

'No!' I exclaim. 'As enlightening as it was, I have no intention of participating in one ever again. No, thank you.'

'Not even if Will was there?' Vic asks, glancing at Faith. I know that look. They think I'm still moping over him. I haven't thought about him in, well, minutes.

'If I'm meant to see him again, it'll happen,' I reply. 'I'm done trying to make sense of any of that. Besides, I'd rather focus on meeting someone who's actually available and not just forced to do yoga with me.'

I see Faith's eyes light up, while mine narrow.

'Oh God, you've got someone in mind already, haven't you?' I ask.

'Maybe... how do you feel about chiropodists?'

CHAPTER 38

THREE MONTHS LATER

I yell for Charlie to grab her bag so I can drop her at school before heading to work. After the official reopening three months ago, I'm busier than ever. Saying goodbye to Café 12 was the best thing we've ever done as Charlie Brown's is already making a name for itself.

'Remember I have drama club after school?' Charlie reminds me as we hurry outside. 'And Joanne is coming back afterwards so we can work on lines for the play. She'll probably just sleep over since it's the weekend.'

'But I'm stocktaking tonight. I won't be back until midnight.'

'It's fine. We'll double lock the door.'

'Just don't use the cooker or—'

'Mum, I'm fifteen. I haven't burned the house down yet.'

'I know, but Joanne might be a secret pyromaniac. A fire-bug. She looks the type. All those fake nose rings and My Chemical Romance T-shirts – classic house-burner.'

Charlie sniggers and buckles her seatbelt. She knows I'm almost as fond of Joanne and she is. When your child finds her tribe it's the most glorious thing to behold.

'Just be careful,' I say. 'And phone me if you need me.'

She grunts in agreement, putting in her headphones as I drive off.

I pull up outside the school fifteen minutes later and arrive at work just after nine. We don't open until midday now, except on weekends when we open at ten to reel in the hangover casualties with our American style brunch and my fabulous coffee. That machine is still the best investment I ever made.

'Delivery has just been,' Victoria yells when she hears the door. 'Give me a hand peeling these potatoes will you, Tracey's not in until eleven.'

'No problem, let me just chuck my coat in the back.'

Two hours later, food is prepped and I'm making sure tables are clean and napkin dispensers are full. We've hired one new guy, Aaron, to work evenings but at the rate we're going, we'll need more hands by the end of the year.

'Faith is trying to set me up again,' I tell Victoria who's now abandoned the potatoes and scrolling through her phone. 'You heard anything about this one? The foot guy?'

Victoria nods, transfixed by something on her screen. 'Uh-huh... Michael something.'

'Bolton?'

'Hmm.'

'Jackson?'

'Yeah, could be.'

'Great, thanks for your help.'

Tracey arrives and gets set up while I grab a quick coffee before we open. I've barely blown the froth off before Faith texts.

Martin Crawford. Owns a foot clinic in Morningside. He'll be
in tonight at 6pm for coffee and marriage. Really think you'll
like this one.

I told Faith weeks ago that I'd only do coffee on first dates. I've wasted far too many evenings with men who didn't deserve longer than an espresso shot. It's easier to approach coffee dates with absolutely no expectations, than spending two hours getting ready for dinner with someone who's already splitting the bill before you've even ordered. However, I didn't intend for the coffee to be served in my own bloody café.

'Nora, these point-of-sale pads are offline again,' I hear Vic yell from the back of the restaurant. 'Can you reset the router?'

I sigh. Today is going to be one of those days. Still, it appears that I have a date with a professional foot-toucher and who knows where that might lead? Nothing about my life is boringly normal anymore.

Thirty burgers, sixteen paninis, twelve nachos, twenty-seven coffees, four Cokes and one Caesar salad later, I'm exhausted and also painfully aware that this Martin guy will be here soon. I haven't even had time to fix my makeup and I smell like fried onions. Why is nothing simple?

As I start clearing empty tables, the door opens and Jean breezes in. Even though we're attracting a much younger crowd these days, I'm glad she's still a regular. It's unusual to see her here alone, however. I hope her usual crowd are still alive and kicking.

'Got a hot date, Jean?' I ask as she walks towards me. She looks lovely. Hair set, nails done, and a faint whiff of Youth Dew perfume follows her to her table. My mum used to wear it and it gave Faith migraines.

'I've been at the spa on Lothian Road all afternoon, with Veronica. You know Veronica. One with the mole on her chin?'

'I do,' I reply. Veronica's mole is impossible to miss. 'Is she not joining you?'

'Well,' she says, as she takes a seat at the window, 'normally she would, but my son is meeting me here. *Les Misérables* is on at the Playhouse.'

'Oh, how lovely. Is he visiting?'

I've heard so much about Wilbur over the years, I'm actually excited to meet him.

'In a sense,' she replies. 'He got divorced last year unfortunately. Been staying with me for a couple of weeks – back down south tomorrow.'

'Ah, sorry to hear that,' I reply. 'It's never an easy time.'

'Well, Dora,' she begins, cautiously looking around in case anyone is listening, 'I'm quite glad to be honest with you. She was a lovely girl, but never quite right for him. I'm hoping he might move closer to home, find someone more suitable. I keep telling him, he's not getting any younger.'

I love the way the older generation just bombard you with facts about their family. I'm pretty sure if I keep her talking, I'll find out Wilbur's shoe size and national insurance number. Why on earth did she name him Wilbur though? And I thought Eleanora was bad.

'Well, I hope you have a lovely time tonight,' I tell her. 'What can I get you while you wait?'

'Tea, love,' she replies, 'and one of those "Rocking Road" cakes.'

I chuckle quietly. 'Coming right up.'

I prepare Jean's tea and smile as I have visions of Wilbur in a bow tie, escorting his elderly mother into box seats.

· · ·

At quarter to six, I bring Jean her second cup of tea. She's been sitting alone for half an hour.

'Been stood up?' I ask, picking up her plate. I get the feeling I have too unless Mr Foot Clinic took one look at my sweaty face and promptly about-turned.

'I hope not,' she replies, handing me her empty cup. 'My son has never been on time for anything in his life. He'd be late for his own funeral.'

'What time's the show?'

'Seven,' she informs me. 'I haven't been to the theatre since my Harry died but I'm looking forward to it.'

'How long were you married?' I ask.

'Forty-three years.' She pauses to clean her glasses on a napkin. My heart aches a little when I hear this. I can't imagine loving someone for that long and then losing them.

'He *loved* the theatre,' she continues. 'I remember he took me to see *Guys and Dolls* on our third date... He played around, my Tony, but the theatre was always just for us.'

Her phone beeps and she stops to look. 'Oh, it's Wilbur. He got held up, but he'll be here in five minutes. You'd best get me the bill, love.'

'It's on the house, Jean,' I say, 'and I hope tonight is just as memorable as *Guys and Dolls*.'

She beams and thanks me as I take her dishes away. At least one of us will have a fun evening.

I load Jean's plates into the dishwasher while Victoria mouths the words to a BTS song, using a wooden spoon as a microphone. She's been playing it repeatedly on the jukebox for days now.

'It looks like Faith's guy's not coming,' I tell her, watching in amusement. 'I'm kind of relieved if I'm honest, I'd rather do anything else tonight. I'm just not feeling it.'

'Maybe you can go out on the town with Jean?' she replies,

now deep into a choreographed routine. 'I mean, you have the same dress sense.'

I grin, whipping her with my dishtowel. 'Nonsense. I think you'll find that *my* grey cardigan has pockets, unlike hers.'

As she laughs, her face suddenly changes to one of intrigue. 'Oh my. Either Jean's son is a hottie, or some random dude just decided to hug our favourite grandma.'

As I turn to look, I suddenly forget how to breathe.

'Nora, you alright?' I hear Vic ask, but I've already dropped my dish towel as I walk towards Jean's table. She sees me and waves me over.

It can't be.

Jean beams with pride and introduces me to the man sitting beside her. The I only knew for a week but feel like I've known forever. 'Dora, this is my son—'

'Will?'

I hear Victoria gasp behind me.

It's him. It's really him. Shorter hair and he's lost a few pounds, but it's him. He stares at me in disbelief. 'Nora?'

'You two know each other?' I hear Jean ask. 'How extraordinary.'

We both nod, unable to take our eyes off each other. As he stands to face me, I'm instantly transported back to last year. To bootcamp. To the moment we said goodbye. To that kiss.

'Well, what a coincidence!' she chirps. 'Wilbur, I'm just going to use the ladies' and then we really should leave. I don't want to miss the opening number.'

I step aside to let Jean pass as she hums 'Look Down' from *Les Mis* quietly to herself.

'Wow,' he says, exhaling loudly. 'How are you?'

'I'm great,' I reply, which is a lie because my heart is beating out of my chest right now. Impending seizure does not insinuate 'great'. 'But I think I need to sit down.'

I take Jean's seat and glance over at Victoria who's doing a terrible impersonation of someone trying not to stare. She mouths, '*Is that THE Will?*'

I nod covertly.

'Shit,' Will says, 'I can't believe it's you. This is too weird. You work here? My mum knows you?'

'I own this place,' I reply. 'Your mum's been coming here for years.'

'This is too weird,' he repeats.

We both sit for a moment, waiting for the world to make sense again and aware that Jean will be back at any moment, and he'll have to leave.

'I've thought about you often,' he says softly. 'Admittedly, my mum wasn't part of the scenario but...'

I laugh a little louder than intended and he smiles.

'Yeah, I've thought about you too,' I admit, pulling my gaze away from his dimples. 'You know, every now and then.'

Every now and then? God, it's taking everything I have not to blurt out that I've missed him every single day.

'I wanted to get in touch,' he says. 'I even looked you up on Facebook. Turns out there are eight Nora Browns on Facebook, all private and none with your picture.'

I cringe from the outside in. 'Um, did you see one with a cat holding a gun?'

'Seriously? That was you?'

I nod. 'My daughter finds it hilarious to change my photo to random shit she finds online. A couple of weeks ago, I was Kanye West.'

He leans back and sighs. 'Maybe I should have just messaged them all. But I wasn't sure if you even wanted to hear from me.'

'I did,' I reply. 'Then I read your article. It sounded like you were glad bootcamp was over and patching things up with your wife... but your mum tells me you're now divorced.'

He rolls his eyes. 'Of course she did. I'm not sure there's

anyone within a fifty-mile radius she hasn't shared that particular nugget of information with.'

'Sorry, things didn't work out,' I say. 'I know you wanted it to.'

'I did,' he responds. 'I really did. But then I went to that stupid fucking bootcamp and met you.'

My eyes meet his as he tentatively moves his hand on to mine.

'I should have tried harder,' Will says, his face visibly pained. 'But then what? Crassly announce my divorce and expect you to give a shit after all this time? I didn't want to disrupt your life because mine now had a vacancy... I wish we could have had longer at bootcamp. Maybe—'

'Are you kidding?' I exclaim. 'Will, I'm grateful it wasn't longer!'

Caught off guard, he frowns. 'You are? Why?'

'Because the way I felt about you after one week... well, any longer and I'm not sure my heart would have ever recovered.'

'Sorry to interrupt, do you work here? I'm looking for Nora?'

My head snaps around to see a man in a denim jacket, stinking of cologne, with wide eyes and a look of anxiety which is universally recognised as Blind Date Face. It takes me a moment to click.

Martin Crawford. Foot clinic. He'll be in tonight at 6pm for coffee and marriage.

Oh God, he brought flowers! My stomach isn't just doing somersaults, it's like the freaking Cirque du Soleil. I move my hand away from Will. Why is this happening, right now?

'Yes,' I reply, smiling meekly. 'That's—'

'Me! I'm her. Nora Brown, at your service!' Victoria swoops in like an eavesdropping ninja, quickly inserting herself between us. 'Michael, right?'

'It's Martin actually.'

'Are those for me?' She takes the bouquet before he has time to respond. 'Well, aren't you just the sweetest?! Faith didn't tell me you were as cute as a button!'

God, she's really hamming it up here.

He looks at me again briefly and then back to Victoria. 'Wait, *you're* Faith's sister? She didn't tell me you were—'

'Black?' Victoria replies, frowning.

'American,' Martin responds, his face now burning. 'She never mentioned you were American.'

Victoria laughs loudly and links arms with Martin, slowly pulling him away from our table. 'Oh, I grew up in America, different fathers, obviously. Have you ever been to the States, Michael?'

'Martin...'

Their voices slowly fade out as Vic takes him to a booth at the back of the diner. I turn to Will, who looks both bewildered and amused.

'I'm not even going to ask,' he says.

'I wouldn't even know how to explain if you did.'

'Are you ready, Wilbur? We must shake a wicked hoof if we're to get there on time.'

We both turn to see Jean exiting the bathroom. His face looks visibly pained.

'You're leaving tomorrow?' I ask. 'Your mum mentioned it.'

'First thing. I found a place to rent in Manchester.'

'I'm feeling a sense of déjà vu here,' I say, my stomach taking up permanent residence in my feet. 'Bad timing.'

'Horrible timing,' he replies.

I stand to let Jean get her coat, my legs unsteady enough to make me grab the booth for support. I can't believe he's leaving again.

'Shame you can't join us, love,' Jean says, 'but it's been sold out for weeks. You two could have had a proper catch-up.'

'Not to worry,' I reply. 'We're open 'til ten and then we're stocktaking. Just have a lovely time and tell me all about it when you're next in.'

Will stands as Jean makes her way outside. 'It was great to see you, Nora,' he says, coming in for a hug. 'Really great.'

I move in and wrap my arms around him. It's been almost a year, but nothing has changed. I breathe him in like oxygen.

'Be happy, Will.'

'You too, Nora.'

This time I don't watch him leave.

CHAPTER 39

'Are you sure you're up for this Nora?' Victoria asks as she locks the front door. 'I'm pretty sure I can handle it if you need to leave.'

While I might have spent the past three hours quietly blubbering, I feel that counting tins of coffee and toilet rolls might just be the distraction I need. Seeing Will was so unexpected, it almost doesn't feel real.

'I'm fine,' I reply. 'Was just a shock seeing him... all this time I've been serving his mum tea and cakes... it's unreal.'

'I must admit, I didn't expect tiny Jean to produce such a towering specimen,' Victoria adds. 'What is he? Like six-foot-ninety?'

'Not sure,' I reply. 'Six-two maybe? But I'd rather not—'

'I mean, I know you told me he was fine, but *damn*, Nora! Your infatuation makes a hell of a lot more sense now. I'd have challenged the wife to a duel.'

'Great,' I reply. 'But can we not talk about—'

'How delicious he is?' she responds, smirking. 'Because I think that's a reasonable and necessary conversation to have.'

'Nope. It's not happening. I'm here to work.'

'Fine,' she says, with a sulk. 'You're no fun. I bet Will is fun—'

I ignore her and start on the first inventory checklist of the night. It's not that I don't want to talk about Will, it's that I'm afraid if I start, I'll never stop. I've come too far for that.

'I must admit, I felt a bit sorry for Martin,' she admits, checking off the contents of the freezer. 'I doubt he'll be asking Nora for a second date.'

'Not into annoying Americans who keep getting his name wrong?' I say, smirking. 'And what the hell was that laugh you kept doing? Sounded like a snorting hyena.'

'Not my finest moment,' she says, 'I was just trying to be as off-putting as possible. Shit, I'd better message Faith before he does.'

'Thanks,' I say. 'For stepping in. You're my hero.'

'I am,' she agrees, 'and this hero needs music. Something to perk us up a little, *oui?*'

'Definitely,' I reply, 'though can we skip the K-pop?'

'Nope,' she replies. 'Those boys were put on earth to make us happy. Once you learn their names, and some dance moves, you'll be much more invested. Trust me.'

Eleven thirty rolls around and we're almost finished; the only stock revelation is that Victoria appears to be eating more cake than we're selling.

'Look, if you want me to be happy here, I need the cake. Take it out of my wages.'

'Vic, you do the wages.'

'Bit of a dilemma for you, then,' she says before pausing. 'What is that noise? Do you hear that?'

I nod, turning in the direction of the thumping. It's coming from the front entrance.

'Should we go and see?' I ask, meaning me remaining here while Vic investigates.

'Nah, probably some drunk,' Vic replies. 'Ignore it.'

'Nora! Are you in there?'

'Friend of yours?' she asks.

I shrug. Between the rain coming down and the noise outside, it's hard to tell.

'Definitely some drunk,' Vic says, getting to her feet. 'All your friends are drunks.'

'You're all my friends.'

I grab the shutter keys and reluctantly accompany her to the door.

'We're closed, dude,' Vic informs him. 'It's late. Come back tomorrow.'

'Sorry, I'm just looking for Nora.'

Vic unlocks and pulls the shutter up to reveal a very tall, very wet Will.

'Um, I'll just be in the back,' Vic announces.

'What are you doing here?' I ask. 'Is everything OK?'

'Not really,' he replies, starting to pace backwards and forwards.

'What's going on?'

He hesitates and purses his lips, wringing his hands together like knows what he wants to say but the words just aren't coming.

'Nora, I don't know what the fuck is going on here, but I'm a little freaked out, you know?'

'OK...'

'And you know I don't buy into any of that universe crap, but even I can't explain this,' he declares, almost oblivious to the rain that's currently soaking him to the skin.

'I'm not sure what you mean,' I reply. Is he on something?

'It's like, I think about you and later that day, a song comes on that we listened to at bootcamp... or I think about you and soon after, I'm finding bootcamp brochures that I swear I threw away months ago. I mean – I think about you while I'm driving to my mother's house, and you appear! Here! Right in front of me! It's freaking me out!'

'You want to come in? Where's your mum?'

He nods and pushes past me, taking the same seat he had earlier. I remain standing. 'I dropped Mum home, after the show.'

'Hi, Will!' Victoria yells, a huge grin appearing on her face. 'You want to get out of those wet clothes?'

I shoot her a look and she slinks off into the back room.

'Who is she?' Will asks, watching her leave.

'No idea,' I reply. 'You were saying... actually I'm not sure what you were saying.'

'I know I'm not making a lot of sense,' he admits. 'And I know you've moved on, but I couldn't just leave without seeing you again. I have to know.'

'Know what?' I ask.

He inhales deeply but I hear it catch the back of his throat. 'I have to know if what we had, what we felt, back then, is still there.'

'Will—'

'Because I think it is. When we hugged earlier, it was like coming home. I know that sounds cheesy, but it's how I felt.'

Now I'm the one pacing. 'What we had back then was amazing,' I say, feeling my eyes well up. 'I fell hard, and I hope you did too, even a little.'

'You know I did,' he replies.

I shake my head. 'I don't. The only thing I know is that, despite everything you felt for me, it wasn't enough.'

He bows his head. 'It wasn't like that.'

'I need to be enough... but, Will, I had to move on. Do you know how hard that was?'

He nods. 'I do, and I'm glad you moved on, truly I am because I never did... and I wouldn't wish that on anyone.'

'Why are you doing this? If this is some rebound situation...'

He rubs the back of his neck and sighs. 'You once said that "sometimes, no matter how hard you resist, there are people that you are just fated to adore". I didn't quite get that until now.'

My words. He remembered my words. I bite my bottom lip before it betrays me.

'I'm doing this because somehow we've managed to come together again, and I'm scared I won't get another chance.'

'But you're leaving tomorrow.'

'I'll come back. I'm freelance. I'll base myself here, I can work from anywhere. If you want me to? Don't you get it, Nora? I don't just adore you. I love you.'

'Love me? How can you love me?'

He smiles. 'Look at you. How can I not?'

As those words leave his mouth, I dive across the table and into his arms. His lips meet mine and we kiss like nothing else matters.

As his hands begin to wander, I prise my face from Will's momentarily. 'Look, before we take this any further, I really need to say something.'

'Is it that you love me too?' he replies. 'Because you technically haven't said it back yet and I'm getting a little concerned.'

'I'm serious. I really need to get this off my chest.'

'OK, shoot.'

I take a deep breath. 'So, it's been eating away at me all day and I'm just going to come out and say it.'

'What?'

'Wilbur.'

He smirks. 'I was wondering when this would come up.'

'Your name is Wilbur. Wil-bur. Willlbbuurrrr!'

'OK, get it out of your system.'

'I thought Will was short for William! How could you keep this from me?'

'For this very reason. You finished now?'

'Absolutely not.'

He presses his mouth against mine and this time I let his hands wander freely.

'Hey, Romeo and Juliet,' Vic yells from the kitchen. I didn't even notice her sneak back in. 'There's a time and a place for everything... hands where I can see them!'

Even with Will's mouth on mine, I can't help but laugh. While that seems like a lifetime ago, those words still ring true, probably more than ever. There is a time and a place for everything and it's exactly this moment. I don't know exactly how we got here; fate, luck, sheer coincidence, I don't really care. All I know is that we're here and I'm grateful.

Hear that, universe? I'm finally grateful!

A LETTER FROM JOANNA

I wanted to say a huge thank you for choosing to read *Bootcamp for Broken Hearts*. If you enjoyed it and want to keep up to date with my latest releases, just sign up at the following link. Your email address will never be shared and you can unsubscribe at any time.

www.bookouture.com/joanna-bolouri

There's a little place near Argyll in Scotland, where you can rent log cabins with hot tubs, which overlook a beautiful loch. The days are quiet, the night skies are black and the hot tub lids are ridiculously heavy if you're attempting to open them alone.

Sometimes I'll go there and write and sometimes I'll bob about in the hot tub at night, staring at the stars while I ponder the universe.

Bootcamp for Broken Hearts was born during one of these ponderings, where I wondered whether the universe really does have a plan for everyone, and can we shape our reality just by imagining what we want?

If you manifested this book into your reality and if you enjoyed reading it, I would be very grateful if you could write a review. I would love to hear what you think, and it makes such a difference in helping new readers discover my books for the first time.

If you have any questions or comments, please do get in touch with me via Facebook or Twitter, as I love chatting to my readers.

All best wishes,

Jo

facebook.com/jbolouri
twitter.com/scribbles78